25699   3/6

THE BREAK IN THE CIRCLE

THE BREAK

IN THE CIRCLE

a novel by PHILIP LORAINE

author of AND TO MY BELOVED HUSBAND

THE M. S. MILL CO. AND WILLIAM MORROW & CO.

NEW YORK, 1951

CONTENTS

PART ONE

Arc

1 – WHAT LINDA SAW . . .

IT WAS STRANGE, SHE THOUGHT, HOW EVERYDAY, QUIET THINGS suddenly brought happiness flooding into you—how bitter memory could suddenly draw back and leave you free again.

She sat down on the low stone wall, leaning against the grey bulk of her cottage, built, as were all the houses in Wainport, to withstand the two winds: rumbustious buffetings from the west and cruel, sand-streaked attack from the east. She felt the grey stone warm against her back; she stared at the wet towels and the yellow-edged tablecloth, which she had just pegged to the line, watching them flap against a blue spring sky, thanking them for this unaccountable happiness.

Was she escaping at last, she wondered? Escaping from those far-reaching, damnable tentacles of the past which clung so avidly despite the passing of time. For so many months she had lived with her own private misery that this sudden sense of freedom took her by surprise; she hadn't supposed that she would ever feel free again. Divorce, with all its legal trappings, had never appeared to her as something which would flay the emotions—not until it had appeared, monstrous and menacing, in her own life. Divorce had seemed to be the way in which maltreated women cast off their husbands; it had never presented itself to her imagination as the possible ending to her own marriage. The shock of finding that Stephen no longer loved her—that he had, for months, been taking his pleasure elsewhere—came to her like a physical catastrophe. She had felt as shocked and shattered as on the occasion when she had driven her car into a tree after skidding on an icy corner. Indeed that shock had worn off more quickly; her broken arm had healed more quickly than the broken spirit which followed the crash of divorce.

But now, at last, on this bright May morning, she was suddenly happy, suddenly free; and the knowledge of it, after so long a captivity, brought tears pressing at the corners of her closed eyes. Yet she had to smile at herself because she knew that in a moment, when the tears no longer blurred her vision, she would turn and look across the cove. She was aware of the young man there, as indeed she had been aware of him now for weeks—a sharpening of awareness when she passed him in the village street, or when they met face to face in the post office, or when, as now, she could sense his presence across a few yards of sunlit water; he would be sitting cross-legged on the fo'csle of his little boat, splicing a rope.

To begin with she had been angry that he—that any man—should be able to reach into the deep cave where her bruised feelings had run for sanctuary. She had sworn to herself that never again would she allow such a thing to happen. Yet he had done it—without the least exertion on his part either.

It was strange, she sometimes thought, that they hardly knew each other: a nod, a wave of the hand, a few words about the weather or the tide. She might never know him any better, and yet she would always be grateful to him because it was he—agile, alive, disturbing—who had performed this delicate operation on her inmost heart and transformed her from a lump of cold clay into a human being once more.

Or was that all a fantasy? And was it only Time, the great healer, who had come to her aid. Perhaps this young man, Alan Morgan, was just any young man anywhere. Yes, perhaps that was it.

And yet, as the idea struck her, a chill crept into the day, and with it a sudden panic that he might after all not be sitting cross-legged on his boat across the cove. At once she opened her eyes and turned.

Idiot, she thought, aware of her heart thumping. *You shouldn't let yourself feel things like that.* But she was glad that she had felt it all the same.

The sun had lifted now, and he was no longer a black figure against the intolerable glitter of the ebbing tide. He always anchored his boat in what was known as The Pool—a troubled piece of deep water, unlike any pool she had known, caused by the swirl of river and tide against the old jetty. Now, in the pull of the ebb, she could see the white-painted hull swinging to and fro as if eager to be free and under sail.

He stood up and stared reflectively at the tide. His faded blue jeans were rolled up almost to the knee, disclosing brown legs. He pushed back his dark hair, examined the palm of his hand (*A splinter*, she thought, wincing) and set to work again. She saw him lift the heavy rudder and lower it gently to the dinghy; then, with that agile casualness which fascinated her, he followed, cast off the painter and was at once whipped away by the fierce current. In a moment, however, the walnut shell of a boat was under control, and he began to pull, not towards the jetty as usual, but straight for the tiny crescent of sand which lay beneath her. It lay "beneath" because her little house had been built at the water's edge on a terrace of grey stone to prevent it slipping into the tideway; thus, sitting on the wall which flanked the rough platform, she gazed down into The Cove.

The Pool and The Cove had amused her on her first tremulous visit to Wainport; it was not so much grandiloquence as pure misnomer. There were others—The Headland, a bluff strip of shelving sand; The Quarry, an imperceptible dip in the dunes; The Castle, an old and battered watchtower. They arose, she had realised after a time, from an old, long-lost importance. The straggling village had once been a vital township: Wainport, the port at the mouth of the Wain. But now the river had silted up; the flat estuary meandered through marshes of its own making, and the sea was a mile away.

His little boat grounded a few yards from its objective; she watched him jump out and drag it after him, the keel marking its shape in wet sand. Once, ten minutes ago, before this freedom suddenly released her, she would not have sat there gazing idly down on him; for he disturbed her with his catlike agility, his lean darkness, his independence, his silence. He seemed in fact to be all that Stephen had never been; Stephen was a dependent man—a man who needed to be watched, to be coerced, coaxed, cossetted, all, of course, without his being aware of the fact himself. Awareness tended to bruise his immense vanity, his sense of male importance.

The young man shouldered the rudder and set off up The Cove to the village street; in passing, he glanced at her and nodded. It was a direct glance and it told her that he had been aware of her all the time; for some reason the knowledge made her blush with faint anger. Any other young man, knowing that a pretty woman sat lazily watching him, would surely have spoken, even if only to comment on the ubiquitous weather.

But this young man—oh no. Oh no, not Mr. Alan Morgan.

He merely nodded and strolled unconcernedly away towards what Wainport still called The Shipyard: it consisted of two tottering sheds where old Ted Clumper repaired what craft the men could not repair themselves, and where occasionally he built a small sailing boat for some rich customer who had heard of his skill from some other rich customer.

She watched the young man go, balancing the rudder with one hand and examining the palm of the other.

Alan Morgan. She leaned her head on the rough wall and gave herself up, not for the first time, to idle speculation. What was he doing in Wainport, for instance? Certainly nobody in Wainport knew. Had he a private income, and, if not, how did he manage to live? It was said that he occasionally hired out his boat and himself at St. Anselm's during the summer: trips for a week, for two weeks or a month. It was impossible to picture him among the prosperous middle-aged couples at St. Anselm's.

He stayed with Mrs. Trigg at Rose Cottage next to the church. Mrs. Trigg was deaf; obviously the main fount of village gossip was stemmed at source. And, now that he had been with them three years (a quiet, well-behaved gentleman, they all agreed, who kept himself to himself) their curiosity had grown blunted.

Indeed, as she well knew, she herself had supplanted him as the object of interest in Wainport: Mrs. Linda Ward-Hamilton, they knew that much from her letters. Divorced! Heaven alone knew where *that* had come from; she supposed that some newspaper she never saw had found something interesting in the shabby proceedings. In any case it was enough for Wainport: Mrs. Linda Ward-Hamilton, divorced. It made a luscious mouthful. And yet it was not a gossipy village. It lay in no lush agricultural dell, where other people's business might hang heavily on the still air; Wainport knew the sea, and the sea's anger. It lay between

7

marsh and estuary, between west wind and east wind, and the blood of Wainport people was stern blood, sailors' blood, smugglers' blood. They must struggle for existence, and other people's business could, on the whole, mind itself. She had recognised this quality, had made sure of it before she went so far as to buy the lease of her cottage on its man-made rock.

But this Morgan, this Alan Morgan, roused her. She sensed in him . . . What was it that she sensed?

Reclining in the warm spring sun, she shook her head as if to clear it. Gulls rose off the estuary and burst into soaring flight against the pale sky.

Whatever he might do at St. Anselm's he was never merely an "all-aboard-for-the-Skylark" sailor. She had seen him on a savage day in March bring his white boat smacking into the lee of the jetty under full sail—beating up the estuary for dear life, almost in the teeth of a blustering westerly gale. And in that case "for dear life" was no easy phrase. Within an hour the wind had increased to demoniac fury, driving fierce rain before it; the distant sea became a maelstrom in which no small sailing boat could have lasted a minute. And the gale went on for three days.

If she was sure in her mind, then, that he did not take fat visitors for trips at a seaside town, she was equally sure that he was not wasting his time. So silent, so independent, so insolent a young man did not waste time; if he came and went, which he did frequently, roaring through the village in an ancient Lagonda, he came and went to a good purpose.

These thoughts were not exactly new ones; she had pondered over them before, half-irritated, half-excited by his presence at the door of her retreat.

But at this moment speculation, though she could not know it, was dying; and whether she wished it or not she had already become part of that young man's life, and he of hers.

A large black car, a tourer with the hood down, had swung off the road and was purring to a standstill beneath her.

A voice said, "Hullo. Er, excuse me."

"I should be careful of that sand." Linda pointed. "You may get stuck."

The man in the car squinted up at her against the light. "Back wheels on the road." He gestured. "Perfectly safe."

He was a type she knew and could pigeonhole immediately. A military moustache, reddish-yellow in colour, clashed horribly with the deeper red of his face. Under the checked cap, which he had touched as if in salute, she suspected he would be bald. His age might be anything between thirty and fifty. He was undoubtedly a major.

"Lovely day," he said. "Awfully sorry to trouble you, but I'm looking for a chap called Morgan—Alan Morgan. Old feller up the road said I might find him hereabouts."

It was at this moment that she saw his coat. It was made of fine tweed and it lay on the seat beside him, neatly folded with pocket uppermost. And in the pocket was a gun.

The shock of this discovery made her glance away towards the estuary; it seemed an eternity before she could look back again to reassure herself. Yes, there was no doubt about it; from her vantage point above him, and because perhaps of a slanting reflection or the thin material, or because he had put his hand on it a moment before, thus pressing down the tweed, she could see, quite clearly, the shape of a revolver.

"Yes," she said, to gain time. "That's his dinghy down in The Cove there. He's . . . What did you say your name was?"

They both knew that he had not so far mentioned his name.

"Hobart," he said. "Major Hobart."

9

"He's . . ." Her thoughts floundered for a moment longer and then were steady. "I'll get him for you."

The major saluted again. He was clambering out of the car as she slipped off her perch and turned from him.

She ran—there was no need to run, but her feet disobeyed her—across the terrace and down a flight of steps to the street. The house lay between her and the car now, but she continued to run: along the road, round the corner and down the long slope into Ted Clumper's yard. Clumper and Alan were examining the faulty rudder. As she joined them the old man said, ". . . have it done by this afternoon for you. Why, here's Mrs. Hamilton, what's it to be, ma'am? A nice little dinghy, eh?"

She stared stupidly and old Clumper laughed benevolently. Young Morgan, on the other hand, only half-smiled.

"There's . . ." She took a breath. "There's someone to see you."

"Me?" He hardened; she saw every nerve, every tissue contract into a wary tension.

"A Major Hobart."

"Never heard of him." He did smile now, a warm slow smile which took her entirely by surprise. To Clumper he said, "This afternoon then. That's very good of you, Ted."

"Anything to oblige, boy, anything to oblige."

"Hobart, eh?"

They walked together up the ramp. At the top, not looking at him, she said, "He's . . . got a gun in his overcoat pocket."

She knew only a second later that there could never again be ordinariness between them. She had destroyed ordinariness in eight words; a whole card-house of conventions had toppled and collapsed. She bit her lip, wishing now that she had minded her own business. Perhaps after all she had imagined the whole thing.

10

But he laughed. "A gun!" He laughed, he mocked her, he was more friendly than he had ever been before. "Oh dear, I'd better be careful then." After a moment he added, "D'you suppose it's an enraged father? A shotgun wedding would delight dear old Wainport, wouldn't it?" He even mimicked the Wainport accent: " 'It's always them quiet ones, Mrs. Clumper. Still waters run deep, that's what I say.' "

No, she could not smile; she had seen the ugly shape, muffled by the soft material but still ugly. She said, "His . . . His car's round by The Cove."

He nodded genially and left her to climb the steep steps back to her domain. Halfway up, her legs suddenly refused to hold her; she stumbled and nearly fell.

All this comes, she thought wryly, *of living on A Height.* She was wishing, now, that she had not looked down and seen the major's overcoat. And yet those wilful, disobedient legs led her to the edge of the terrace once more.

The coat had been thrown into the back seat, and the two men were standing down by the water's edge, idly tossing pebbles into the tideway. Again she doubted herself; it was such an ordinary scene: a car with a coat in the back seat, two men standing on a strip of warm sand, and behind her the idle flap and smack of the clothes hung out to dry. The quiet village, the spring sky, the gulls squabbling over something beyond the jetty.

Then certainty returned. She was sure of what she had seen, and she realised with a sense of shock that she was sure not only because of what her eyes had told her, but because . . . Oh, but it was absurd! And yet the knowledge of it taunted her; she could not turn away from it. There was something expected, something *natural* even, in Alan Morgan's visitor arriving with a revolver in his pocket. It was the death of speculation; all the time, hiding at the

11

back of her mind, had been the clear knowledge that he was dangerous.

The major, leaning indolently against the door of his car, was startled because the young man's voice, taut and bitter, spoke into his ear. No other sound had heralded that catlike arrival.

Glancing down, the major saw why: bare, brown feet.

The voice said, "For Pete's sake don't start waving a gun about. This is an English village."

Since Major Hobart had, in his surprise, half-drawn the revolver from his jacket pocket, to which he had transferred it in Linda's absence, he coloured abruptly. A deep, wonderful flush spread over his corrugated neck and to the tips of his pointed ears.

The young man liked that; this silent arrival and the savage voice were old tricks which seldom failed him. Already, because he was a fool, this man was in his power. The sense of that power tingled in his fingertips, warmed his stomach and went to his head like a gulp of brandy on a cold night. Power, to Alan Morgan, was just such a physical delight, even though, paradoxically, he did not delight in physical power. He went on:

"Haven't you realised yet that women see every damned thing there is to see? What sort of an idiot do I feel when a female I hardly know comes and says, 'There's a man to see you, with a gun in his pocket.' Gaw' strike a light! Come on." He walked away so that the major must follow obediently.

Now I, thought Alan Morgan, *would have stayed by that car at all costs; I wouldn't go whinnying after a bad-mannered fellow young enough to be my son.* He was sick with a sudden despair; whereas he had despised the major from the start, he now found that he hated him—hated him for his weakness.

"Who told you where to find me?" he demanded, half over his shoulder.

"Well now," said Major Hobart, evidently determined to be friendly, "that's not the sort of question . . ."

The young man faced him abruptly, dark eyes watchful. "Joe Johnson? Trigger Parks? Pete Lawley?" He laughed —a snort of contempt. "Davey Meridith."

Major Hobart was not adept at hiding his feelings. The young man laughed again. "Don't believe too much Meridith tells you. He's dirt."

"You may be grateful to him for this."

"Me, grateful to Dopey Davey! That's rich."

Hobart glowered from under bushy red eyebrows. "Dopey meaning stupid? He didn't strike me . . ."

"Dopey meaning dope." The young voice was contemptuous. He raised finger and thumb to his nose and sniffed. "If ever they put Davey Meridith inside, he'll go stark staring crazy. *And* he knows it." He picked up a pebble and lobbed at a somnolent seagull perched on an old mooring post. The major followed suit.

"Well, what did the muck-heap lead you to believe I'd do for you?"

Hobart stared. He had bright blue eyes with veins of red crisscrossing the whites. *By George,* he was thinking—and Alan knew he was thinking it—*the feller's a gentleman.* Doubtless the word he used was *sahib.* The hazy eyes were perplexed, outraged.

"I, er . . . I'm acting for another person," he said.

"Of course." The contempt was absolute; it raised Major Hobart's anger.

"Look here, young feller-me-lad," he blustered. "I advise you . . ."

13

"Keep your bloody advice," said the young man evenly. "And don't stand there snorting fire. At least five people are now watching us, and one of them knows you've got a gun in your pocket. What's your business?" He was wondering how much or how little time, and money, it had cost this man to find him. It was a warning in any case: he must move.

Hobart was silent for a time. He picked up another pebble and aimed it. The seagull seemed almost to sigh; then it spread beautiful wings and rose effortlessly from its perch. The major's stone struck the top of the mooring post where the bird had been sitting.

"I represent," he said ponderously, "an exceedingly important man."

The other nodded absently. "They all do."

"I should be very surprised," Hobart continued with an effort, "if you have ever been approached by anyone even half as influential."

The young man gave his abrupt laugh. "I constantly perform small murders for the Prime Minister and the Archbish of Cant." He bowed. "But pray continue."

"This person," said Hobart, "wishes . . . I've advised him not to." He frowned, tussling with a problem of his own. "However, he wishes to see you in person."

"Ta-ra. Ta-ra." He examined the major disbelievingly, as if expecting him to be someone he already knew disguised for a joke. Finally he said, "You're perfect. How much is your Prince offering me, and for what?"

"It, er . . . It concerns a journey," replied Hobart evasively.

The young man grinned. " 'You will meet a tall dark stranger, and go on a journey,' " he said, mincing. And suddenly the grin vanished. He took a pace forward so that for a moment his dark eyes, fierce with an inexplicable fury,

14

were close to the major's apoplectic face. "Are you clever," he demanded, "or a jackass? I can't decide."

Hobart gobbled, his resemblance to a turkey growing stronger.

"Whichever you are, I don't like you. And your Personage must be a poop to send you to see me." He stepped back. "Now," and he picked up a large stone. "Facts. Come on." He flung the stone and it flew straight as a bullet to crack against the mooring post.

Hobart controlled his temper with an effort. "You'd better not use that tone of voice when you meet . . ."

"When I meet your employer . . ." He lingered on the word. "I shall use whatever tone of voice I choose—according to the money he offers me. Where does he want me to go?"

"Germany."

The young man nodded. "That's not difficult. What for?"

"To fetch something."

"Hell! What? An elephant or a . . . a packet of pins?"

Hobart crumpled. "I don't know what, and that's a fact. He should have told me." He stirred the sand with a disconsolate toe.

The dark eyes fixed him again. "No one in their senses would tell you anything they wanted kept secret. My opinion of your owner has gone up. I'll see him. When and where?"

Hobart took a card from his pocket and held it out. "Tomorrow at eleven-thirty. Ask for me."

"Gaye and Mountview Ltd.," said the card, "Electrical Engineers. Incorporating Simpler Electrics, Vandermein Time Switch Inc., North West Heavy Electrical Units Ltd. 13 St. Clair House, Piccadilly." It told him nothing, as was doubtless intended.

"I'll be there," he said.

15

Hobart cast a wary but disparaging glance at the bare feet, the faded jeans, the torn shirt.

The young man smiled charmingly. "It's all right," he said. "I'll put on my sea boots and my pirate hat. I know how to dress for an occasion."

The major snorted and turned away towards his car, stumping importantly across the sand. Alan Morgan watched him, frowning. Then, suddenly, he burst into a sprint. He ran in complete silence until a foot separated him from the pompous tweed back; then he said, "Boo," in a loud hard voice. The major wheeled on him, hand darting to jacket pocket; there was panic in the pale eyes. Obviously his nerves were not as good as they had been.

"You fool," he shouted. "You blithering young donkey, I'd like to give you a damn good hiding."

"Well, put your gun away," said the young man wearily, as if tired of the game, and he turned back to the river. Before Major Hobart had reached his car, the dinghy was afloat, already dwindling downstream.

As soon as she saw him standing in the doorway—no bell-ringing, no tap on the knocker for Mr. Alan Morgan—she knew that he had come because of the major's gun. His appearance was only a crystallization of her thoughts. She had known in a flash of intuition that everything had changed between them—that they could no longer disregard each other; and now, as proof, he lounged against the open door, setting foot in her house for the first time, uninvited and yet casual.

"Hullo," she said.

"Hullo." He regarded her carefully. Behind him the sky across the river was lurid with sunset so that she could not see him distinctly. He, on the other hand, could see her extremely well, for she was bathed in the thick golden light of the dying sun.

He decided that he had never examined her before, merely noting her as a pretty woman. Now he saw that she was not pretty; there was something deeper than prettiness in the exact poise of her head, in the straight nose, the generous but firmly controlled mouth, the grey eyes which answered his stare so steadily. He liked the artful nonchalance of her hair, cut in Byronic curls but, unlike the wicked lord, startlingly fair—and, in this sunset glow, all on fire with red and gold lights.

The scrutiny over, he said, "Do you like jugged hare?"

"Very much."

"Do you put port in it?"

"Of course."

He held out a hare, a loop of string holding its stiff legs. "Today's bag. Bit of luck really. Where shall I put it?"

She was entranced—both by this abrupt generosity and by the suspicion that if she had confessed to not using port in the cooking, the gift would never have been made.

When he had hung the hare in her larder, they moved back towards the terrace. In the kitchen, however, he hesitated, then turned upon her that flash of white teeth which was his most engaging grin.

"What's the matter?" She felt as if someone from another world had wandered into her house. The soundlessness of his bare feet and the aura of . . . not quite independence, but more *aloneness* which surrounded him. "What's the matter?" she said again.

"Would you give me something to eat? I've only had a bit of bread and cheese since breakfast."

"Certainly. What?"

He continued to smile. "I'm awfully hungry."

"Well, you're in luck. It so happens I've got some ham."

17

She boiled him two eggs, put them on a tray with bread, butter and the ham, and carried it out to the terrace. He made no move to help her, but watched all her movements with great attention. She knew, in spite of their light conversation, that he was assessing her, that he had been doing so ever since he came in at the door. She had never been assessed quite so coldly before; it was amusing and yet ominous.

On the terrace, however, his mood changed. He sat with the tray on his lap and ate slowly—not at all like a very hungry man, although it was obvious that he needed the food. Strangely, she felt no surprise at seeing him there; it was so clearly an ordinary occurrence for him to descend on a stranger, make a gift, demand food and eat it at his leisure that she too found it ordinary. In his world, she perceived, there were many things which seemed casual to him but which would leave her astounded.

Suddenly, just when she was lulled to the point of daydreaming, he said, "Why did you think Major Hobart had a gun?"

She paused a moment, recollecting, before she spoke.

"I told you, I saw it. I saw the shape of it in his pocket."

"But why should you think I cared?"

She glanced away at the marshes, darkling under the first twilight. This was a question she had anticipated—but only in her wildest thoughts; yet it did not surprise her that those wildest thoughts should be the rough coin of his everyday life. So, carefully, she replied, "You've always struck me as being a . . . a man who might have enemies."

He laughed. "What? With my charm?"

"Charm?" She knew at once that her sarcasm was cheap —that there had been no real arrogance in his claim, only a pretence at arrogance to rouse her. Quickly she added, "Yes, I suppose you have. When you care to use it."

18

"I've very few enemies really."

"Then," she said, suddenly sure of herself, "you added one to their number today."

A pause under the deepening sky.

"You think so?"

"I'm quite certain." She remembered that last absurd, humiliating gesture. "Boo!" shouted in a small boy's voice, and the major wheeling round on his frayed nerves, hand flying to pocket.

"You were watching?" he said finally.

"Yes."

"And what did you think? That I behaved like a bad-mannered schoolboy?"

"Yes."

He nodded. "You're right, I did." He stood up, pushing his tray along the wall. "Yes, you're right. But somehow . . ." He stood, perplexed, looking down at her. After a time he said, "I'm . . . antisocial, I'm afraid. I loathe conventions, fetishes, tribal dances. They kill freedom."

"They're necessary."

"Are they?"

"Of course." She gestured. "The conventions have been very carefully worked out over several thousand years in order to keep a . . . a sort of decent veneer of civilization."

"Ha!" He exploded into speech. "And what d'you find if you peel off a bit of the veneer, eh? Oh, the dirt and the pettiness, the bugs crawling over each other to get away from the light." He stood, legs apart, arms akimbo—an angry buccaneer. But still she was not surprised; she had known that his philosophy would be like this.

"I loathe civilization," he said. "The white races are dying on their feet, dying of civilized constipation. They've no guts any more."

"Nonsense," she replied evenly.

19

"Is it nonsense?" He put a foot on the wall beside her and bent forward, peering at her face in the twilight. "Millions of atrophied little insects, catching the same train every morning, working to earn money for someone else, catching the same train every evening, going home to 'The Nook' and a parasitic little wife who starts nagging about new curtains for the front room, because the Smiths have got new curtains. Dear God!" He broke off as if ashamed of his passion. "Do what everyone else does," he muttered, turning from her. "Dress like everyone else. Eat, live, *think* like everyone else. I tell you," he said, turning back, "if Drake or Marlborough were alive today they'd be in prison."

"Drake and Marlborough were clever men. They'd be just as great today as they were in their own time, only they'd get there by a different process."

He stared at her.

"And as for the 'insects'—" She held up the gaily printed edge of her skirt. "I'm grateful to them for this, and for my food and furniture and soap and . . . and all my other civilized amenities."

"Fine." He laughed. "And down we go—drowned in a flood of amenities—too weak and spoiled by our amenities to realise . . . to realise what we're capable of achieving."

"Every man can't be an individualist. We can't all be leaders."

"No, no, no." He came and sat beside her. "I don't mean that; it's deeper than that. What we're losing is faith in ourselves. People don't have the strength to *be* themselves any more." He looked closely into her eyes and added, "I hate weakness. I despise it."

She thought suddenly of her divorced husband and had to agree. "Yes," she said, "weakness is a terrible thing."

He had come, she realised, not quite for the purpose she had supposed, and the realisation made her unsure of herself suddenly, and unsure of him too. His proximity was alarming, of course, but for the very simplest of reasons; long ago—after she had been in Wainport a month—she would readily have admitted that she found him attractive. A woman of any experience at all knows instinctively and swiftly whether or not a man attracts her.

But, she argued, it would be unforgivable and humiliating if he took her in his arms and kissed her, as she wanted him to do—and, unless her faculties misled her, as he *would* presently do unless she stopped him. It would be humiliating because her pride told her that his motive, if indeed he did kiss her, would be of the basest—far baser than that of mere physical hunger. He would do so in order to make a dishonest pact between them. She had seen a gun in a man's pocket and had run to warn him; he was annoyed that this should have seemed to her a natural thing to do. And so, to seal her lips, to seal a conspiracy of silence between them, he presently meant to make love to her.

She stood up, therefore, and moved away to the far side of the terrace. Not quickly enough, however, to avoid seeing his smile.

The smile enraged her—that and the renewed knowledge, now that she had broken away, of how much she had actually wanted to be kissed.

"I've a lot to do," she said. "I'd better get on with it."

He shrugged and stood up. "Pity. The moon'll be rising in a few minutes." The grin broke into an abrupt laugh. He was mocking her. "We could have gone for a sail. I like sailing this time of evening."

Only then did she realise how much she would have liked to sail with him—to escape for a little while from her solitary woman's world and to share his wider solitude of tideway and marsh.

21

He picked up the tray, and together they returned to the door of her house.

"Thank you," he said, "for my supper. I was very hungry."

She nodded, too full of anger and frustration for words.

He held out the tray and she took it. Then, when her hands were entirely full, he leaned across and kissed her on the mouth, pressing her head back against the wall. It was a long and intimate kiss.

"Thank you," he said again, and was gone, his bare feet making no sound on her stone steps.

She went into the sitting room and dumped the tray untidily on a chair. Her hands were shaking, and she pressed them tight against her cheeks—cool hands, burning cheeks. Thus she stood, lost in contemplation of the carpet.

After a long time she gave a deep sigh, ran the hands through her curly hair and went across to a small Chippendale mirror over the mantelpiece. The grey eyes regarded their reflection a trifle contemptuously; she noticed how the colour on her cheeks was heightened, how the spring sun had already touched her skin with faint brown.

All right, said a prim little voice inside her. *You wanted him to kiss you and he kissed you. That's nothing to get tremulous about; you're supposed to be grown-up now.*

She was aware of her heart still thumping a great deal more energetically than usual.

I hope, said the prim voice, *that you don't imagine you're in love with this extremely doubtful young man, because nothing could be more absurd—or more unsuitable.*

"Um," said Linda aloud.

2 – "YOU LIE, MY LORD"

HE LIKED SPEED AS MUCH AS HE LIKED POWER—AS MUCH AS he liked to pit his skill against the fickle sea. The bright spring morning was still cold when he swung his big grey car too fast, round the corner by Linda's house and away across the marshes where even the least important roads were straight.

Linda, who liked to rise early herself, suspected that the noisy bravado of his skid-turn was intended to wake her from luxurious morning sleep. As it was, she stood at the window sipping her coffee and watching him dwindle in a dwindling cloud of dust until the roar of the engine was once more absorbed by birdsong and the cry of gulls, until only the dust—a pillar by day, perhaps—indicated that he had turned right at the Wallchurch road and was probably going to London. It never entered her head to doubt that his journey was directly concerned with the major's visit, and no less directly with what had been in the major's pocket. Any doubt which she might conceivably have cherished had been dispelled by that brief, disturbing statement of his philosophy: the philosophy, she had decided, lying awake in the small hours, of an anarchist.

As he drove, he sang; he shouted his song to the reeling hedges, the marching telegraph posts, the changing landscape. He was glad to be on the move again, and he looked forward to whatever tussle of wits this day would bring. For too long now he had been inactive—necessarily inactive and for the very best of reasons. All winter he had lain fallow, but promising himself that in the spring . . . And now, here, he was borne on the intoxicating wings of speed towards an unknown and possibly dangerous future—un-

23

known and possibly dangerous, but of his own choosing. That was how life ought to be; that was *living*. And yet . . .

Yes, there had been other spring mornings, though he prided himself on being proof against nostalgia. But the seasons played odd tricks; that first flurry of green across the elms, or chestnut boughs heavy with pink candles, or the sudden dead-sweet scent of syringa—all could catch at the throat, at the heart. Could and did.

Even now, swerving expertly between two lumbering lorries in order to avoid collision with a milk van, he remembered waking to a spring morning in his familiar room at Ladeleigh—the first morning of holidays. He remembered how the white ceiling had glowed with a pale green light of its own, the reflection of bright sun on rain-washed lawns. He remembered leaping out of bed, struggling into old clothes, shorts and a shirt, and running barefoot, with last night's rain—a drop for each blade of grass—drenching his legs. And there, on that enchanted morning, he had stood under the Japanese cherry tree, shaking a snow of petals about himself, and had heard the first cuckoo, far away in a magic haze of eternal spring.

Yes, Ladeleigh would keep returning, wafted gently on the revolving seasons—on a scent, or a sigh, or a sunset. It would take him savagely unawares and shake him rudely so that his clever mask and nostalgia-proof armour fell clattering at his feet, and he remembered. For he had loved Ladeleigh, and his father and mother, and his brother Michael, and he could not cast off that love however he might try, whatever deeps of humiliation and sorrow he had experienced since their day. Death made no difference; for they were all dead now—his father, his mother and Michael, and the lovely house too—all dead, and yet at the scent of syringa on a still evening they clutched at his heart and made him a child. He was no longer the steel-taut young man who

24

held his life, and sometimes the lives of others also, in firm hands; master of himself and therefore (or so he reasoned) capable of mastering those who could only vacillate. He became once again a child at Ladeleigh, standing with wet feet amid a soft snow of falling petals, hearing the first cuckoo far away on the other side of the valley.

In the evenings it was difficult, impossible sometimes, to combat those memories. But in the mornings, particularly at high speed, or at sea, or engaged on a dangerous enterprise, he could beat them back, subdue them, force them into the attic rooms of his brain and lock the door. And there they would stay—for a week, a month, half a year— until some creeping reminder stole in and turned the key. Then, again, memories would come tumbling out to shame him.

Yes, they never failed to shame him, because he knew, beyond all argument, that the child had been made of gold —all sunlight and generosity and high ideals—whereas the man was at worst a leaden image, at best a steel one.

This morning he was strong, sure of himself and full of excitement. The past was not important and the future was all. He drove a little faster, knowing that soon he would reach the ragged fringes of London's dirty skirt, would be embroiled in a maddening muddle of the purposeless "civilization" which he despised: a mess of self-important little men, of giggling girls, of witless youths on brakeless bicycles, of harassed mothers with shopping baskets, dogs, infants, prams.

So much did this muddle infuriate him that he often left his car at Bert's Garage on the outskirts and continued his journey by train. And, since the beautiful morning seemed to have brought out every man, woman and child in the metropolis like some awful rash, he decided to do just that today, and so swung the Lagonda into the quiet concrete yard of Bert's establishment.

A gangling youngster whom he had never seen before emerged from the office, looking expectant.

Alan said, "Where's Bert?"

"Inside."

"Well, why the hell doesn't he come out and see an old pal?"

Surprisingly the boy said, "Oh cripes!" and scurried back to the office. Something was obviously afoot; something usually was at Bert's place. Alan waited.

Presently the boy reappeared, holding a large spanner, and began to open up the bonnet of the car. For a while he tinkered aimlessly, his corn-coloured hair falling forward to impede him.

A few minutes of this pantomime passed in silence. Then the boy emerged and turned back to the office. "Mr. Walker," he wailed plaintively. "Oh, Mr. Walker, come an' have a look at this distributor head."

Bert, at last, appeared at the office door, frowning. He nodded to Alan as though he had never seen him before, and peered into the engine for a while. Then he straightened up and leaned on the door of the car.

Alan said, "What's wrong?"

"Plenty. You bin up to anythink?"

"Not since last October."

Bert sniffed. "Someone has. There's a bloody copper been goopin' round here a fortnight now. Stupid mucker." He was staring, as he talked, a fraction of an inch past the young man's left ear. "'ullo, 'ullo." He whistled through his teeth.

"Where is he? On the other side of the road?"

Bert nodded. "An' he's just popped in his flippin' 'phone box too. Looks like you're being passed on, boy." He ran

26

a hand through black, wiry hair and cocked an eye at the man in the car. "You *sure* you bin a good boy?"

"Good as gold."

"Gold's good, all right," replied Bert, picking his teeth reflectively.

"Any news?" enquired Alan.

"Gawd, how should I know? Never had no one near me this last two weeks." He nodded across the road. "Not with him acting bloomin' watchdog, not muckin' likely." He grinned, suddenly at ease. "Puts you in the clear, Al, anyway. No one who'd been busy'd come within a mile of here these days." The grin faded. "But I wouldn't mind betting a tenner he's passed you on somewhere. I wonder where?"

The young man gestured to the boy to close up the bonnet. "I'll tell you where," he said. "S.D."

"What the flippin' hell's S.D. when it's at home?"

"Special Department, my old darling."

Bert grinned again. "Trust you to have something special after you."

"Lovely fellow called Farquarson. Francis Farquarson. Francis Kenneth Victor Farquarson."

"Gawd!" said Bert. "Quel moniker!"

"He collects old china and silver snuff-boxes and looks like a schoolmaster."

"Sounds nice," said Bert, grinning. "You must introduce us sometime. What's he after you for?"

"For Activities," replied Alan, slipping the gear lever, "outside The Law."

"Ah." Bert picked his teeth reflectively. "Well, if I were you I'd keep your activities moving, old cock, and go home."

"Home? Why?"

"Because monkey-face over there's plotting something with one eye on your number-plate."

"I can take it. They haven't got anything on me."

27

Bert sniggered. Alan gripped his arm and leaned towards him. "Evidence, Bert. Ever heard of evidence?"

"Strikes a bit of a bell. Why?"

"Because that's what they haven't got as far as I'm concerned."

Bert said, "Ah."

"And it's evidence," Alan added, "that puts you inside—or strings you up on the end of a bit of rope." He nodded towards the closed doors of Bert's garage. "I bet a clever copper could find enough evidence in there to keep you out of harm's way for a while, eh?"

Bert's eyes narrowed. Alan released his arm. "Well, they could take me to bits, Bert boy, and search until they were dizzy, and they wouldn't find a thing."

The big grey car swung away, leaving the garageman scratching his curly hair in bewilderment. You could never tell with Al Morgan, he was thinking. Everybody said the same, even Johnny MacBride; and MacBride should know if anybody did, because they had worked together—on and off—for years. If anybody knew what drove Al Morgan it ought to be Johnny MacBride; and yet he often said, "Al doesn't work with me, Bert, Al works with Al, and it's a good partnership, I can tell you. Maybe it's the only partnership that doesn't lead to trouble."

The premises of Gaye and Mountview Ltd., 13 St. Clair House, Piccadilly, were, to say the least of it, luxurious. They gave more the impression of *haute couture* than electrical engineering. Behind a grey desk in a grey-and-salmon-pink reception room a honey-blonde of petrified gentility welcomed him with guarded politeness.

"The name's Morgan," he said. "I have an appointment with Major Hobart."

She reached for the nearest of four grey telephones and

dialed with a pink pencil on which was inscribed in gold "Gaye and Mountview, At Your Service."

"Helloo," she said faintly. "Eu, Mejor Hubart, ai hev a Mr. Morgan for you . . . Raite away, Mejor."

She turned upon Alan a dazzling smile, and presently, as if by magic, there appeared a slick young man wearing, of course, a grey uniform.

Hobart, sitting behind a massive desk, clad in a sober suit of blue worsted, struck Alan as being more out of place than Hobart in tweeds at Wainport. Clearly he needed khaki to complete the reality.

He rose stiffly, registered surprise at the almost aggressive smartness of the younger man's clothing, and subsided again.

"On the tick," he observed, glancing at his watch with an aggrieved air.

Alan did not answer but leaned on the windowsill. He had nothing to say that would not be insulting.

"I'm afraid," said Hobart, "that my, er . . . that the gentleman in question is engaged at the moment."

"I can wait ten minutes."

"Yes. Hrrumph, er . . . Yes."

"You'd better tell him."

"Well . . ."

Turning, the young man became aware of the fact that the major was frightened of his employer. He had coloured, and as usual the pink of his face clashed horribly with the red-yellow of his moustache. The flush spread upwards over his balding pate and disagreed with the hair which surrounded it. *Altogether,* thought Alan with a pang of something like pity, *a most unattractive old bozo.* Aware of his own physical assets he invariably softened towards those who lacked them.

Major Hobart was saved from taking distasteful action by

a peremptory buzz from the office intercommunication on his desk. He flipped the switch and said, "Yes, sir."

His tone was so deferential that Alan was struck with sudden curiosity, sudden excitement.

"Where's Morgan?" demanded a disembodied, yet primely authoritative voice.

"Er . . . Here, sir, with me."

"Bring him in then." The voice implied, by its tone, ". . . for heaven's sake, you tiresome idiot."

The major said, "Yes, sir," again and stood up.

Alan regarded him with pity; it saddened him to see any grown man so abject, so completely another man's creature. "Who is this King of yours?" he enquired idly. But the answer dispelled idleness in a word.

"Kellandale," said Hobart, as reverently as if he had mentioned a deity—which, of course, he had. Yet, when he searched the young man's face for some sign of wonder, he found nothing. One of the first things Alan Morgan had learned under Johnny MacBride's tutelage had been to control his facial muscles. But his mind was electrified to galvanic activity; in a few seconds it flashed upon the screen of memory all that he knew of Lord Kellandale: a melee of combines and cartels, of acknowledged powers, and powers only half-hinted at, of enormous wealth and enormous prestige and enormous influence in unexpected but strategic places. Kellandale was the newspaper on five million breakfast tables; he was last year's Derby winner; he was the detective story on the bookstall, the penknife in a schoolboy's pocket or the packet of soap flakes in his mother's shopping basket. Kellandale's life blood was the sap of the rubber tree, was oil spouting from the well, was the continuous gush of a particularly scented fizzy drink to which teenagers the world over had become addicted. The brain reeled before any computation of Kellandale's *admitted*

30

connections; what went on beneath the surface was, perhaps mercifully, beyond comprehension. It was characteristic that his name had never been mentioned apropos Gaye and Mountview Ltd.

Hobart had by this time led Morgan down a corridor and had paused before what, from his expression, was evidently The Door. He knocked daintily and opened it.

Kellandale, rising to meet his visitor, was so exactly like the cartoonists' idea of him that Alan was momentarily dumbfounded. The big head—head of an Emperor—set upon the stocky body, the black, straight brows, the blue, bright eyes and the almost childish mouth above a mighty chin— they were all so well-known that any awe he had felt a moment ago was swept away, and he smiled.

Kellandale was possibly unused to the smiles of young men (too often they merely cowered) and his own smile in answer held something of uncertainty, which went strangely with the heavy power of his face. He seemed aware, also, of the shortness of his legs, for it was with apparent relief that he sat down behind the desk once more. Standing, he was a stockily built, ungainly man with a large head; sitting, he became an absolute ruler. From the waist up he was superb, and from the waist down almost ridiculous.

All this—and the blank, impersonal office with its uninhabited smell—Alan noticed at once. He became wary; his whole body tingled with expectancy, but he lounged a little in the deep leather chair because he suspected that lounging young men no less than smiling young men were something rare in Lord Kellandale's life.

For a while they regarded each other in silence, each recognising the other's mettle. There was still enough of plain Reg Harper, who had started life in the pits, left in Kellandale for him to appreciate hardness and individuality in the young. Surrounded as he was by servile youth, he felt a strange lifting of the heart to find that independence of spirit, arrogance and a sense of adventure were still to be found in connection with bright hair and hard muscles.

He said, "Hobart disapproves entirely of me giving away my identity to you."

"Hobart would," replied the young man evenly.

Kellandale grunted. "I'm a bad leader. I can't be sure that an order's been given properly unless I've given it myself. Always interfering."

Alan smiled at this. "I only trust myself," he said. "I find it pays."

The older man glanced at him sharply and away again. "Yes, it pays. You're a bit young to know it, all the same."

"I've learned the hard way—by experience."

"The best way." He turned his massive head and stared at the sky—puffs of white cloud sailing serenely on a pale sea. "You're probably the only person, in your . . . particular line of business, that I'd approach in this matter."

"I wonder why?" said Alan, knowing why, and clenching his hands against it.

"Because you're a . . . a gentleman. You come of a fine family, you went to a fine school—then to Cambridge . . ."

"I ran away from Cambridge," observed the young man in a dry, cold voice.

Kellandale nodded. "Yes. To go to sea."

"I was only a kid—therefore a fool. But you know what wars are." He seemed to be searching his memory for some clue which would make sense of the excitement, the bravura, of those early days of war.

"You liked the Navy?"

He glared. "We'll not discuss it, sir, if you don't mind." He refused to be impressed by this careful display of biographical details.

32

Kellandale stretched out an imperceptible claw. He said, "I see. You liked the Navy very much."

The young man stared at him with blank eyes.

"I," observed Kellandale, enjoying himself, "am not a gentleman, as you see. If an advantage presents itself I take it, mean or not. That's why I've got a lot of money."

It was impossible to say whether this naïveté was real or feigned. No one had ever been able to decide. It was part of the Kellandale legend.

But two can be naïve as well as one; Alan said, "I liked the Navy, yes. I bear it no grudge. As for a certain gaggle of ancient flag officers, that's another matter."

Brutally—for he intended to have the upper hand at any price—Kellandale said, "A court martial is the nastiest form of justice, in my opinion, because it prates so much about loyalty and honour."

"No," said Alan, dangerously quiet, "you are certainly not a gentleman."

Kellandale's hand gripped the edge of the desk. Otherwise he betrayed nothing.

The young man was quick to notice such things, however; he had been trained in a hard school. Follow a straight left with a right hook, MacBride always said. He followed:

"I must say, sir, I don't quite see why you feel you must have me under your thumb before you tell me what you want me to go to Germany for." (Kellandale stiffened: Alan had suspected that to mention Germany had not been part of Hobart's orders.) "I shall go—*if* I go—because of what you pay me, not because I admire you personally—or fear you, or love you, or whatever this wrestling match is supposed to make me do."

Kellandale stared. Finally: "Hobart said you were insolent."

"Hobart, in my opinion, is a fool."

33

"But useful. Loyalty and devotion are useful."

Alan could smile now. "Oh yes, and honour. Particularly in a court martial." He stood up suddenly, knowing that the older man would remain seated. Was there, he wondered, some psychological chain linking those absurd legs, supporting so magnificent a torso, and the Kellandale lust for power?

Standing, he said, "I'd like your money but I'm in no way reliant on it. If you want me to go to Germany for you I'll go; if not, we're simply wasting each other's time."

Kellandale stared for a full minute without answering; the blue eyes were almost hypnotic, so bright and unwinking. Then he smiled, a grim, slow smile of real pleasure.

"Yes, I want you to go. You're an impossible young man, as Hobart said, but that's probably why you're right for the job. Sit down."

Alan sat down.

"I want you," said Kellandale after a moment's thought, "to go and bring back a friend of mine. I gather that there are means of doing such a thing without worrying the authorities, and—" he glanced sideways—"that such a venture would not be . . . entirely new to you."

"Not entirely."

"You speak the language well, I take it."

"More or less perfectly. I had an uncle and aunt who lived in Austria, spent most of my school holidays there. The Austrian accent's a help as a matter of fact, makes me difficult to place."

Kellandale nodded, satisfied.

"I want to assure you that there's no *political* angle to the business. If I'm going to involve people in politics I always tell them. This man is, as I say, an old friend of mine, as well as an old business associate; he was once able to do me a good turn." He paused, caught up in some memory.

34

"Now he wants to leave Germany in order to join his son in Brazil. The son married a Brazilian before the war and Paul has not seen him since; there are children." He gestured. "You know how it is, particularly with Germans. Family feeling. Paul wants more than anything to see his grand-children." Again he brooded, then sighed. "As I say, he once did me a good turn. I feel I should repay it."

Alan knew that he was now expected to speak; he knew, also, what he was expected to say, and—because on this oc-casion he wished to know the answer—he said it.

"A man in your position has only to lift that receiver, get through to the Home Office, and ask for your good friend, the Secretary. The whole thing would be settled in five minutes."

Kellandale nodded. "A man in my position. Yes." He leaned forward. "Do you know what would happen if I did that? There'd be a hue-and-cry." He beat the desk with his fist. "Do you suppose that *any* move I make is taken at its face value? No. And quite properly not, too. Some years ago I was unwise enough to support a certain group who wished to save Kurt Schwartz; you've heard of Schwartz, the philosopher? The very sight of my signature alarmed my friends in the Government to such an extent that they started quibbling. Could there be a political significance?" He laughed sourly. "A political significance! That poor, harmless old man! While they were dithering, Schwartz was taken away, lined up with a lot of Communists and shot." Again he thumped the desk. "Any unusual action I take is noted down and examined. I am suspect—eternally and irre-trievably suspect. In the past on occasion—" he grinned boyishly—"I've put my finger into the political pie, and I don't pretend; I've never pretended. I'm a bloated capitalist par excellence, and I use workers, millions of 'em, for a funny old-fashioned purpose: I make 'em work." He sat back in

35

his chair. "If they couldn't discover a shady reason for my asking to get a German out of Germany, the press would damn soon invent one. Paul would find that life wasn't worth living—in Brazil or anywhere else—and I'd have to spend a lot of money denying rumours in order to keep people happy and preserve what is sometimes called public goodwill. I need public goodwill. Paul has got nothing to do with politics, I've promised you that, but Germany has, and so have I. The mixture would be fatal."

The young man, lounging in his armchair, frowned at the sky. He longed to turn to this man, this all-powerful, unbelievably rich man, and to say, *You're a liar, Lord Kellandale.* The argument was entirely convincing; no single word of it was untrue in all probability, and yet he, Alan Morgan, knew that in some devious way it all added up to a lie.

The question was: How much did he care? How much did it matter what Kellandale's motives were, or who this Paul might be, so long as the money was good? And he had no doubt now that the money would be more than good.

He wanted that money, and he wanted the excitement. He was filled with a sense of his own strength and ability, longing to pit them against whatever dangers might be implicit in this journey; he knew in his bones that there would be danger. And yet . . . and yet . . . Cooped up in a stuffy office watching those white clouds surge in from the west, he knew only a desire for freedom, for excitement and the sea—a desire to escape into that world where he was alone and dependent only on his own resources. And so he did not say, *You're a liar, Lord Kellandale.* He simply said: "Yes, I see. Very well, I'll do it."

The man behind the desk held out a photograph. "This is Paul Schröder. It's important you should be able to recognise him."

It was a curious face—a blank oval on which the features

had been fixed without regard for co-ordination. The light eyes—blue, it was stated in the list of characteristics pasted to the photograph—were too far apart, and their distance from the nose necessitated an endless sweep of eyebrow. Had the eyebrows been dark they might have linked nose and eyes into some sort of unity, but they were fair, almost invisible. And then the nose which should have been aquiline and long, joining eyes and mouth, and making some sort of division of the big face—the nose was short, tip-tilted, and the upper lip in consequence seemed never-ending: seemed, in fact, to sprawl away to a rounded, characterless chin. It was the face, Alan realised with a faint tingling of wariness, of a man who couldn't be trusted. Powerful in its components, yet weak as a whole. The face of a genius—or of an idiot. Once again, as he studied it, caution came tugging at his sleeve. *Don't go*, it whispered. *That man would let you down in an emergency.*

But he returned the photograph and said, "Couldn't very well miss him, could you?"

"He's tall," Kellandale continued. "Six foot two, and very fair." He drew a wallet from his pocket and extracted a thin sheet of paper which he unfolded.

"Schröder has been living in Berlin. Next Saturday he is going to stay with an old friend of his, a Frau Lantz, at a small country town called Neulingen, about fifteen miles southeast of Hannover. You'll need to remember her name and address: Frau Lantz, 17 Ludwigstrasse, Neulingen. They will be expecting you." He glanced up. Alan nodded.

"Do I need to give you any more information?"

"None. Except how much I'm to be paid."

Kellandale smiled grimly.

"It's important to me," he said, "as a matter of . . . of loyalty, if you like—a matter of friendship—that Schröder shall reach this country safely."

37

He paused, and Caution stepped up to Alan's shoulder again. *Isn't it clear?* came the craven whisper. *Isn't it abysmally clear that he is lying? All this friendship twaddle . . .*

"For that reason," Kellandale continued, "I am willing to pay you well." The hard, blue eyes were unwinking again, hypnotic. "I'm willing to pay you in direct proportion to the trouble you take . . ."

You see, cried Caution in sudden panic. *He means in proportion to the trouble you're going to walk into. You fool, you fool!*

But Kellandale's steady voice beat down all opposition. "A thousand pounds in advance. And a further sum, to be agreed upon by the two of us on your return—that sum to be not less than another thousand."

They stared at each other, striving in one last exertion of will power to read the other's thoughts. And in that moment of silent conflict Alan knew, as certainly as if Kellandale had spoken it in words, that he had been right all along: that there was a lie hiding in that forest of speech, and that there was danger waiting for him at Neulingen. He could not have been more certain had the man behind the desk said what his blank eyes so clearly stated:

Yes, I am offering you twice—at least twice—as much as the journey is worth on the surface. As to why I am offering so much, you may guess as you will. Obviously I have not told you the whole truth, but you are a hired adventurer, why should I tell you the whole truth?

Slowly, haltingly, the young man said, "I . . . I accept that, sir . . . on your own terms."

The tension between them was as taut as a quivering cable between two ships in a rough sea; the small impersonal office sang with tension.

Kellandale's eyes narrowed slightly. "On my own terms, what do you mean?"

38

"I mean," Alan replied carefully, "that I'm perfectly ready to do what you ask . . . as long as it's agreed that I am paid according to the . . . the difficulties I happen to encounter."

"That's what I said, isn't it?" snapped the man behind the desk, switching off the power of his eyes.

"Was it? I'm sorry. I'm a bit silly when it comes to business matters."

At this—as Alan had intended—faint colour touched the tips of Kellandale's ears. It was a long time before he spoke again.

"I think," he said gently, "that we understand each other."

"I think so too."

"Good. It's not necessary for me to add that this whole exploit will never be mentioned in connection with my name. In the event of any . . . difficulties, you are entirely on your own."

"Yes."

"In fact you are on your own from the moment you leave this room." He raised his head and gave the young man a blank look. "If any . . . any rumours were to arise, I should squash them. I should deny all knowledge of you or your actions."

"Of course."

"And if," he added heavily, "things were to go awry—which won't happen, of course—and you were to make any ill-considered remarks . . . You understand?"

"Perfectly."

"I would not hesitate to destroy you." He laughed, as if to rob the remark of its ugliness. "I think you would expect it."

"Yes. I'd expect it."

Kellandale observed him with something surprisingly like a twinkle in his eye. "It's strange," he said, "but our respective . . . professions have much in common."

"I've always thought so, sir."

"That's probably why I trust you, we're alike in so many ways. And yet I'm going up, whereas you're going down."

The young man flushed.

"I," Kellandale continued, in explanation, "have just bought a house very like the one you once knew as a child. If it had been in better repair I might even have bought Ladeleigh."

Silence.

"I looked at Ladeleigh, you know. The Army and the Allies damaged it shockingly."

Alan was on his feet before he knew it. "I don't wonder," he said, surprised at the calmness of his voice, "that so many people dislike you so intensely."

Kellandale seemed to brush this barb aside.

"Don't tell me you're a sentimentalist. I don't believe it." He also stood up, a trifle ponderously, and came round from behind his desk. "As I was saying, my son is at Cambridge now—not unlike you in some respects. He is a pretty good imitation of a gentleman already." Again the naïveté flashed out; he looked almost benign as he stood there thinking of his son. Reg Harper, one-time pit boy turned lord and millionaire.

But a furious anger pounded in Alan's head, and found vent in words. "I wonder," he said, as casually as the anger allowed, "I wonder what makes you so determined to be top dog, always." And he let his eyes wander slowly down the big body to those short, disproportionate legs. And, faintly, he forced himself to smile.

Kellandale turned abruptly to the window, and his big hands were working—clenching, unclenching, clenching, unclenching. The young man was exhilarated by the sureness of his aim—he had fired, after all, in the dark—but he knew a light touch of fear also.

40

Without turning Kellandale said, "That's all, I think. When you return, get in touch with Hobart here. On no account approach me. You understand?"

"Yes."

He turned then, perfectly under control, but cold with repressed fury. He prided himself on being proof against the taunt of his damnable legs; dear God, hadn't the cartoonists made them a commonplace joke? But, he realised, no one had ever drawn deliberate attention to them—not for twenty years or more. He hated the irony which made it impossible for him to show his anger to the insolent, unforgivable young man who confronted him, still smiling; the only young man among the thousands he employed who could not be antagonised—could not be dismissed—could not, with any safety, even be told what a damned insolent young man he was. And well he knew it.

"Good-bye," said Lord Kellandale. "Good luck."

Alan met the blue eyes steadily. "Thanks for the luck," he said. "I have a feeling I shall need it."

He turned, but some ominous overtone in the taut young voice had caught inexplicably at the older man's imagination. He said, "Wait a minute."

When Alan turned back, Lord Kellandale was fumbling with his wallet again.

"Here. Take this." He held out a thin white envelope. "I hadn't meant to give it you, but this . . . this thing is important to me. I owe something, and I like to pay my debts without fail. Take it." He watched the young man carefully. "Now listen. If, while you're in Neulingen, you find yourself in any . . . trouble, you may open that envelope; inside you will find the name and address of a man who will help you. If you are forced to open it, you will destroy the contents at once. Understood?"

"Yes."

41

"On the other hand I would prefer to get the envelope back as it is—unopened."

Casually, because at every point he knew he must counter the man that faced him, Alan thrust the envelope into a trouser pocket. *You have not,* the gesture said, *got the better of me, my lord.*

"And the money?" he enquired.

"I'll have it sent." The contempt which Kellandale induced into his voice was not quite genuine—perhaps because he found nothing contemptuous about money.

They neither of them spoke again; they parted in silence and anger. But the young man knew, as he went softly down the carpeted corridor, that it would be Kellandale who would suffer because, whatever he might say, it mattered to him a great deal that Herr Paul Schröder should reach England safely—and his reasons were not purely sentimental either.

To the genteel lady at the reception desk Alan said, "Is there a back way out of this place?"

"Eu yiss," she replied, waving her pink pencil vaguely. "When you stip out of the lift, take first left, second raite. It comes out in Paton Street."

"Thank you so much." He smiled. "My wife is waiting at the front. You know how it is."

Her eyebrows shot up so high that they threatened to become lost in her hair.

There was no harm in going out the back way. Had not my Lord Kellandale himself said, "You are on your own from the moment you leave this room"?

Besides, somewhere out there in the bright streets, Farquarson would be waiting for him.

3 – STRAIGHT AND CROOKED MEN

HE HAD LEARNED NEVER TO AVOID FARQUARSON. IF HE KNEW,
or even suspected, that Farquarson was looking for him he
went out of his way to be found quickly; otherwise that
quiet, undistinguished but infinitely cunning man was apt
to appear at the least desirable moment. He was apt to
catch you talking to somebody in whose company you had
no wish to be seen, or he stepped quietly up to your elbow
in a post office, knowing as well as you did what the parcel
you were handing across the counter really contained.

For this reason, as soon as he left St. Clair House, Alan
went straight to the quiet Square where he had parked the
Lagonda, pausing on the way only to buy a couple of shirts
so that, parcel in hand, he might have an adequate excuse
for returning to his car.

As soon as he turned the corner into the Square he saw
that he had been right: Farquarson was sitting in the driving
seat, a newspaper balanced on the wheel, eating something
out of a paper bag. Alan approached carefully, keeping out
of view. Then, for a time, he stood leaning against the
Square railings, watching.

Farquarson was slightly plump and very fair—he looked
somewhat like an overgrown pink baby. His features, like
a child's features, were ordinary and hard to recall once he
was out of sight. He dressed without care, a fat, pink, overgrown and untidy infant. But his eyes were another matter;
for through them, unless he was careful, flashed the razor-
edged sharpness of his mind. In their soft brown depths,
it was possible to see quite another Farquarson whose name
was spoken with a lowering of the voice, a quick glancing
towards the door. The rest of the man might give an impression of laborious ennui, but the eyes were a contradic-

tion; they proved some of the ominous stories told about him.

After a time Alan became aware that the two driving mirrors of the Lagonda had been set at unusual angles to give a maximum back view to whoever sat in the driver's seat. In one of them he met Farquarson's bright, brown eye.

"I wondered," Farquarson said, "whether you were contemplating violence on my pairson." It pleased him to produce one word occasionally and pronounce it with a flourish of his otherwise imperceptible Scottish accent: it was a pleasantly absurd habit, and it strengthened in some subtle way his resemblance to a schoolmaster. It was the kind of trick that a dominie might have cherished.

"Contemplating," Alan said, "but not violence."

Farquarson nodded. "And how are you keeping?"

"Very fit." He moved up to the car and leaned against it. "And you?"

"Fair. Fair." He took a ham sandwich from the paper bag and bit into it.

"You've prepared a siege, I notice," Alan said.

"Well, how could I tell when you'd put in an appearance —an erratic young lad like you."

"Here I am, all the same. Fire away."

Farquarson, munching, examined him with interest. "Have you retired?" he asked finally. "Taken my advice like a wise laddie, eh?"

"Yes," said Alan promptly. "It got boring."

Farquarson nodded. "Purely an adventurer, that's what you are. I wouldna call you a crook at all."

"So you said before."

"Pity," he continued evenly, "about poor John MacBride."

Alan's heart missed a beat. It was an old trick of Farquarson's this—to slip in a punch below the belt when all

44

seemed quiet and friendly. He forced himself to keep silence.

"But there." Farquarson put a crust back into the bag. "There, as I say. Poor MacBride was never an educated laddie like yourself. Pairsonally I had no respect for his brain whatsoever. And he slipped up. Of course, he slipped up." He glanced at the young man's face and was irritated to find it blank. "Och," he added, "I agree with you, it's of no interest. No interest whatever."

Alan was searching his memory in a frenzy to find out when he had last had word of Mac; in his bones he knew that Farquarson was lying—for some devious purpose of his own. MacBride *was* clever, as clever as the rest of them put together, a genius, not only at evasion, but at finding new lines where evasion would pay. It was he, 'way back in the old rough-and-tumble days, who had organised that endless chain of soldiers and airmen, each one returning from the Continent on leave with a couple of wrist watches strapped round either ankle or with a bottle of wine, declared and paid for at the customs, full of Chanel No. 5. It was he who saw the lovely simplicity of sending a grey-painted launch, manned by naval ratings into French ports for small cargoes of dutiable goods. No. He was sure in his mind that MacBride had not slipped up. To Farquarson he said, "A fellow like you oughtn't to have to tell wopping great lies. I may not be living in London but I know what goes on."

Farquarson rubbed his nose. "Smart, Al, that's what you are. Smart." His guilelessness was fascinating. "I'm thirsty. I'd like a beer."

They went to a quiet pub off Jermyn Street.

"All right," Farquarson said over his tankard, "I'll lay my cards on the table." This was the moment, Alan knew, when the smooth sandy man in a creased suit and an overcoat too heavy for warm spring weather was at his most dangerous. "You didn't believe me about Mac. I wouldn't expect a clever young lad like you to believe such an obvious fabrication. Dear me, no." He stared disconcertingly, and Alan found himself colouring.

"*Pre*-cisely," said Farquarson. "Dear me, it's a great pleasure to be talking to someone intelligent for a change. That's what I deplore about my profession—it leads one to consort with nitwits. However . . ."

Yes. Alan saw now that the lie about MacBride's arrest had simply been Farquarson's way of laughing at his own lie about having "retired".

"Ah yes," he was saying now. "They say you have a fine boat down there at . . . at . . . Bless my soul, don't tell me, I'll have it in a second."

"Wainport," said Alan harshly.

Farquarson blinked. "Ah yes. Wainport. A fine boat."

"A *sailing* boat."

Their eyes met.

"Aye, so I was told." He brooded.

It didn't matter what he had heard about Wainport, but did he, Alan wondered, know where the *Bonaventure* had spent her winter? If he did. . . .

Swiftly Alan said, "I sold my old boat. I didn't want to, but I needed the money. The *Bonaventure*, you remember?"

"Ah, do I not? A lovely craft."

"Fast, too," added Alan, watching intently now. "Chap took her to the Med, I believe. Nice trip that—across France by river and canal. I'd like to make it one day."

Farquarson flashed him a straight look of sudden intensity. "Why not take it now?" he said. Even his voice had changed.

After a moment Alan said, "Why now?"

"Because if you don't you're going to get into trouble."

46

He held up a fat hand to forestall speech. "I know, I know: you've had a nice quiet winter. So has MacBride. But it's spring now, and you won't sit quiet much longer, either of you." He leaned forward. "I know you both and I know you well; I know you so well that if I'd been able to make certain pairsons act when I told them to . . . *If* . . . Then you wouldn't be here talking to me today."

It was a threat. It was the nearest to the true Farquarson, the man behind the eyes, that he had ever approached; and he knew that what had been said was true: it bore the imprint of truth as surely as the story of MacBride's arrest had been palpably a lie. He felt the chill fingers of fear caressing his spine.

Farquarson had leaned back once more, peering gloomily into his beer. The moment of plain speaking was evidently over. Now they would return to evasion and counterevasion.

"And so?" he contrived to say, evenly.

"And so," replied Farquarson, never taking his eyes off the amber liquid, "and so I advise you to take that trip." He glanced up. "I like you, Al my boy, and it's my opinion that prevention really is better than cure. Colonel Patchway agrees with me."

Patchway was Farquarson's chief. He sat, an unseen almighty spider, in the centre of the web of Special Department.

"By the way, laddie, he wants to have a word wi' ye."

Alan was taken unawares by this fantastic statement. Mentally, he recoiled. It had been said that S.D. occasionally picked recruits from the other side of the fence, but surely they couldn't imagine that he, Alan Morgan . . . He smiled at the thought.

"Not angling for my soul, are you?" he enquired. "You and the Colonel?"

Farquarson ignored him. "Any time this afternoon," he said. "Now that's generous. The Chief's a busy man."

"He must want me badly."

"You're too good for this game, Al. A chap with your schooling and family . . ." He broke off, as if suddenly aware of anger in the young man's eyes. "We understand what made you go this way, of course. That court martial was a mistake, no doubt about it. . . ."

"Have you finished with me?" Alan said. "Can I go now, please?"

Farquarson nodded. "That's a raw wee temper you've got hidden away, laddie. I wonder it hasn't tripped you up long ago." He pushed his beer away—almost a full tankard. "I hope you'll get to see the Colonel. It might be to your own advantage."

"I'll try. I've a lot to do."

"Have you now?" said Farquarson idly. "Well, keep off the drink; it never did anybody any good."

Alan stood up and looked down at him. "Now what the hell does that mean?"

"Your friend Bob Smiles was drunk when he made a fool of himself. Six years, they gave him."

"No friend of mine."

"No?"

"No."

Farquarson could look dazed sometimes—vacant, mental almost; it was an expression to be wary of. Alan left him sitting in the corner, brooding over a pint of beer he would not drink. As soon as the young man had gone, however, a complacent smile spread over the policeman's face.

Alan was glad, after the silent menace of that too-gentle, too-knowing schoolmaster, to lose himself in the chatter and clatter of Berwick Street Market. In the bright sunlight the tiers of fruit, flowers and vegetables glowed and glittered, emanating a brilliant light of their own. He luxuriated in the impersonal faces and the impersonal stares, in the colour and the smell, like a boy let out of school.

Rocky was standing by a stall, arms akimbo, shouting obscenity at someone across the narrow street. Alan came up behind him quietly and said, "I want a nice carrot for my donkey, please."

The young man turned, eyes wide, brown face startled under untidy black hair. "Strike a bloody light," he said. "Creepin' up behind a bloke like that! Thought you was a flattie." He grinned, eying the smart suit. "What are you on now, anyway? Taking a duchess for a ride?"

Alan grinned back; it was impossible not to when confronted with Rocky. His plain face, tip-tilted nose and bright eyes had the innocence of a child's. He said, "Care for a drink, Mr. Rockingham?"

"Don't mind if I do. Half a jiff." He peered through the screen of gladioli at the back of the stall and shouted. "Alf. Hey, Alf— I'm going for a drink. All right?"

"Thirsty bastard," replied the invisible Alf. "Don't be long. Got to sell this lot today."

They strolled away through the crush and glitter of the market.

Alan said, "Heard anything about MacBride?"

"Yes. Saw him yesterday. He'd got that redhead with him again, so I guess she must be his missus." (So much for Farquarson.) Rocky helped himself to a grape off a barrow in passing and avoided the feint which its owner directed at him. He was small and wiry, restless with energy and high spirits; he seemed to be well known in Berwick Street—people waved at him and smiled, always they smiled. A large Italian woman was haggling over asparagus.

49

He pinched her ample bottom in passing and was sworn at good-naturedly in her native tongue.

Alan knew that he could trust Rocky: there was a bond between them—a double bond, in fact. In the first place both had served in the Navy and could use to each other an assortment of slang which placed them slightly apart from the rest of MacBride's team. There was more to it than that, however. He remembered the scene in the boat-house vividly: the light of the hurricane lamp on the ring of faces, the slapping of water against the wooden walls and the creak of hawser as the *Bonaventure* jerked in impatience, the song of wind in the eaves and under the doors, the rattle of window and spatter of rain. Even the smell of pitch and seaweed was clear in his memory . . .

MacBride had stared round in silence at the men's faces. "All right," he said. "Dawson's gone, as you probably know. I'm not sorry and I don't suppose you are." The wind buffeted the wooden walls and roared away down the estuary. "I daresay you've been wondering who Mr. Morgan here is. Well, he's your new skipper. He came along on the last trip to have a look at you and he knows what's what, I can tell you." Again he stared round the silent faces. "He knows what's what," he repeated, "and he didn't like what he saw."

There was a murmur, then—a grim mutter of complaint. The eyes were switched to Alan, hostile, resentful.

MacBride said, "He's going to pick the men he wants and that'll be the end of it. All right, Al."

He had stood then face to face with the sullen men, and he was pleased, perhaps surprised, to find that he did not fear them.

The first that he had picked was Rocky. He did this because he had watched him working, watched him sure-fingered and quick over the recalcitrant engine while they had wallowed uneasily in the basin at Le Havre. He recognised then—long before he knew that Rocky had been in the Navy, even before he knew that the others led him a dog's life—that the boy could be trusted and was not afraid of work. Only later, from snippets of talk and from what Rocky had told him, he discovered that this had been a turning point in the little Cockney's life; by such accidents, by such trivial accidents, were these things accomplished. Rocky found respect, and Alan found a life-long ally because of that sullen moment in the boathouse . . .

They turned into a pub, loud with the chatter and clatter of market midday. When they had retired to a corner with their pints Alan said, "Rocky, I've got a job on."

The bright eyes glanced up. "With Mac? I thought . . ."

"No, not with Mac. This is on my own."

"Same stunt. Smuggling aliens?"

"Hardly. It's one bloke."

"V.I.P. eh?"

"More or less. Are you on?"

"You bet I am."

"Don't you want to know what's in it?"

Rocky shook his head. "Selling fruit gets me," he said. "Anything for a change."

"Anyway, there'll be a couple of hundred quid for you, maybe more."

Rocky became wary suddenly. "What the hell is it? New York and back?"

Alan laughed. "As far as you're concerned it's Antwerp and back—keep an eye on the boat at old Poiret's place for a day or two in between."

"Someone must be forking out."

"Someone is."

The brown face under the shock of hair broke into its grin. "It'll be a pleasure, skip. When do we start?"

"We get the boat first—or rather you do."

Rocky bit his forefinger thoughtfully. "Going to use the old *Bonny?*"

"Yes. She's been laid up at Turner's place all winter; he says she's in fine condition. Nothing you won't be able to fix up in a day's hard work."

"You can trust Rocky, skip."

Yes, he could trust Rocky—that was the point. There was something very reassuring about that trust, something reassuring about the compact, wiry little man with the anchor tattooed on his left forearm, his eyes very bright under the uncontrollable forelock—reminiscent of one of the smaller, hairier dogs. When he walked—and his walk was springy, cocky—the forelock bounced up and down over his forehead.

"What's the rest of the dope, then?" he said. "Who's the passenger?"

Alan was drinking. He lowered the glass and stared at the froth in it. "I've got to go into Germany and get him," he said. "I don't know who he is."

Rocky whistled. "Why can't he walk out, same as the rest?"

"I don't know. It doesn't matter. I'm being paid to get him, that's all."

The other took this, or the tone of voice in which it was said, as a warning. He shrugged but he was still frowning. "And I stay in Antwerp?"

"Yes, you stay in Antwerp, amongst all those lovely ladies."

"Lovely, maybe, but too expensive for this boy." He grinned. "So I'm the gash hand."

"Far from it. You're in charge of the motor, God help you. I'm not touching it."

Rocky sighed. "You don't treat 'em right. You can't get temperamental with an engine—they don't understand. Gentle and easy does it."

52

Alan flicked his glass so that it pinged. "*You* do it, Rocky, that's all I care." He straightened up from the wall against which he was leaning. "All right then, you're on?"

"Sure, I'm on. Good oh. 'Special sea dutymen to your stations.'"

A strange shadow crossed Alan's mind. Abruptly he said, "You should've stayed in the Andrew, Rocky."

"Me?" He brushed back the forelock, staring up. "Me? Gawd forbid—all spit and polish in peacetime."

But Alan only said, "You should've stayed in. Anyway, what the hell made you take up this racket?"

"Swelp me," said Rocky. "What's come over you, skip? Sally Army been at you?"

Alan laughed then, but the shadow still lay over him; he hated himself or the world. What was it, in any case, that made a man step outside the limits of the law: circumstance, or inclination? Which had got at Rocky, the little man that people loved, little man with an upturned nose and an anchor on his arm, who had been mentioned in dispatches three times, who had a girl called Vera in Campden Town?

He said, "How's Vera, Rocky?" in order to hide from the mood which pursued him.

"Vee?" Rocky blew his nose. "I ditched her, skip."

"You did?"

"Too true I did. Found she was messin' around with another feller." He grinned. "Well, skip—ought to be getting back to me bleeding grapes, I suppose, or our Alf'll be having twins on the pavement. I'll nip along, and get going on the *Bonny* this evening."

"That'll be fine. Bring her down the river to Wainport tomorrow afternoon. You remember Wainport?"

"Certainly I do. Smashin' piece called Eileen in the post office."

53

"Eileen's married." He smiled, and Rocky grinned back. And there was something so frank, so open, so utterly uncomplicated about that grin that he couldn't help saying, "What made you take it up anyway, Rocky?"

"What? The Life of Kerrime, you mean?"

He nodded.

Rocky rubbed his chin. "Dunno, really. Yes, I do. Can you see me going back to the timberyard after five years in the Andrew? Saying, 'Yes, Mr. Crowthorne,' 'No, Mr. Crowthorne,' every time the old bastard shows his head? D'you know, I went down there the day after I was demobbed—remember it like it was yesterday—and the geezer on the gate says, 'Have you a union card, Rockingham?' Sounded like a blinkin' gunnery instructor, and I told him so. I said, 'No, have you?' and he says, 'Of course,' classy-like. 'Well,' I says, 'I'll tell you what to do with it.'" Rocky grinned. "And I did, and I walked straight home without even going in. That ends instalment one of how Eric Percy Rockingham took the wide and crooked . . . So long, skip. I'll let you know how it goes." And he turned away, strutting along the pavement towards Berwick Market, his forelock bouncing over his forehead as he went.

Alan, leaning at the door of the pub, saw him pluck another grape from the same barrow, dodge the same friendly blow, pick up a carrot and throw it; then he was lost to view in the crowd.

Alan strolled away in the opposite direction, bored with his own feelings. It was unreasonable, he told himself, to be angry, to let that insinuating melancholy catch hold of him, merely because a petty crook of his acquaintance wasted an essential honesty on what he mockingly called "a Life of Kerrime." Was it circumstance? Was it Rocky's sudden hatred of officialdom ("Have you a union card, Rockingham?") like his own hatred of it ("This is not the behaviour, Lieutenant Morgan, that we can tolerate in an officer of the Royal Navy")? Oh, the hypocrisy of it, the bloody hypocrisy! Why had Kellandale had to drag it all up again from the deep well of half-forgotten memories? For months now all that bitterness had lain dormant. But now he could no longer subdue his anger; he let it surge through him. The president of the court martial had said, "Your attitude is not reasonable, Lieutenant Morgan. No one is going to pretend that all men are perfect; in war-time particularly there will be certain . . . er, certain lapses from discipline. But you are charged with wholesale smuggling. That is another matter entirely . . ." In fact the officer could have said, "It is one thing to commit a crime, quite another to be caught." And yet it was reasonable and just that he should be punished; the Navy was always reasonable and just and he could bear it no malice. What he resented was the hypocrisy: the neat wrappings of forms in triplicate tied up with red tape which proclaimed to the world, "This young officer, whom we had trusted, has been found guilty of behaviour unbefitting to his uniform, be-haviour well-nigh unheard-of in His Majesty's Armed Forces. He will therefore be dismissed the Service just to show what honourable men we are." Could they not have been honest? Could they not rather have said, "This fellow Mor-gan's a bloody fool. We all do a bit of quiet fiddling on occasion—who wouldn't?—but if the idiot has got to get caught red-handed, then it's time he learned some discre-tion. Out you go, my lad!"

He had wandered down into Piccadilly Circus Under-ground Station, and for a while he stood watching the crowds. Grim-faced, grey-faced, harassed, they flowed up or down the escalators in a passionless, lifeless flood. Apathy ruled them, apathy enveloped them; their minds were only fixed on bills to be paid, rises in salary to be wangled, bath-

55

room ceilings to be replastered, winter vests to be purchased for Harold now that summer was here and they'd be cheaper. *The business of living*, it was called. Business of living, indeed! Was that living? The week of slavery and the week-end on the Co-operative Society's tennis courts or in Epping Forest tripping over the lovers?

His anger left him suddenly and he was glad—glad for himself, glad for Rocky—that at least they were free men; and if they did make profit from the gullibility and greed of the crowd, what of that? If this, this creeping trail of shadows, was the crowd then, Heaven knows, they deserved it. He despised them, hated them even. Dear God, how complacent! He slammed into a telephone box and dialed the number Farquarson had given him. He wanted to get to grips with something. Better, oh better far, to accept the threat, to accept the challenge, to go out and face danger, than to wallow among the sloths. (Outside the glass door of the box they swam to and fro like pallid deep-sea fishes.)

A woman's voice said, "S.D.3, Secretary speaking."

"Is that Colonel Patchway's office?"

"Yes, sir."

"Mr. Farquarson told me that the Colonel wanted to see me. Morgan's the name."

"Yes, Mr. Morgan, he said you might ring."

"I'd like to come this afternoon."

"One moment, please."

The clatter of a typewriter came to him distantly, and a man's voice saying, ". . . anyway he wants it at once. You'd better . . ." A telephone rang.

After a moment she returned. "Colonel Patchway is very busy today, but he could fit you in at seven this evening or in five minutes' time, whichever suits you best."

"I'll come now."

56

"Very good, Mr. Morgan. You know where we are, do you?"

"Whitehall?"

"Oh no." She seemed amused. "Amaryllis Street, off Belgrave Square. Number one."

"All right. Five minutes."

He slammed down the receiver and pushed out of the box, ran up the subway stairs two at a time to the surprised ejaculations of some of the sloths who were caught there in a helpless, ineffectual clot of parcels and infants, dodged across the street and grabbed a taxi from under the nose of an important looking man with a brief case and a neatly rolled umbrella.

Lying back as they moved off, he felt better.

Number one, Amaryllis Street, was not quite what he expected of a Government office. Some pains had been taken to make it habitable. The hall did not seem to have been changed since its conversion from a private house. Upstairs, however, the dull portraits of somebody's ancestors and the gilt console tables gave way to chromium and light oak; it was businesslike but not bleak. The secretary was plain—"a sensible girl"—but she had shrewd eyes; he wondered how much she knew: whether the shrewdness was a carefully affected pose—he had met women engaged on secret work before—or whether she did indeed have access to Patchway's famous dossiers. He suspected the former. Presumably S.D. knew better than to trust women —other than their accredited and reliable female agents, of course.

She said, in a faintly surprised voice, "Colonel Patchway will see you now, Mr. Morgan."

He wondered whether Farquarson was kept waiting; he hoped so.

The room into which she showed him was large—the

drawing room of a bygone era, presumably. Far away in a dazzle of sunlight sat a man at a desk. Alan advanced towards him. The face was distinguished, heavily lined, a long face scored by two parallels, the deep hollows of the cheeks and the deep furrows dropping from nose to edges of mouth. A straight nose between these made it all into a mask of perpendiculars—a disquieting mask with dark, quick eyes. Colonel Patchway looked more like a well-known Harley Street specialist or a leading K.C. than a soldier—perhaps because his strange life contained more of medicine and law than it did of the military. His hair was fine and grey, scanty as if it had never been otherwise. He looked weary, and his voice when he spoke was weary also.

So this was the great Patchway. He did not look formidable, but then neither did Farquarson. He said, "One moment. Please sit down." Then he continued writing, the sunlight catching his hair. A bluebottle buzzed and tapped about the ceiling. There were roses on the desk, blood-red, full-blown, drooping a little in the heat of the sun.

He finished writing and looked up. "Excuse me," he said. "We're exceedingly busy."

Alan smiled.

"Of course. That must amuse you." He pushed away the papers before him and leaned back, closing his eyes. Obviously he was dismissing one subject and considering another. Finally he said, "I suppose it's rather unorthodox asking you to meet me like this. What I'm going to say is more unorthodox still. However . . ." He flicked open a pale blue file—one of the famous dossiers, no doubt. The bright eyes were quick and sharp in the tired mask.

"I have a theory, which you will probably think absurd, that prevention is better than cure."

Alan said, "Well, it's a theory."

The other screwed up his mouth and shrugged; he did not

58

raise his eyes from the blue file. He said, "What I'm going to say will seem personal, if not insulting. You may even lose your temper, they often do. I haven't the time for tactful pleasantries."

"I prefer it neat."

"All right, you can have it. Your court martial now—did it . . . cause you much unhappiness? Family and so on, I mean?"

Alan was surprised, but in his present mood not inclined to intimacy. "No," he lied. "I don't hold much brief for my family anyway."

Patchway nodded. "Then I would be wrong in supposing that you took to . . . to your present way of life as a direct result of that incident."

"As a result, possibly."

Colonel Patchway began to tap his lips with a pencil; the eyes were fixed in a point of concentration. "I said at the time that it was a mistake. It's always a mistake to sacrifice an individual to a policy, but . . ." He shrugged and embarked at a tangent. "You went to an exceptionally fine school. You did well. You even appear to have worked at your University. In fact, you're a well-educated and intelligent young man."

"I was."

"And . . ." He gesticulated. "Well-born also. With a fine record of service in the war."

"For what it's worth."

There was another silence. Then, "Morgan, isn't it about time you pulled yourself together?"

Alan was angry suddenly with this omnipotent, super-schoolmaster. He said, "Is it?"

"You know perfectly well what I mean."

Alan grinned. "And you know what I mean too, sir."

The other stared, hard and long, and there was at that

moment such . . . almost, compassion in his eyes that the young man was startled. If possible, the voice had become more weary when next he spoke. "Listen, listen," he said. "Don't go off into heroics and all the rest of the belligerent hard-luck claptrap. I know it, I know it backwards: the world owes you a living; you were made an example, a scapegoat, an Aunt Sally; you don't want advice, you don't want a job on a stool in the city, you want to get your own back. Oh God, don't tell me. They come in here and they sit where you're sitting now and they trundle it all out. . . ." He broke off suddenly and rapped the desk with the flat of his hand. A rose petal fell. "*After* they've been caught," he added. "They sit there and they cry, some of them. Debenham—you probably knew Debenham—well, *he* wept. Lot of good it did him I must say. He shot himself in the end, you know."

Alan said, "I shan't oblige you either by shedding walrus tears or by shooting myself." He was angry. "But I appreciate the psychology."

"I'm not trying to frighten you."

"Well, what are you trying to do?"

They stared at each other—a tense, hostile stare. Another petal fell from the rose.

The older man pressed his fingers into his eyes and smoothed the skin outwards; he was obviously overworked to the point of despair.

"I'm trying to warn you off," he said.

"Why, in God's name?"

Patchway held up a rose petal and looked at it. The crimson glowed like velvet against his long dry fingers.

"Because," he said, "I knew your mother, and . . . and had a great respect for her."

This struck the young man like a slap in the face, and, like a slap in the face, it left him momentarily shocked into a vacuum before the sudden rush of temper; and his temper took the form of a tone of voice. He said, "Strike a bloody light, I might have known it."

The fury and the cruelty in the words were real, almost tangible. They brought a quick flood of colour into the older man's face.

Alan stood up; he was trembling. "You'd stop at nothing in this little mutual-admiration group of yours, would you? No wonder the poor victims weep all over the place."

"I didn't mean. . . ."

"I don't give a damn in Hades what you didn't mean, but it just so happens that you've pulled the wrong knob this time."

"You'd better go." He showed no anger.

"I'll say I'd better go, and then you can put Farquarson onto me and let him arrange one of his 'accidents'."

Patchway pressed a button on his desk.

Alan stood in silence facing him. He said again, "No wonder they weep. You'd have to either weep or puke."

The lined face was haggard suddenly. He said, "Farquarson told me it wouldn't be any good. You know what this means?"

"Certainly I do—the end of a beautiful relationship. From now on it'll be a matter of evidence." He heard the door open behind him.

Patchway said, "Well, it's your own choice."

"Yes, it's my own choice and it always will be. Individuals versus bureaucrats." He turned, looked at the man who waited expectantly by the door, and laughed. "Send him away. I'm not dangerous. I just happen not to like sentiment; I'm going anyway."

Patchway said, "All right, Jameson."

The door closed, a shade regretfully perhaps.

Alan said, "What amuses me is that though you're on

61

the side of the angels you have to use our methods." He laughed. "You'd find it far more profitable to come in with us, you know. Or do they pay civil servants these days?"

Patchway picked up the rose petal again. "You," he said, "could also come in with us."

"Ha." He beat his fists together. "I wondered if that would come. Informer, eh?" He felt on top of the world for no very good reason. "I'd rather cry my eyes out for the edification of the good dog Farquarson. I imagine he's a sadist of sorts."

Patchway said, "Good-bye."

"Tell me I've signed my own death warrant, please. Things won't seem complete otherwise."

"Isn't that a little previous?" He tore the petal in half.

"A little. But surely the fact that I haven't done murder wouldn't deter Farquarson in the execution of his duty?"

The long brittle fingers tore the petal again, wearily destroying beauty; and yet the former compassion—there was no other word for it—had crept back into his face. "You mean," he said, "that you haven't done murder—*yet*." He did not, even then, look up from the torn petal. It was as if he could see, without the use of his eyes, the spasm—was it further anger, or was it by any chance fear?—which crossed the young man's face.

4 – LADY WITH A WANDERLUST

As soon as she heard the knock on the door she knew who it was, and as soon as she opened the door, still struggling with the belt of her dressing gown, she knew that he was drunk. Not riproaring drunk, nor rollicking drunk—nor, she was glad to notice, in a state of amorous alcoholism. He was just very, very drunk, dismally and resignedly so. He peered at her, his grey eyes owlish in a pale face. And how his excesses had washed the lines from that face; it was almost boyish, if flabby, and for the first time since she had known him it was relaxed.

"Well," she said. "You knocked. Come in."

He came in. "You were in bed." It was an accusation, but presumably leveled at himself. "I'm most awfully sorry." He contrived a thin pure *s* with difficulty, and he was amazingly steady. She rather admired him in his cups, for he had evidently stowed away a great deal of drink.

He smiled. "I can't pretend," he said. "I'm stinko. Stinko profundo." He frowned. "Profundissimo." And he sat down heavily in her only kitchen chair.

Linda filled a kettle and put it on to boil. "D'you want food as well?" she enquired.

"Lady, you're too kind. As well as what?"

"As well as Alka Seltzer and coffee."

He blinked. "No. No, I think I'd better not eat." He stood up and walked, a trifle unsteadily after sitting still for a time, to the window over the sink.

"Beautiful," he said. "Isn't that beautiful?"

She joined him, and observed that he had driven the Lagonda down The Cove almost to the water's edge—luckily it was high tide—and had left the headlights on. The powerful beam shone straight down the estuary where a fresh wind ruffled the river; each wavelet glittered into a crest of jewels under that bright glare.

"Yes," she agreed. "Beautiful. Now go and switch them off."

He peered at her again. Doubtless she seemed to him a wavering object, forever receding and advancing. "Aye, aye," he said. "Aye, aye, sir."

She watched him run down onto the sand, leaping into

the air like an excited child. He tried to reverse the car onto the road, succeeded in digging the back wheels up to their hubs in sand, switched off the lights and returned to her, whistling "Cherry Ripe." By that time the kettle was boiling; she put a great deal of coffee into an earthenware jug and poured boiling water on top of it. Then she put three Alka-Seltzer tablets in water and made him swallow the fizzing mixture. By the time he got to the coffee, speech had begun to return to him.

Linda said, "Did you have a nice day in London?"

"I did not." He glowered, passed a hand over his eyes and shuddered. "There's a conspiracy," he said suddenly, tripping over the sybilants, "to make me look a cretin."

There didn't seem any adequate answer to this, so Linda kept silent. He fixed her with slightly crossed eyes. "Do people keep dragging up your past?"

It did not occur to her that the question was rhetorical; her "Yes, frequently" became entangled in his "No," and they both stared stupidly.

"They do?" he said.

"Yes."

Obviously this admission achieved momentous proportions somewhere inside his fuddled brain.

"Doesn't it make you mad?"

"It makes me unhappy."

"Unhappy." He stared. "Why? Is it such an unhappy past?"

Fantastic conversation, she thought, enjoying every minute of it. "Unwholesome in parts," she admitted.

"Like the Curate's egg?"

"Exactly."

"But my past isn't like that. I was happy, that's what makes me mad. No one minds being reminded of *un*happiness," he pronounced with sudden crazy insight. "But to be

64

reminded of happiness—it's like . . . it's like those people who keep saying, 'Oh, but you should have seen Nijinsky, you should have heard Caruso'."

Linda stared in amazement; it seemed to her at that moment as if he would never stop producing new facets of himself. Then, with a sense of shock, she realised that she knew him hardly at all, as yet.

"Who's been flinging your happy past in your face then?"

"Oh . . . people. It's not them that gets one down; it's *it*."

"*It?*"

"The past." He grinned fondly into his coffee, remembering something. "I'll tell you what," he said, slowly. "They talk about the chain of life, don't they? Each year, they say, forges another link. I heard an old geezer on about it in a pulpit once." His brow clouded. "What was I talking about?"

"The chain of life."

"You're as intelligent," he said, "as you are lovely. May I kiss you again?"

"No."

"No, I thought not. The chain of life. Yes. Well, I don't know how your chain's made up but I often see mine lying around; the first part's made of gold and the last part's made of tin, and they're joined together by a dirty old piece of string. That's the war."

Something in all this gibberish touched her. She recognised the dim shape of his life hovering in a miasma of drunken nonsense; she touched for a moment upon whatever lay behind his arrogance and his loathing of society—touched upon it and then lost it.

"You had a divorce," he said abruptly.

"Yes."

"Did you . . . love the . . . your husband?"

"Once."

65

"And he did the dirty, and you were miserable?"

She nodded.

"I'd like to wring his neck." For the first time he had expressed a heartfelt sentiment regarding herself; the knowledge warmed her strangely.

"Your chain's silver," he said. "It gets a bit tarnished in one place, and maybe there's a dud link somewhere but it's silver all the way through." His eyes were clear at that moment, shining with a warmth and kindliness which took her by surprise. It seemed that he must always take her by surprise. In any case before she could assimilate the compliment he was away on another tangent.

"Gawd," he said. "I'm getting sentimental. I tell you what. Let's both pull our chains, shall we?"

They laughed together merrily over this: he at the absurd joke, she because he had produced it with such a naïve air of naughtiness like a small boy unsure of the propriety of what he is saying.

However, Linda laughing and in her dressing gown, was an attractive sight; his face clouded suddenly and he caught her wrist. For a time, they observed each other in silence. Linda tried to draw her hand away, without success; she found herself wondering whether she was ever going to be able to allow herself to give way, even slightly, to this maddening young man, or whether he was always going to queer the pitch, by being drunk or by having his mind fixed on an unworthy ulterior motive. She knew now, from the hot cloudy look of his eyes, exactly what was going to happen.

"Listen," she said equably, "if you try any amorous tricks, Alan Morgan, I'm going to sock you."

He grinned amiably and she caught an extremely strong whiff of rum. His expression—oh, how *ridiculous* men were, she thought in her fury—said quite plainly, *All the girls put up a bit of a tussle; it helps their self-respect.*

66

"No. Listen," she said again. "I shan't slap you, I shall sock you."

He chuckled and made a swift encircling movement.

Linda, true to her promise, socked him.

"Now," she added, "you'd better go."

He sat back amazed, feeling his nose and upper lip as if in disbelief; there was a faint stain of blood on his teeth.

Linda held the door open.

He stood up with dignity and set a course towards it. Only then did she realise quite how drunk he really was. However, he steadied himself and faced her.

"I'm . . . I'm extremely sorry." His eyes were blank again now. "A beastly day," he added vaguely. "Ought to have more self-control but you know how it is, you had a bad time too." With which he turned and reeled away into the darkness.

As she closed the door she heard the unmistakable sounds of vomiting.

Her immediate inclination was to run to him, to hold his head with soothing words. Her second thoughts were more cautious, more feminine, but, she couldn't help feeling as she trailed wearily up to bed, much less interesting.

Alan, the paroxysm over, stood listening in the road. There was no sound. He tiptoed round to the kitchen window. Darkness.

Then he saw the light in the bedroom—a warm, pink, entirely suitable light; he saw the shadow move across the curtain. He stumbled to The Cove and sat down carefully on the dry sand, his back against one of the wooden mooring posts. Presently there were no more shadows. And presently the warm square of window flicked into darkness.

But long before that, Alan Morgan was asleep.

Away over the marshes a curlew called once and was still. A light breeze moved on the estuary.

Shortly after five o'clock the following afternoon a long lean motorboat came chugging quietly downriver.

Linda, watching from her terrace, knew instinctively that this was what Alan had been waiting for all day. She had watched him at work on his little yacht, *Honeydew*, or sitting on the jetty edge splicing rope, and had sensed from his bearing that he waited.

As soon as the motorboat came in sight he jumped to his feet and waved. The salutation was returned by a stocky little man with a mop of black hair, who evidently knew something about boats also. He brought his craft neatly alongside the jetty and together they made fast.

Linda went on with her sewing and continued to observe. Perhaps the scope of her observations would have surprised the two men on the other side of The Cove, for she was not entirely ignorant of the sea and ships.

Bonaventure. The name was written in red across a shapely grey stern. Yes, but why grey? Why that particular shade of battleship grey? She knew how he liked a boat to look; the little *Honeydew* was evidence of it, with her glistening white paint, rust-red at the water-line, and her glittering brass. But the launch *Bonaventure* was painted all over that warlike grey.

Linda frowned, studying the flared bow, like the bow of a destroyer, and the rakish lines of her. A fast boat. An exceedingly fast boat.

Alan was lifting the engine hatch now, and, although she could not see into it, the length of the thing was enough to suggest that the engines themselves were not small. And there were two propellers, because she could see them clearly through the still water in the lee of the jetty.

Her heart had suddenly begun to beat faster; it behaved these days as if it had a will of its own. *Where is he going?*

68

she wondered. *And why must he have a fast boat, painted so that she is hard to pick out at sea?*

She noticed now that there were tarpaulins draped on either side of the cabin, and that the tarpaulins bulged unevenly. The independent part of herself had a quick answer for that too: it had a quick answer for everything to do with Alan Morgan. *Petrol*, it said now. *A craft that size, built for speed with big engines, would need a lot of fuel—particularly,* it added craftily, *for a long journey.*

"Damn," said Linda out loud. She stood up and went into the house.

"Damn, damn, damn," she said, pacing about her tiny sitting room, aware of that renegade heart beating furiously under her breast. Her brain was a pandemonium of conflicting thoughts and ideas. "Why should I care where he goes, or why? Because you love him. I do not. You do. Don't, do, don't, do . . . He's a crook; something happened to him long ago—during the war, perhaps. He went sour. He became so violent inside himself that he can only relax when he's drunk . . . What does that matter—he's a crook, isn't he? . . . I don't care what he is."

And the prim voice of her conventional upbringing chimed in to say, *Now really, this has gone quite far enough; you're behaving like a child.*

"But," she said aloud, "I love him."

Staring, appalled, into the Chippendale mirror she saw how the blood mounted to the very tips of her ears, then ebbed, leaving her pale.

Yes, it was true. She had known it, of course, in her deepest heart for weeks. She loved him. Nothing that he might say or do could alter that salient fact.

She stood in the small room deep in thought, watching the two men bending over the *Bonaventure*'s engines. Gradually her expression changed; her beautiful poised head went up; the firm chin asserted itself; a glitter danced behind the gentle eyes and she began to smile.

Then she turned decisively—how decisively, she could not know—went upstairs to her bedroom, and sat down at the dressing-table. . . .

When she said "Hullo," both Alan and Rocky jerked up together like marionettes on the same string. Alan shaded his eyes and stared up at her, his face wrinkled against the glare of the sky. Linda returned the stare amiably; she knew that in a faultlessly tailored white blouse and a butcher-blue linen skirt, and with a certain amount of recent attention paid to her face, she looked as fresh and calm as the spring evening around her.

Alan, who had so far only seen her on his own terms, if on her ground, had difficulty in hiding his appreciation. It was evidently one thing to surprise her tidying her sitting room or rumpled from sleep—quite another to meet her in the field, as it were, of battle.

She came down the jetty steps and jumped lightly onto the *Bonaventure*'s deck.

"I won't be in the way," she said, and in the same breath, "Where are you going?"

Rocky cleared his throat.

Alan said, "Er . . . yes. Linda, this is Rocky. Mrs. Ward-Hamilton, Rocky."

Linda gave the little man her sweetest smile, which, she knew, was quite a smile, and said, "Mrs. Fiddlesticks. Linda."

Rocky grinned.

"Well," she repeated, "where are you going?"

"Nowhere. Yet awhile."

Is he, she wondered, *doing a bit of quiet smuggling? I wouldn't be surprised. And how good and strong those shad-*

70

ows under the cheekbones are. And how brown he is already.

She sat down on the deck. "I must say I think this boat's a hideous colour, but I suppose it's convenient."

"Convenient?" His voice hardened.

"Useful. Doesn't show dirt and so on."

The two men were back at the engine now. She watched them for a moment in silence and then said, "I'll tell you why I asked where you were going. I suddenly had an idea it'd be fun to pop over to France, and I thought that if . . ."

He came towards her along the length of the boat. "Yes?" Something in his eyes quelled her, but she managed to add, "Oh, I just thought I'd love to go with you."

He stood over her, staring down. "What gave you the idea I might be crossing the Channel?"

How dangerous is he really? she wondered. There was a hardness about him now—about the grey eyes and the taut voice—which frightened her a little. She stood up to face him.

"Nothing *gave* me the idea. It was just . . . an idea." She met his glare unflinchingly. After a while—indeed, after what seemed a very long time—he smiled; it was difficult not to smile when confronted with so feminine a performance.

He said, "The pub's open. How about a drink?"

"Yes. I'd like a drink."

To Rocky he said, "We'll be in the local, Rockabye. Come on up when you've finished. You can't miss it because it's the only one."

Rocky said, "Aye, aye, sir," and grinned again at Linda.

When they were on top of the jetty, Alan took her arm and held it. "All right. So you've got all sorts of ideas. What are they?" His voice was genial; the charm was at work.

"Ideas?"

71

"About me. About the *Bonny* there. About where I'm taking her on Friday."

Friday! The day after tomorrow. Panic started up in her heart; she knew then that she *could* not be left behind. A great surge of knowledge—a compound of fear, of intuition and love and excitement—swept over her so that for a moment she needed his support to keep her on her legs at all.

"Hey," he said. "Steady. What's up?"

"Danger," she said, and stared blankly.

"What are you talking about?"

The wave receded, leaving her weak.

"Nothing," she said. "I . . . I had a . . . a sort of feeling. A presentiment."

His grip on her arm increased and then relaxed. "A presentiment of danger?"

"No." She shook her head to clear it. "I'm a fool."

But he himself, talking to Kellandale, had known just such a feeling. He drew her to a standstill. "Listen. Just what are you thinking? What've you been dreaming up, over there in your . . . watchtower?"

"I want to go with you," Linda said.

Because he still held her arm they were close together, and their relationship had suddenly changed. A kind of hopelessness in her voice touched him; it was as if they were both lifted on that wave of uneasiness, and deposited on another plane.

"I want to go with you," she had said—without excuse or reason—and her eyes were determined, yet soft. He guessed instinctively what her excuse and her reason were, but he shied away from so personal an admission. He did not want to become involved in this woman; he did not want to become involved in mankind as represented by her. He wanted to be alone.

"You can't come with us," he said.

She backed away. "You don't trust me."

Again the wave lifted them, carried them over yet another fence, pressed them closer together.

"It's not that . . ."

Oh, damn the woman, he thought. *What is she forcing me to say?* He shrugged and said it. "You're right. There may be . . . danger. I'm not taking you into it."

Still without looking at him, she said, "You'll be taking me into it whether I'm there or not."

Then she turned and walked away.

He watched her go, blue skirt swinging defiantly, head up, bright hair glinting in the soft sunlight of evening.

He caught up with her just before she turned into the village street and drew her firmly into a corner by the Old Customs House.

"Don't be a fool." He shook her gently. "You've been stuck in this place too long, all by yourself. Get out of it sometimes."

She stared at him for a time and then said, "Grow up, Alan Morgan, for Heaven's sake."

"Meaning?"

"You know perfectly well what I mean. I'm not a girl. I don't have to be sent off to stay with Aunt Sarah because I happen to have fallen for the wrong man."

He sighed heavily. "Well, you *have* fallen for the wrong man."

She laughed. "Did you ever know a woman who cared a hoot in hell about that?"

He moved towards her, touched by her self-sufficiency, by her straight-forwardness.

"If you try to kiss me," she said, "I shall do it again."

At this he got angry: he didn't want all this feminine complexity. He swore.

Linda laughed.

73

Then he grabbed her, pinning her arms to her sides, and did exactly what she had warned him not to. He kissed her and he went on kissing her until all rigidity ran out of the soles of her feet and she stopped struggling. When he released her she lay back against the wall of the Old Customs House and stared at him.

"All right," she said finally. "Now may I go home?"

"Certainly."

She went. He watched her with admiration. He was still standing in the lane watching her when Rocky joined him.

"Hi, Skipper," he said. "Lost her?"

Alan looked at him ruminatively. "I don't know," he said.

FIRST SEASCAPE

THE SUN BALANCED ON THE EDGE OF THE MARSH, A RED DISC against a pink, clear sky, as the *Bonaventure* slipped quietly down the estuary on the flow. The evening was warm and perfectly still—an infinity of peace—of rippling tideway, russet- and sand-yellow saltings, calm sea beyond, vast heavens above.

The bird sounds of the marsh and the distant excitement of gulls were compound of that stillness; the only alien noise was the quiet throb of *Bonaventure*'s powerful engines, now throttled back to a mere flutter hardly as loud as the ripple of water at her bow.

Alan and Rocky were silent, lapped in the great contentment that sea- and boat-lovers know when the land casts off its dull shackles and they are once again free of it.

Presently the marsh on either side gave way to low, undulating sandhills, and they in turn slipped into the gentle sea, reappeared, vanished, reappeared once more where a tired wavelet lapped over with a sigh. Then it was all sea. The *Bonaventure* shuddered, dipped to the calm swell and rose on its crest.

The sun had gone now. The flutter of powerful engines increased to a throb, to a grumble, to a steady, controlled thunder. The flared bow cut through the next wave and lifted on two fans of white spray. Rocky grinned appreciatively and winked to no one in particular. But his wink was returned, far away to port where sky and sea met in a darkening line, by the red eye of the Crowl Sands Light.

Alan said, "Rocky?"

"Skip."

"Come here a minute." And when Rocky joined him at the wheel, "Take over, will you? I want to settle a bet."

Rocky stared at him. "What bet?"

"Watch and you'll see." He opened the cabin door and pushed it well back; then he switched on the small bulkhead light and waited.

"You bonkers?" enquired Rocky.

"Maybe." He pointed. There was a disturbance behind the half-drawn curtain of the starboard bunk, and presently a foot appeared.

Rocky stiffened, thinking of police, but a curly blonde head made him relax into laughter.

Linda straightened up with difficulty and faced them, pushing back her hair. "You knew," she said furiously.

Alan did not answer. He turned back to the wheel.

Linda came up out of the cabin.

"Switch the light off," he said sharply. She obeyed. And to Rocky, "Nip aft to your blessed engines a minute, chum."

Linda said, "Aren't you angry?"

"I've no reason to be angry."

He scanned the darkling surface of the sea, and his face, so consciously impersonal, maddened her. Realisation dawned. "You *meant* me to come."

He cocked an eye at her, dark brow raised. "And *you've* no reason to be angry either. You wanted the trip, and you've got it."

"You left the boat on purpose; you expected me to stow away; you meant me to come."

He turned on her then. "All right. I did. What of it?"

"And if . . . if I hadn't walked into your little trap?"

"Trap! Who the hell's talking about traps?"

"I am."

They were both irritated now. He turned back to the sea and said in a hard, cold voice, "If you hadn't taken the matter into your own hands I should have invited you to join us. Put it that way."

"But I asked and you refused . . ."

"That was before I'd had time to think."

She stared.

"To think," he continued, "how angry you'd be if I left you behind; and how if . . . if certain people started asking questions about me, you might feel disposed to give them a few answers."

"You haven't got a very good opinion of me, have you?"

"On the contrary. It's my opinion of certain female characteristics that's not very good."

She was miserable suddenly, seeing how cold his profile was in the evening light. "You think I'd have . . . betrayed you to the . . . the police?"

"Perhaps not consciously. But you have truly appalling ideas about the sort of life I lead."

"Don't be a fool," she snapped. "You're a crook and I know it. It doesn't make any difference." Her voice faltered and he glanced at her sharply.

"Who's the fool?" he said, and then, seeing her misery, "Oh damn! I didn't mean to hurt you. Can't you see I've got a job to do and I'm not taking risks? I didn't kidnap you; you wanted to come."

She did not reply, because she could not admit the justice of what he had just said.

"You wanted to come and here you are. Now you'd better make yourself useful. Go below and brew up some kye."

"Kye?"

"Navy for cocoa."

He laughed and the weight lifted from her heart. She thought, *Yes, he's right. I'm the fool.* However base his reason for wanting her company, the fact remained that she was with him. As she returned to the tiny cabin she remembered walking with him up the ramp from Ted Clumper's yard; she had said, "There's a Major Hobart to see you; he's got a gun in his pocket." She had known, at that moment, with those fumbling words, that she had bound herself ineluctably to this dark, dangerous young man—and she had been right. There was no point in regretting or in thinking *If only*. . . . The two of them must go on, linked, to whatever the outcome of this adventure would be.

Above her, Alan shouted, "And let's have some rum in that kye, miss. There's a bit of an east wind."

She laughed, suddenly happy, and shouted back, "Aye, aye, sir."

In the stern, Rocky winked at the Crowl Sands Light—and the red eye winked back.

PART II

Semi-Circle

1 – ILLEGAL ENTRY

MONSIEUR EMILE HAGENAUX WORE A BATHROBE OF GREEN-AND-white-striped Turkish toweling over a pair of lemon-yellow silk pyjamas. The result was not flattering to his complexion but was, in some way, appropriate to his personality. His bright, black eyes, small in the pallor of his moon face, watched the young man with a mixture of caution and friendliness, bred of long years' association with unreliable people. The dome of his bald head shone like polished ivory against the crescent of sleek, black hair that circled it. The hair, the eyes, a small line of black moustache and a ridiculously prim mouth were all the features he possessed. All else was pallor.

"And so," he said, "you wish to pass discreetly into that detestable country."

"I do—and out again."

Hagenaux laughed; his long body quivered with a strange paroxysm; he wiped his moustache carefully.

"My friend, my friend, you do take your pleasures dangerously, don't you? Here, in Belgium alone, I can put you in the way of twice the amount of money your present patron will pay you for this . . . this quixotic adventure. It's like a schoolboy story." He waved fat expressive hands and poured out more coffee for both of them. "I don't complain.

81

It is easy to procure you the papers and to get you over the frontier—that is nothing. I merely say that you are wasting your talents—risking them, is that not so? This man Farquarson, I do not like the sound of him. Here the police are always busy with this and that. Another croissant? I insist. The situation is ideal. Beautiful." He kissed his fingertips delicately.

Alan thought that, if ever Hagenaux deigned to descend to blackmail, half the distinguished men and women in Europe would have circles under their eyes. His brain was a human filing system, he never forgot an item of gossip nor an indiscreet confidence. His wife, a plump and behenna-ed lady, lived a life of her own in Brussels. Few of her acquaintances ever gave a thought to her husband beyond supposing him to be dead. It was generally accepted by those who knew she had one that they were divorced; this was not legally the position. Madame Hagenaux was simply employed by her husband at a handsome salary; she was more use to him as an agent than she had ever been as a wife. All this Alan knew because Hagenaux himself had told him. They liked each other, admired each other, though the older man could only abhor the younger's lack of finesse.

Now, waving one hand and lifting his coffee cup to the absurd mouth with the other, he said, "I am getting old, it must be faced. But I am unique in my way, am I not? Unique but no longer, shall we say, agile. Together, you and I, ah but there is nothing we could not do."

Alan smiled. "In the meantime," he said, "Germany."

Hagenaux sighed gustily. "That island." He clapped a hand to his forehead. "God help me, but that island of yours is responsible for much. Your ancestors were plundering the Spaniards, no doubt, when mine were making chaste ladies accessible to lascivious princes. Mine is the more useful inheritance, my friend: subtlety, the flick of the wrist and

82

see . . ." He cupped a plump hand in the air. "The plum falls into the fingers. So. Whereas you. . . ." He gazed to heaven. "Look at you. You are still a pirate when with the figure, the aristocratic nose, the English tailoring . . ." He snapped his fingers. "You are 'in,' as they say. The women will like you because you do not care for the devil, and the men will think you a good fellow because you know a horse and wear the tie, the discreet one. Is it not so?"

Alan laughed and selected a peach.

"Instead, but yes, you frighten my little Josef who says to me, 'There is a *sans-culotte* to see you.' He hides now in the kitchen." Hagenaux banged the table with a large fat fist, setting the silver jangling. "You—are—wasting—yourself." He sat back and stared, tiny eyes hard and brilliant.

The younger man said, "Germany, Emile."

Hagenaux groaned. "I could say damn you, couldn't I? I could say 'Go and find some other fool to smuggle you into that snake-pit . . .'"

"Why don't you?"

"Because I am not a fool. Half the rats on the dockyard can manage the frontier for you, and the papers. Also, I lose your friendship." He leaned forward. "All I ask is that you consider what I have said."

"I will. In fact, I have. When this job's finished I'll come back and discuss it with you, perhaps."

"Perhaps! More likely you will marry and settle down on a farm. Oh yes, I know the English; they are not consistent. They do not know their own damnable worth. No, don't say 'Germany' again with that long-suffering look. I have finished. Now go to the bathroom and wash yourself, shave yourself. When you come out I will have made the arrangements for your schoolboy joke. They will take ten minutes."

The bathroom was immaculate in white-and-blue tiles.

On a shelf were ranged bath salts, bath essences, bath oils and a variety of talcum powders in blue jars.

Alan, lying back in scented splendour, gazed at his feet and thought of other bathrooms which he had experienced all too recently: the writhing maze of dusty pipes, the constipated plumbing systems, the shabby holes in the linoleum and the scaly texture of the baths themselves. There was no avoiding the comparison and the meaning of it, even though he had been avoiding the decision, which they demanded, for two years—ever since the day, in fact, that Hagenaux had first made his suggestion.

He knew that once he had joined Hagenaux—and "joining Hagenaux" could be a metaphor in this respect—he had severed the last link with all that he had been; in fact—and now, lying in the magnificent bath, he laughed at himself for it—it was a futile echo of the sportsman's eternal argument about amateurs and professionals. Alan Morgan, hiding in Wainport or engaged in a little quiet smuggling, bullying ephemeral Hobart or fencing with Farquarson over a glass of beer, was still a dilettante, an amateur. Still, just. That, of course, was why Patchway had sent for him because he knew, out of all that bitter experience, that there was a young man on the brink, but still within recall. But Alan Morgan living in a smart flat in Brussels, with a blue-and-white tiled temple for a bathroom, was another matter; and he, like any old duffer in a Pall Mall club ("damn feller's turned professional") was still wrapped around with the Englishman's sporting preference for the amateur.

Hagenaux, almost as if he sensed all this, made no further mention of his plan; he had become businesslike, efficient. Josef, the little manservant, was helping him dress, but when Alan strolled into the bedroom, he said, "Run, Josef, run; the brute Englishman will eat you."

Josef smiled pityingly, gathered up the striped dressing

84

gown and the yellow pyjamas, and withdrew quietly. Hagenaux, his fat legs encased in immaculate fawn trousers which
balanced breathtakingly on his waistline, was struggling with
a bow tie. He took an envelope from the dressing table and
flung it onto the bed. "There are your papers all in order:
Werner Sagan of Hartberg in Austria. Near enough to the
Hungarian frontier to explain any accent you may have."

"And . . ."

"Listen to me." He waved a fat hand. "The firm of Strelitz
and Sonneberg have re-opened their factory at Mülheim—
look at the map there . . ."

"I am."

Hagenaux swore at the tie. "Heavy industrial machinery.
Your papers describe you as a draughtsman—nice and vague.
On the journey to Hannover you can be on your way back
from applying for a job; on the return, the reverse. Not that
anyone will ask you, the whole place is full of young men
drifting about after jobs—always on the move, always con-
vinced that somewhere they will find . . . what?" He turned,
arms raised enquiringly. "What? They do not know what
they hope to find." He peered at himself in the mirror again.
"Their souls, perhaps, for they have certainly lost them—*if
they* ever had any."

"Beethoven," said Alan. "Goethe, Bach."

Hagenaux shrugged. "The Nazis would have shot all of
them. However . . . it is not our business what they search
for; sufficient that they are always moving." He laughed his
subterranean laugh. "It is a useful habit. As I have said
before, Europe is in a state of priceless confusion. It is most
satisfying. The Russians . . ." He laughed again. "They all
make it so *easy* for us, my friend. There is money to be
made out of those Russians—they are stupid. I am meeting
a man today who. . . . No matter. Now, as to the frontier,
it is child's play. You will take a train to Liége, a dirty

place; you will arrive there . . . let us say, before four o'clock this afternoon." He smiled. "In time for the weak tea, perhaps. You will find the road which leads to Spa and take a tram along it as far as the Leopold Bridge. Is that clear?"

"Yes."

"There you will continue on foot until you come to a small factory owned by Monsieur Bonneville. You cannot miss it because the name is written in letters as high as a man across the wall that faces you. Bonneville. Good. You will arrive there between half-past four and a quarter to five. Do not be late or early. Opposite the factory is an open space—derelict, tin cans, children, dogs: you know it well—and there you will see parked several lorries. One of these will be dark green and on the side of it you see 'Soufflon' in red. Get into this lorry and stay there until the driver speaks to you. Don't smoke and don't make a noise." He fixed the young man with his beady eyes. "You understand?"

"Perfectly."

"Of course you do." He had tied the bow to his satisfaction. Now he took an immense jacket from the bed and heaved himself into it. "For me," he said, "it is all preposterous—not the kind of game I appreciate. However . . ." Again the shrug. "It is a matter of taste." He adjusted a spotless handkerchief in the breast pocket, having scented it liberally first. Then he filled his cigar case.

"Where is your boat?"

"At Poiret's."

"You have a man to look after it?"

"Yes."

"Poiret is a reliable fellow." He offered a cigar and shrugged at the refusal. "Good. Tell me, my friend, this . . . patron of yours. Why does he wish the man brought out of Germany?"

"Because he owes him a good turn."

86

Hagenaux pursed his tiny mouth and looked excessively prim. The eyes were brilliant.

Alan said, "You don't believe it?"

"My dear boy—" he took a natty fawn hat from the wardrobe and admired it—"my dear boy, who am I, a mere Frenchman, to judge the motives of the fantastic English? Why do you risk yourself playing Boy Scouts' games when there are such fruits for the picking, merely by raising the hand?" He did so. "Why does a rich and powerful man take so much trouble to repay a favour? Why?" He gesticulated. "Because you are both English. *But—*" he held up a plump forefinger—"is it so simple as all that? The English are not fools, they only look it, they are as I say, fantastic."

Alan grew tired of the fat Frenchman's rhetoric. He said, "Does it matter? He's paying me well enough."

Hagenaux stared at him, grave suddenly. There was a pause.

"One does not realise," he said finally, "that you are a most serious young man. Like many serious young men you take your own life too lightly."

"What do you mean?"

"To you, I see it clearly, it does not matter whether your powerful friend tells the truth or not. Your duty is clear to you . . ."

Alan glanced up.

". . . you fetch the man from Germany and ask no questions. Admirable." He placed the hat delicately upon his bald head. "Admirable, but oh how stupid." He gazed benignly at the young man and shrugged. "Is there anything else you want? You've got the papers and the money; you know the route."

"Yes, there is something else." He took Hagenaux' plump arm and led him to the window. On the other side of the street was a café: small tables crowding under a striped awning. At one of the tables sat Linda, toying with a cup of coffee. Alan pointed.

Hagenaux grinned appreciatively. "Charming, yes, but what of it?"

"Her name's Linda Hamilton, she'll be staying at the Trois Couronnes. I'd like you to be able to recognise her. I shall give her your telephone number in case she gets into any sort of trouble."

Hagenaux swore gently but explicitly. "You are not, my dear boy, you are not working with a woman, God help you."

"No. She's a friend of mine."

"You trust her?"

Alan glanced away. "I . . . No. But I could if necessary."

Hagenaux sighed. "My dear infant, when a man can say that, it means he believes the lady to be in love with him."

"Does it?"

"Always. And so you brought the beautiful Miss Hamilton over in your boat."

"Mrs. Hamilton. Yes, I did."

"Then you are twice a fool."

Alan considered this in silence for a moment, and, to Hagenaux' surprise, replied, "Yes, I think I am. However—" he laughed—"she'll be staying at the Trois Couronnes. I just wanted you to know."

"Charmed, dear boy. So I am to become involved in your woman in order to preserve our friendship?"

"This is probably the last you'll see or hear of her, Emile. Relax."

"One never sees or hears the last of a pretty woman." He gave a vast Gallic shrug of resignation. "Now, shall I give you a lift down to Poiret's?"

"No, thank you. I must get the lady settled."

Hagenaux rolled his eyes to heaven in an agony of the

88

soul. But he smiled as they parted and said, "Good luck, my friend, and *bon voyage*. You deserve to fail, but I don't suppose you will."

Alan joined Linda at her table in the sunshine.

"Was the interview satisfactory?" she enquired.

"Oh yes. An old friend."

She regarded him in silence for a while. Then she said, "Wouldn't it make things easier if you trusted me?"

"No, it would not." He glared. Not only did he regret having brought her, but he was beginning to be slightly ashamed of himself. He had taken it for granted that if there was any danger it would lie in Germany, but now he was not so sure. Hagenaux had only echoed the warning he himself had felt in Kellandale's office. Already it seemed to him incredible that he had ever believed anything that Kellandale had said. Of course, there was more in the matter of Paul Schröder than met the eye. A man of Kellandale's eminence did not have to resort to employing an adventurer, a crook, unless what he needed doing was criminal— and if a man of Kellandale's eminence proposed to commit a crime, then the crime would be big, as big as the man himself. "This is not a political matter," he had said, but that was manifestly absurd. Whatever Kellandale did was on such a scale that it could not help having political repercussions.

And so Alan, watching the girl opposite him, was ashamed. She loved him—or thought she did—and she was happy, happy merely to be with him. And wherever he was, on this particular trip, something told him that danger would not be far away.

Yes, he was ashamed.

"Listen," he said. "I'm not sure what's going to happen now. In any case you've got to keep out of it. Don't go near Poiret's place, or the boat, or Rocky. Don't identify yourself with them at all."

She frowned at this intensity. She had never known him to be intense before, and it was alarming. "But I shall hear from you?"

"Yes. I'll let you know when we shall be going back, and where to meet us." He essayed a smile, but it was not entirely convincing. "In fact your time's your own. A nice little holiday."

Linda did not smile. "I'm . . . I'm going to worry. I'm worried now."

He caught himself being a trifle pleased about this, but stifled the feeling at once.

"Can't I help you at all?" she said.

"No. I'd rather not. There . . . may be danger and I don't want you to be involved."

"It's rather absurd," she said. "I'm worried about you, and you're worried about me."

He glanced at her sharply. "As a matter of fact, I wish to hell I'd left you behind."

"I take that as a compliment."

"Fine." He was not looking at her now. "It is one."

A flare of tenderness passed through her—tenderness and fear hand-in-hand. She leaned forward and touched his arm. "I'm glad you *didn't* leave me behind. If you're in danger I'll be in danger too."

He turned, and their eyes met.

"Idiot," he said gently. "We'll talk about that when I come back." He stood up abruptly. "The hotel's up that street to the left; the room's booked, and I don't propose to show my face there. It's comfortable. You'll like it. Just enjoy yourself until you hear from me."

"Oh yes, I'll enjoy myself, wondering what sort of mess you're in."

90

But his moment of tenderness had passed. He took a card from his pocket.

"This is the name and telephone number of the man I've just been to see. I shan't tell you anything about him; the less you know the better. If . . . if you should need any sort of help ring him up. Mention me."

She sighed. "I'd rather be trusted."

He did not reply, but bent and kissed her lightly. Then he turned and walked away.

Linda watched his lanky figure down the bright street. He did not look back, and presently he turned a corner and was gone.

Sitting alone in the sun she thought how extraordinary it was that all this seemed so natural, in fact so ordinary. *Am I*, she wondered, *the stuff that gangsters' molls are made of?* Or, on second thoughts, were gangsters' molls simply women who happened to love the wrong men? Yes, he was a crook, and she loved him. She would, quite without scruple, aid and abet him; already she was in all likelihood an accessory after some fact or other. And yet it was all ordinary; and in some strange way, in spite of the anxiety for him which troubled her, she was happy.

This, she thought, *is the loveliest thing about being a woman—and the most degrading—this acceptance of a man with all his faults and failings.*

Her conscience (prim and acidulous in its permanent Sunday-school dress) taunted her a little it was true: *If you were a decent woman—if you were even half a woman —you wouldn't be content with such a worthless creature; at least you'd make some effort to reform him.*

And the answer to this really did take her by surprise. *Don't worry,* she could reply to her conscience, *don't worry a bit. I shall reform him.*

She sat for a long time in the sunshine, appalled by this discovery.

Monsieur Poiret's establishment was situated on the east bank of the Scheldt slightly below the main industry of the docks. It consisted of a narrow inlet at the end of which was what Papa Poiret called The Factory; here, in a large, ramshackle shed, small sailing boats were built with the same care and pride which the old man's father and grandfather before him had lavished on their trade. The left side of the inlet consisted of a sloping ramp up which various craft were hoisted on rollers for scraping and repainting, while in the basin itself, awaiting repair or merely harboured there under Poiret's eye, were others—motorboats, cabin cruisers, dinghies and small yachts. Towering above all this and forming the right bank, was the dizzy, dark cliff of a warehouse. For the rich amateur yachtsman Poiret's was the ideal place to keep his boat because it was safe from the visitations of small hooligans; for other, less reputable citizens such as Monsieur Hagenaux, it proved an excellent hiding place for craft engaged in various private enterprises.

Alan found Rocky, attired in bathing trunks, seated with his back to the stumpy mast; he was drinking coffee from a cracked mug and struggling with the morning paper, intoning the French aloud with phonetic pronunciation. Maurice, old Poiret's boatman, was listening from the jetty, puzzled but entranced.

Rocky glanced up and grinned. "Bloody language," he said cheerfully. "How was Fatty?"

"He never changes." Alan jumped down into the boat. Maurice, the entertainment over, returned to his work.

Rocky lay back in the sun, shading his eyes. "When are you off?"

"This afternoon."

"Don't hurry, skip. This is my summer holiday. Smashin' tart in the newspaper shop across the road too. Says she'll teach me French in no time."

Alan smiled at the resourcefulness of the English sailor abroad. For a moment he had wondered whether Rocky would manage all right by himself with his extremely limited command of the language; he realised now that he need have no such fears.

He went below to the tiny cabin and pulled out an American army haversack. In it he packed the few tins of food he had acquired since leaving Hagenaux and a generous supply of coffee ("Coffee, my friend, is more useful than money"). Also among his luggage were a carton of American cigarettes, an English soldier's gas-cape, one of the shiny peaked caps so much patronised by Germans, his Lüger and a spare pair of socks. ("Avoid the wet feet, my friend; one cannot be heroic with wet feet." This with a rumble of mirth.) He dressed himself in an old pair of khaki trousers and pulled a thick blue sweater over his shirt. A pair of ancient brown boots completed the fancy dress.

"You look," said Rocky, "like an out-of-work sanitary man."

That was tribute enough to the efficiency of Hagenaux' advice. Lolling at the wheel of his huge black car he had said, "It is the uniform, my dear friend, the uniform of the dispossessed. Each article has its history written upon it—the trousers begged from an American, the boots stolen from an army truck, the cape bartered for one's mother's engagement ring. But yes, it is tragedy. It requires only the tragic mask which you do not have. The skin is drawn tight and polished, so. The lines are all downwards and deep, and the eyes are blank. You understand, one sees nothing in really tragic eyes."

Standing on the deck of the small boat, staring down at

93

Rocky spread-eagled upon the cabin top, he remembered Hagenaux' words. He had not known that there was quite this sensibility behind the pallid, fat face; it made the complacency, if not relish, with which he had spoken somewhat unnerving. He knew also that the Frenchman was trying to provoke him in his own subtle way: the English championship of the underdog, particularly when the underdog was an erstwhile enemy, never failed to delight him. Hagenaux, born in Alsace, was governed by no such complication. For him the German undefeated was loathsome and dangerous; defeated, he was merely contemptible.

"Well," said Rocky. "What's the orders?"

"There aren't any. Expect us when you see us."

The unknown German stood with them on the deck of the small boat.

Rocky scratched his chest and waved away a fly. "I wonder who this bloke really is?"

Alan started; an echo of Hagenaux crossed his memory. "I told you . . ."

"You told me what your boss said, skip. Old chum of his youth, or some such tripe."

"You don't believe that, then?"

"No bloody fear, I don't—not with no blinkin' businessman, I don't."

Consciously echoing the remark which had moved Hagenaux to such rhetoric, Alan said, "Does it matter? He's paying us well enough. I don't give a damn about anything else."

Rocky's reply was as representative as had been the Frenchman's. He squinted up against the sun. "Ah," he said, "*I* don't give a damn, but you do, skip. That's your trouble—you give a damn about too many things."

"I do, do I?"

94

"Too true you do." He sat up and prodded the haver-sack. "You got everything?"

"I hope so."

"I can't feel it." He stared brightly.

"It's there all right. I'm not such a silly twit as to pack it on the outside."

Rocky saluted. "Aye, aye, sir. Got your warm vests?" He avoided the brown boot. "I feel kind of responsible, see, skip."

Alan took out his wallet, removed the plain white envelope which Kellandale had given him and tossed the rest onto the deck. "Hang onto it, Rocky. Lock it up if you like."

"Money?"

"Hagenaux changed me some."

"Good old Fatty."

Alan mused, again staring at the glitter of sun on the river. Outside the basin a timber boat hooted impatiently and a fussing tug pooped in answer.

"Well," he said, "I'd better get going. If anything goes wrong, you've got Hagenaux' telephone number."

"Yes."

"And if there's any change of plan, mind you ring Linda. She might . . . she might worry."

Rocky grinned. "You old heart-breaker you, skip. Any-way there won't be any change of plan, and everything'll be fine and dandy."

"Yes, everything'll be fine and dandy." He said it firmly but doubt nagged at the edges of his mind.

"Stop fussing," said Rocky. "I bet you mucked 'em about in that M.T.B. of yours."

"I'd have smartened you up, Leading-Seaman Rocking-ham." He clambered up onto the jetty and walked away, slinging the pack onto his shoulder. At the gate he turned and looked back. Rocky waved the newspaper.

Again—in spite of himself—that maggot of doubt moved within him. He turned out into the street.

The journey, a mere forty miles, proved uneventful. Having no wish to talk to his fellow travellers, he at first feigned sleep, and then—after his restless night at sea in the small boat—fell asleep in reality. And he dreamed. He dreamed of Ladeleigh. He was a child again—a child and terrified. He ran in a panic of terror along the dark, paneled passages, walls and pictures and tables towering above him; he ran down the broad sweep of stair, across the marble paving of the hall, his feet clattering, and out into the drive; he ran, breathless, choking, down the avenue, and the elms seemed to open before him in a dark tunnel of green foliage. And still he was pursued, though he knew that whatever pursued him was far away. He kept saying to himself, *There's no need to run, there's no need to run,* but nothing would stop that headlong flight. *It's only a dream,* he said to himself. *Stop, stop, it's only a dream,* but he heard his own voice crying out—a long, high-pitched wail of terror. . . . And then the engine was hooting and the wheels were clanking over innumerable points, and the chimneys of Liége were pointing grey fingers to the sky, as if accusing God of the squalor from which they sprouted.

He glanced guiltily at the other occupants of the compartment, his dream so real to him that he felt that they too must have shared it—or, at least, that he had betrayed himself by grumbling and groaning in his sleep. The fat woman in deep mourning still stared morosely out of the window, however; the bibulous professional gentleman, probably a traveller in something, was intent on a typewritten folder.

The train clanked regretfully into Liége station and came, hissing, to rest.

Alan was pleased to find that his appearance raised no interest in the streets—pleased and at the same time depressed. Hagenaux' phrase came back to him, "the uniform of the dispossessed." He paused, catching sight of himself reflected among the smirking dummies of a cheap outfitter's window. *The dispossessed*, he thought, seeing the shabby, unfamiliar figure between genteel young men with pink cheeks and fixed idiot-smiles. *Am I dispossessed really?* This idea made him think suddenly of Linda—it was a natural juxtaposition of ideas. He remembered her as she had prepared food for him on that far-distant evening—capable, gentle, possibly possessive. He thought again, *Am I dispossessed really?* It was a chill thought.

A shop assistant's face, pallid and pimpled, appeared amongst the dummies and reached for a peculiarly revolting green shirt. Their eyes met through the window.

Alan thought, *To him I am a tramp, staring at finery I shall never afford to wear. To me he is a pathetic little snot whose clothes I would not be seen dead in. So what is real?*

The assistant withdrew, the wax models stared back coyly.

There were three hours to be passed before he was due at Monsieur Bonneville's factory just over the Leopold Bridge. He would have liked to drink because the day was hot, sultry, with lowering grey clouds upon the horizon and the sun a bronze disc in a colourless sky, but he needed a clear head, and so turned into a cinema.

No less sultry and oppressive was the third-rate French film through which he was now forced to sit. A dark, overblown lady with a mouth like a freshly torn wound was having an affair with a brutal taxi-driver. It was a matter of glowering looks, low corsages and the man's face, in close-up, resembling a wild beast in sight of meat. It seemed that the lady's husband was a diplomat and too busy to give her all the attention she demanded; by the look of her, even the taxi-driver would be hard put to it. For some reason, doubtless explained at the beginning of the film (he had missed the first fifteen minutes) the brunette Medusa wished her husband disposed of, and the poor taxi-driver, maddened by her taunts, achieved this with his bare hands on a railway station against a background of fog and express trains, for symbolism, in ferocious close-up. In the meantime Medusa, whose real preference in mates now revealed itself as a slim, blond, and effeminate *jeune premier*, betrayed her brutal taxi-driver to the *Sûreté* and sailed for America, the young man of her choice following meekly like a lamb to the slaughter. The name of this epic, revealed under the end title, was *The Lapdog*.

Alan, unrelieved of his mood, repaired to a nearby café and ate a large meal—his last, he could not help feeling, for a day or two. Then, after making sure from three people that he was taking the correct tram, he started off towards Spa.

Now that his journey had begun in earnest, the doubts and moods of the morning deserted him; he was excited, tense with expectation and with the effort of concealing what he felt. The Bridge, which he had been afraid he might miss, was large and quite unmistakable. Before he had reached the far side he saw the name Bonneville, in black letters on a white strip, painted across the face of a tall, blank building like a Lancashire cotton mill. He strolled more slowly, lit a cigarette, leaned against the bridge and stared at the oily water below.

Small boys, like frogs, were hopping and sprawling on the grey grass of the bank. A large clock, deep-toned, struck the half hour, and others—a jangle of voices—chimed in

98

after it. The small boys stood in a row and relieved themselves into the river, shouting obscene comments. A man in a barge shouted back.

When the last clock had finished its discourse, he turned and strolled once more towards Bonneville's. The patch of waste ground came into view, scattered with broken bricks and patches of coarse grass. There were seven lorries there parked higgledy-piggledy like abandoned toys; the green one with *Souchon* written on it in red caught his eye at once. He wondered, as he had wondered when he first heard the name, what *Souchon* meant. His heart began to beat more quickly, and he knew that this—this quickening of awareness—was what he lived for.

He walked slowly towards the lorry, his eyes moving swiftly across the grimy building which enclosed the waste ground. Children were playing King of the Castle on a refuse dump, and a fat woman in a red skirt was beating a carpet in her backyard.

A little way from the lorry he paused, leaned against a baker's van, bent to his shoelace, eyes always on the alert. He felt that all the world was watching him—a million eyes pricking the small of his back. Then, quickly, he moved across to the lorry and climbed the tailboard. The canvas flap was untied but heavy. He pushed it aside and rolled into the darkness within. Nobody shouted, no footsteps came running, no whistle blew. He laughed softly to himself, wondering at the bludgeoning of his heart and knowing that it was just this, just this combination of helpless terror and agonized excitement, which led him on, which would always lead him on.

The inside of the lorry was exceptionally dark; no light showed through the painted canvas of the walls and roof, and it was not until somebody moved in the darkness that he realised that he was not the only passenger for Germany

99

that evening. He remembered Hagenaux' injunction to keep quiet and so restrained his curiosity. It was, however, a peculiar sensation, this sitting in the blackness with an unknown fellow conspirator.

At a quarter to five exactly footsteps approached, stumbling a little on the refuse of the waste land. A tin was kicked and went ran-tankling away over the broken bricks. The door of the driver's cab was opened, the whole vehicle lurched as the man's weight tipped it, the door slammed and the self-starter whirred anxiously. The first few yards of the journey, bouncing over uneven ground, were acutely uncomfortable; in a moment, however, they reached the road and turned, not towards Spa, but back into Liége. Inside the lorry silence continued, becoming uncanny. Alan wondered suddenly whether the whole box were not crammed with people; perhaps, on the other hand, he had imagined the single sound which had suggested a fellow traveller. He realised that he was nervous.

For a time they jolted forward, turned, stopped, spurted along for perhaps fifty yards and then, once again, came grinding to a standstill; but as soon as the city dropped away their progress became less erratic, the surface of the road smoother. At five forty-five by Alan's watch, they slowed down and turned sharply. The road deteriorated and the engine groaned in second gear. Presently they came to a stop, the door was heard to open, the driver lurched out, the door slammed, the chains of the tailboard clattered and daylight flooded in.

Alan found that he had indeed a companion, and one only, a fair boy of perhaps fourteen. The smooth, childish face took him by surprise. Apparently the driver, a stocky, unshaven man in faded blue overalls, knew him, for they exchanged a casual greeting and both turned to stare at the stranger. However, there was only interest in the stare, no curiosity. They glanced at his boots and his pack, and accepted him. (Hagenaux had been right then.) He offered them American cigarettes and they smoked, mostly without speaking.

The lorry was drawn up in a clump of poplars through which meandered a narrow, dusty lane. There was silence except for the twittering of a lark, high overhead, and the occasional rumble of traffic somewhere beyond the trees. The bright sky still glared uncomfortably, but the sun was now obscured in hazy cloud. Heat pressed down upon them and rose up from the white dust under their feet.

"There'll be rain," said the boy.

"Good job too." The driver scratched his untidy head and glanced at the stranger. "First time, eh?"

Alan nodded.

"How did you get in?"

He did not answer and the man shrugged. "You have a good introduction," he said, referring presumably to Hagenaux. "That's all I care about, eh, Rikki?"

The boy agreed and lifted a shabby suitcase out of the lorry.

The driver grinned. "Now," he said, "you go up."

"Up?" Alan stared, and the other two burst out laughing. It was evidently an old joke.

"Up," the driver repeated. "Show him, Rikki."

The boy put one foot on the hub of the back wheel and, without apparent effort, swung himself, via the mudguard and the iron stanchion of the back flap, onto the roof. For a moment his legs wriggled frantically, then he slithered out of view.

"See," said the driver with pride. "You'd never know he was there."

Alan imitated him, hung for an awkward second in midair and found himself rolling full length beside the boy.

101

The roof was constructed of canvas over a metal frame; between the girders of the frame it sagged, and in the segments thus created they lay down—Alan, the boy, the precious suitcase. He noticed that the roof did not give beneath him because it was so encrusted with green paint. From his lying position he could not see the earth at all, merely the silver-green of the poplars fluttering in no wind, and the brazen sky beyond. At the end of the roof nearest to the driver's cabin was a rolled tarpaulin. Seeing his glance, the boy said, "For wet weather. We don't use it much. There are no hills and no tall houses this side of the frontier." He kissed his fingertips. "It's easy."

Again the lorry lurched as the driver climbed in; the engine throbbed and they moved away. The poplars slid past over their heads and receded in a swirl of pale dust.

It was an admirable hiding place—admirable in its complete simplicity—but it gave him a feeling of nakedness, of being exposed to every eye. The boy did not seem to notice this; a caterpillar had fallen from the trees and he was playing with it idly, coaxing it along the ridge which divided them. Alan watched the wriggling scrap of green life humping its way laboriously towards the edge. It reminded him painfully of himself; and when it came to the edge, what? Would it fall into the road and be squashed, or would it find another trailing branch of poplar and climb sedately back into leafy seclusion to continue its miraculous life, to weave its cocoon, to emerge quivering ecstatically as moth or butterfly, to propagate, to die? He watched anxiously.

Meanwhile they chugged along under the heavy sky. The earth, as his companion had suggested, did not exist. Occasionally a poplar reeled by, and once, set back from the road, he saw a group of factory chimneys; but there were no houses, or at any rate none high enough to overlook the

102

roof of the tall lorry. The simplicity of the hiding place was doubtless its strongest asset.

Then their driver honked his horn. The boy said, "This is it," and lay flat. The caterpillar, no longer urged along, paused and waved its head as if scenting the air. They were at the frontier. There was a sudden outburst of chatter, and Alan's heart began to pound again; his stomach turned over. Perhaps. . . . But no, the driver was on good terms with the guards; they were all laughing. This, after all, was only the Belgian side; here there would be no difficulty.

Again they moved forward, slowly, and jolted to a standstill. People were speaking in German and English: frontier guards and British soldiers. One voice, unmistakably a townsfellow of Rocky's, said, "Wotcher, cock? Any fags?" and another, further away, shouted, "Nobby, what about my char?"

The chains of the tailboard rattled and the board itself fell with a crash. Alan stiffened. Somebody had climbed into the lorry beneath him. He thought suddenly that his shadow must be visible against the bright sky; then he remembered the darkness within and saw its purpose. Nailed boots clattered on the wooden floor, paused, jumped down onto the road. The tailboard was swung into position and fastened. Somebody shouted; somebody else laughed. The lorry lurched as the driver climbed in, and a moment later they were moving, and he was in Germany. Only then he remembered the caterpillar and turned his head, but the ridge was deserted.

2 – THE MAN WITH TWO FACES

THE RAIN CAME DOWN STEADILY, FLATLY, WITHOUT RESTRAINT as though some floodgate in the heavens had broken open. The people on the platform huddled together under that part of the roof which was waterproof, and stared vacantly across the rails at the broken shapes of bombed engine-sheds. Beyond, softened by gauze upon gauze of rain, the desolation stretched away—tottering façade, twisted girder, heap of rubble. There was almost a design, a monstrous Gothic magnificence about those ruins, as if an eccentric nineteenth-century nobleman had erected them for a morbid "prospect."

The lorry had taken him as far as Mülheim, but the boy had climbed off at Düren not far from the frontier. Then Alan had ridden next to the driver in the cab. He had been glad to do so because the first fat drops of rain were beginning to fall.

"Only fourteen, that kid," the driver said. "Still I suppose you're used to it." He shrugged. "I'm Belgian myself, and we don't love you Germans, as you know, but. . . ." He was a kind man; he had a wife and four children. "It's the things you see," he had said. "They make you think. The kids most of all. I'm a family man myself and I know what's what. . . . Boys like that one, and the girls. . . . Whew! Hardened to it at fourteen; do anything for a packet of fags or a loaf of bread." He had glanced at Alan. "The chap that recommended you said you might be wanting to go back in a day or two."

"I was going to ask you about that."

"Well, I make the journey most days. See that farm?"

Alan stared through the rain which was now falling in

104

earnest. He saw a grey-stone barn and a derelict wind-pump. "Yes."

"It's called Kleinefeld. It's empty but the land's worked by a chap who runs the next one—over there beyond the trees. All you have to do is drop a line to Frau Straus—you can't forget that and the address is easy—Weserstrasse, Mülheim. No number, just Weserstrasse: it's a paper shop. Write any kind of bilge you like, but put the date when you want to go at the top, see—as though it was the date of the letter. Got it? Well, of course, you have. There's nothing to it.

"Then you go to Kleinefeld. Get there early in the morning, and keep an eye open till you see me stop on the main road."

"How about the farmer?"

"Oh, keep out of his way if you see him, but the place is lousy with tramps; he'll only chase you off."

Alan had complimented the driver on the simplicity of all his arrangements.

"Ah—" he had winked—"that's the dodge, chum. As you say, simplicity. Learned it in the army. Never fails."

There was a sudden movement on the platform. A train was coming in. Somebody shouted, "Neuweid, Mainz, Ludwigshafen. Change at Mainz for Saarbrucken."

Alan felt suddenly alone, defenceless. The grey-blue twilight depressed him, the eternal drift of rain across sightless windows and crumbling walls. The only consolation was that his own train, when it came, promised to be comparatively empty.

He was relieved that the people to whom he had talked seemed to accept him as one of themselves. He knew that his German was good and, in its region, colloquial, but that region was away to the South, in Austria where he had spent so many school holidays, walking in summer, skiing

105

in winter. In those far-off days he had been just as much at home with his Aunt Iris and Uncle Franz as at Ladeleigh with his mother and father. But how remote it all seemed now—remote, unreal, like a land of operetta—for even then, impoverished by one war and threatened by total annihilation in peace, there had been an irrepressible gaiety about Austria—to a child, at any rate.

Uncle Franz was dead now, and Iris, his mother's sister, presided autocratically over her second husband's family in New England.

His memories, as much as the rain and the desolation, seemed to emphasise the transitoriness of human endeavour. Sometimes it was almost as though the past bore no relation to the present. He thought of it again as a chain: gold links for the past, cheap nickel ones for the present, and joining them, where war had broken the continuity, a dirty piece of string. The memory of that evening when he had laughed with Linda in the kitchen of her tiny cottage seemed precious suddenly. He found, almost to his surprise, that he missed her. There was too much of loneliness in this deserted, ruined railway station, too much of departure for unknown places, too much of despair. And it was strange how that one word echoed in his mind: *dispossessed*. Was it because of Linda and the pathetic trust she had in him? Was he really dispossessed—he and all those like him, who, because society had slighted them, must sit back and raise their thin, lonely voices against it?

At that moment in the deserted railway station, surrounded by the ruins of man's folly, the memory of all that he had once been stifled him with its desirability. He wanted, passionately and suddenly, to be ordinary again, to allow himself to feel kindness and sympathy and love.

He thought, *Dear God, if I'm not to make a hash of this business, I'd better pull myself together.*

106

Then the train came clanking in, and he was momentarily enveloped in a swirl of hot steam with which his introspection faded, whipped by the cold wind into tatters and wraiths. There were three coaches immediately behind the engine; the remainder of the long load consisted of wagons bearing huge, wooden crates. As he had hoped, there were few passengers. He found a compartment to himself, wrapped the gas-cape tightly round his body and lay down full length, using the haversack as a pillow. Until that moment he had not realised how tired he was. It seemed incredible that only twenty-four hours ago he had been watching the lights of England fading away into night, had felt the cold wind on his face and the first lift and fall of the open sea.

Before the train moved out of Mülheim he was, asleep.

Twice during the night he awoke: once at Hamm—or so he presumed—to the dismal clink, clank, clink of a hammer testing the wheels; once in open country. He thought, *Soon, in a few hours, I will be in Neulingen. I will be knocking at the door of Number 17 Ludwigstrasse and Frau Lantz (she will be long-faced with brown hair parted in the middle) will open it, and I will say, "I wish to see Herr Schröder please," and there—in a room crowded with knickknacks, photographs in silver frames and ferns—the man with the fine features stuck haphazard into a coarse face will be moving to greet me.*

At Buckeberg, the purpose of the three coaches, attached apparently for no reason to a goods train, became manifest. There was a clatter of boots in the corridor, a sudden burble of chatter, and his privacy was invaded by a crush of workmen. From emptiness the compartment was swiftly packed jam-full of cold, swearing and yet surprisingly good-natured humanity. Three-quarters of an hour later, with much

107

shrill whistling and the clank-clank of many intersecting points, they rolled into Hannover.

All things considered he had slept well, and the day that was dawning showed signs of promise. Away to the east there were greeny-blue patches in the cloud, and the rain had dwindled to a fine drizzle.

By the station he found a small fuggy café; it also was full of workmen, but no one paid any attention to him. He procured a greasy mugful of something called coffee and retired to a corner with it. He breakfasted off this, a small tin of sausage and some dark bread which he had bought in Mülheim. Then he shaved with ice-cold water in the station lavatory, and went out to face the day.

It was now eight o'clock, and he decided to go at once to Neulingen and to find Schröder. The first strangeness of his position had worn off; he felt at ease, and that sense of desolation and hopelessness had left him. He was himself again, owing nothing to any man. To strengthen him in this mood the sun found those blue gaps in the greyness, flooding the shattered streets with a cool, yellow radiance which glittered in every quivering drop of water, blazed in the pools and puddles and on the defiant green of tree and grass and willow-herb.

Neulingen, he was told, was twenty or so kilometres out of the city, and for the first three or four of these he was content to walk. He did not want to descend upon Frau Lantz too early; moreover, his bones were still stiff from the seat of the railway carriage, which had been far from soft, and he needed the physical exercise to loosen them up.

However, when he did at last tire of walking, it soon became evident that begging a lift was no easy matter. There was little traffic and what there was seemed mostly of an official nature: a jeep driven by a young British officer splashed him all over with yellow mud, a van belonging to the telephone company swept by with regretful gesticulations, and a vast limousine containing three fat-necked and prosperous gentlemen who might well have been armament manufacturers ignored him grandly. Without much hope, therefore, he waved his thumb at a newly painted fifteen-hundred-weight truck, and was surprised when it came racketing to a standstill and the corporal at the wheel shouted, "Where to?" in excruciating German, adding "Cock" in English for good measure and friendliness.

It was on the tip of his tongue to shout back, "Neulingen, mate," but he restrained himself and replied in sedate Germanic English.

"Hop in," said the corporal. "And keep your head down if we pass any bloody officers."

"Please?" said Alan blankly.

"Down," explained the corporal, with gesture, "if I tell you to."

They moved off.

"Also—" he changed gear dexterously—"you'll have to hop out this side of Neulingen—" he called it *Nuligan*—"because we aren't allowed to give lifts, see. No give lifts."

Alan nodded.

"And the Colonel's a sod."

"Please?"

The corporal translated. He evidently knew the German words of disrespect.

Alan, who had been puzzled by the sign on the front of the truck, an arrow transfixing a red circle, pointed to its replica on the man's arm and questioned tentatively.

The corporal laughed. "You staying in Nuligan?" he enquired.

"For . . . one, two days."

"Then you'll hear us called the Gestapo, cock." With which cryptic comment he fell silent, applying all his energy to keeping the vehicle on the road. In spite of the pock-marked surface he drove at top speed.

Alan, though firm of nerve, was not sorry to get out when finally the town came in sight. The corporal smiled cheerily and shot away in a flurry of mud and a spurt of dirty water.

The first thing that he noticed about Neulingen was that it had not, as he somehow expected, been spared by the juggernaut of war. Evidently a pitched battle had taken place in and around it. He saw the rusted track of a tank coiled by the side of the road (too heavy presumably and too unimportant to be moved, even after so long) and the first houses that he reached were either ruined or pitted with the pox of small-arms fire. Strangely enough, those savage tooth-marks in small white cottages were more violent a reminder of war than the shattered cities. A rambler rose half-covered them.

The town itself was not large. It was compact but curiously featureless, as though it had been built all at the same time by a man without imagination but with a strong sense of utility. There were no picturesque old houses, no graceful town hall, no ancient church. The nineteenth century had given birth to it, and the twentieth, he discovered the closer he approached, had all but laid it waste. Willow-herb, bind-weed and nettles had seeded themselves joyfully, concealing man's handiwork.

The Ludwigstrasse, however, had survived almost intact. As an example of "German Domestic" it was not inspired. The three-storied houses had stucco fronts, grey slate roofs, and four yellow-stone steps leading to each front door. The churchyard occupied nearly all the side of the street, and, though pathetic individual attempts had been made to expose one or two graves, the majority of them were already concealed by the ubiquitous weeds.

He found himself, naturally, at the wrong end of the street

—opposite Number two, in fact. As he walked slowly along, counting, he became aware that excitement had gripped him once more. He was visited with a strange sense of absolute aloneness, for he had hardly seen a soul since he entered the town: only a black-habited nun scurrying across a backyard and a handful of middle-aged women gossiping on a corner. Of course he had not been near the centre of the place, but the old man who had told him the way had stared curiously; presumably strangers were few and far between in Neulingen, and well they might be—there seemed nothing to visit the place for, and it was inconceivable that there ever *had* been. He stopped on an impulse, listening. Yes, it was quiet, all right; somewhere beyond the houses a chicken was clucking in agitation, a lorry was grinding along in bottom gear, a man was sawing wood, the birds sang noisily in the churchyard, and yet a deeper silence held the town. No one moved down all the long stretch of the Ludwigstrasse; no dogs cavorted, no cat tiptoed carefully, no youth went whistling on a bicycle. Yes, it was uncanny; he felt that he was alone in the place, in the world perhaps.

Then, out of the corner of his eye, he saw the curtain of Number twelve twitch nervously. He laughed. An old woman pried behind her lace curtain, suburbia was in Neulingen, and God was in His Heaven.

He walked on more quickly. Fourteen . . . fifteen . . . sixteen. He paused at the foot of the yellow steps and smiled at the house; then he ran up to the door and rapped with the ugly iron knocker. The sound, peremptory and commanding, rang loudly up and down the empty street. He could not get over the peeping eye behind the lace; jocularly he thought, *I am in Hounslow, I am in Bourne-mouth, I am in Laburnum Avenue, Wellington Road, Acacia Crescent.*

The door opened.

111

"Frau Lantz?" he said.

"Yes."

A chill descended on him but for a moment he could not place its source. The woman was small, delicately boned; her hair neither brown nor parted in the middle. She looked frail and old. The eyes were startlingly blue in a pointed, once beautiful face, and the face itself was transparent. He remembered the bullet-pitted houses and was suddenly ashamed of his jocularity. She was old, frail, and. . . . Yes. Something slipped into place in his mind. She was afraid.

More guardedly, but still smiling, he said, "Does Herr Schröder live here, please?"

The reaction of the eyes was startling; they widened, flashed over him, briefly taking in his appearance, and fixed themselves—was it in appeal?—upon his face.

"Herr Schröder," she began. "Well, he . . ."

A man's voice behind her in the house snapped, "What is it? Who is there?"

The old woman said, "One moment. I . . . You . . ." She stood aside, or was brushed aside, and the man faced him. He was thickset with dark, cropped hair; he wore an untidy but not old blue suit.

"What do you want?"

Alan's mind had ceased fluctuating. As always in a real emergency—and he knew this for a real emergency now—it became calm and sharp. He said, "Is there a Herr Schröder living here, please?"

"What do you want?" the man repeated.

"To speak to Herr Schröder." He allowed a note of coldness to creep into his voice. It clearly surprised the other. He, like the old woman, now studied the young man curiously, then he said, "Why do you want him?"

Alan had prepared himself for this. Firmly he replied,

112

"He is my uncle, my . . ." He allowed his eyes to drop. "My only living relation."

There was an instant's hiatus. He realised that what he had said was not merely an excuse; it had taken the man by surprise—so much by surprise, in fact, that he asked a rather peculiar question. "When did you last see Herr Schröder?" Then, as if to cover it, "I mean, are you sure that it is your uncle who lives here? The name is quite common."

Alan struggled with this, but he could not immediately grasp the significance of it. Playing for time and letting pure intuition guide his answer, he said, "I have not seen him since . . . since before the War. I . . . I just hoped. . . ." What he really hoped was that his indecision would appear to be the halting emotion he intended.

The man stared for an instant longer; then he smiled abruptly. "Forgive me," he said, "but these days. . . ." He shrugged. "We have to be careful when people start asking questions. Please come inside. Herr Schröder is upstairs. I'll fetch him."

Alan walked into the narrow hall, aware of the old woman's brilliant eyes. He found the intense stare disquieting and would not meet it.

The man said, "You will wait in here, please," and ushered him into a small room. "Herr Schröder will be down in a minute."

Turning, Alan saw that the woman had moved to follow him but that the man closed the door in her face. This and the aura of her fear were the only two things that counted. The rest, the man's belligerent questioning, was not unexpected. After all Schröder was preparing to leave the country by illegal means; this in itself, apart from the secrets it implied, was enough reason for extreme care. Since he was the "illegal means" in question, Alan could

113

welcome any amount of caution. But Frau Lantz ("an old and trusted friend of his," Kellandale had said) was another matter altogether. What, then, did it all mean? Instinctively he eased the haversack onto one shoulder and loosened the frog which held it shut; he touched the rough butt of the Lüger and felt reassured.

The room was small, stuffy, a dining room but not used. Remembering more of MacBride's advice (good old Mac) he placed himself near to the door so that anyone entering the room would be forced to stand beyond it. He also (MacBride again) noticed the position of the large mirror over the fireplace.

Heavy footsteps were descending the stairs now. He heard the woman's voice saying, "But if what he says is . . ." and then the man's voice cutting in on her. "You had better go back to your room, Frau Lantz."

Alan was tense now, excited. He touched the gun again, then rested his hand lightly on the haversack.

The door opened. The old woman was arguing, evidently refusing to obey her orders. All three of them seemed to come into the room at the same moment—the woman, the man in the blue suit and another, taller, in grey. The woman stood with her back against the doorpost and it was at her that Alan now looked.

The man in grey said, "Good morning. You wished to see me?"

There was a moment's utter silence, broken only by the sound of the distant saw biting into wood. In the mirror Alan noticed the woman give an imperceptible shake of her head, but he knew, without her assurance, that the man in the grey suit was not Paul Schröder.

3 – DEATH AT THE WINDOW

THE SILENCE ENDURED FOR A MOMENT LONGER. HE WAS DEEPLY aware of the three pairs of eyes watching him.

Then he said, "You . . . you are not as I remember my Uncle Heinrich, but we have all changed so much. . . ."

There was an almost audible sigh. The woman looked away suddenly as if to hide some emotion.

"Heinrich," said the man in the grey suit. "My dear boy, I'm afraid there must be some mistake. Paul is my name— Paul Weibach Schröder. As far as I know I have no nephews alive."

Alan put a hand to his eyes and looked round for a chair. He sat down and stared at the ugly linoleum on the floor. "I'm sorry," he said in what he hoped was a broken voice. "I . . . I have come so far too."

The woman said, "Poor lad. And you'll be hungry. We haven't much, but. . . . No, I insist."

The two men glanced at each other. The one in the grey suit smiled. "Yes, I am sorry. Mine is not an uncommon name. You will excuse me; I am very busy." He turned and walked out of the room. The other lingered. Frau Lantz said, "Come into the kitchen. I'll see what I can find."

Alan followed her, and the man in blue tailed along behind. He was sure now that she wished to speak to him, but it seemed unlikely that she would be allowed to do so. The kitchen was bare and spotlessly clean. The old woman motioned him to a chair and spread a folded tablecloth over one end of the table; she was smiling secretly to herself and not looking at him. The man sat down in an ancient wicker chair by the window and picked up a newspaper. Glancing at him, Alan received a momentary impression of his not being a German, but could not analyse the feeling. Their eyes met.

"You say you've come a long way."

"Not far today, but I travelled all night."

The other nodded. "How did you hear that there was a Herr Schröder in Neulingen of all places? We . . . are very quiet here."

Alan had known this would come; he had prepared the only possible answer. "Oh, it was a chance. I was on my way to Bremen in any case, and I remembered my mother saying that Uncle Heinrich used to stay round here in the old days. We came once to see him, when I was very small."

The woman was frying something on a tiny primus stove. He could see, from the corner of his eye, that she was listening intently. He did not try as yet to arrange his thoughts and impressions, but it crossed his mind that it was clever of her not to blurt out whatever she wished to say; he would not have expected such self-control.

The man, however, had not finished his questions.

"That is most interesting," he said, "but didn't you say that somebody had told you that there was a Herr Schröder in this house?" He smiled again—the cold pretence of a smile. "Or have you been to every street in the town?"

Alan knew that there was no reason why he should comply with this cross-examination, but he knew also (MacBride again) that you learned more by answering questions with lies than by remaining doggedly silent. He said, "Ah, that was a bit of luck, I must say. I happened to ask a chap the way—as luck would have it he was a postman—so naturally I said, 'Perhaps you can tell me whether there's anyone called Schröder living in this town?' and he scratched his head, like they do you know, and he said, 'Well, it's funny you should ask. . . .'"

The man broke in—somewhat sharply. "Yes, yes. Of course. Quite a coincidence."

Frau Lantz exclaimed in annoyance and murmured something under her breath. Then she moved towards the door. The man was clearly suspicious; he said, "Can I fetch anything for you?"

"It's only the salt," she said and went out. There was evidently another man in the passage because he heard their voices. He wondered suddenly whether she was on his side after all. For an instant the whole thing seemed preposterous. He had barged into a strange house, imagining all manner of mysteries . . . and then he remembered Kellandale, decisive and powerful behind his desk, remembered the deep, sure voice. Whatever lies he had told—and it now seemed that Hagenaux and Rocky were right—he had been sure of his facts, and Alan trusted them implicitly. Schröder was here in this house and these men were enemies; in all likelihood Kellandale had half-expected them—hence the repeated opportunities that he had been given for backing out; hence the small white envelope to be opened only if there was "any trouble." He felt a slight twinge of anger against the bulky man comfortably entrenched behind his millions, his race-horses and his far-reaching power, but it was only a twinge.

Frau Lantz returned with a packet of salt. She glanced at him with excited blue eyes, and away quickly. Her silence had given way to a twittering solicitude.

"It's only sausage, I'm afraid, but it's all I have. Never mind. Here's bread, and I've plenty of milk so the coffee will be nice. You have no knife, have you?" She placed the plate before him. The man had retreated behind his newspaper but his watchfulness was only accentuated.

"And no salt-cellar," she continued. "I can't find it any-

117

where, so you'll take it from the packet if you need it, won't you? Such changeable weather for tramping the roads."

Her eyes held his as she put the packet of salt before him. The newspaper stirred and she moved away to deal with the coffee.

Alan looked at the packet. The cardboard was of bad quality and greasy, and the pencil had barely marked it, but he could read clearly enough what she had written: "He is here. We do not know these men." He poured a thin trickle of white crystals onto the edge of his plate and pushed the packet away. She understood him at once, picked it up, tore off the top and emptied the contents into a jam jar. Then she crumpled the cardboard and threw it into a bucket under the sink.

He was grateful for the meal, his first hot one for twenty-four hours, but was too occupied with his thoughts to notice it very much. Frau Lantz busied herself with cooking and the man in the blue suit continued to read the newspaper.

Alan realised at once that any sort of coup was out of the question. Whatever these men were up to they were in earnest. Schröder was very likely under lock and key, and the old woman, gallant though she was, could hardly be expected to shine in a rough-and-tumble. It would be a case of two, possibly three, to one. The house was silent, as if deserted, and he was reminded of the darkness of the lorry, the feeling that he was surrounded with people; there was the same feeling at Number seventeen, Ludwigstrasse, as though the first and second floors were packed with professional-looking gentlemen in untidy suits. He wondered how long this discreet villa in its silent country town had been in a state of siege. Of course it was preposterous: the old lady in Number twelve peeped behind her lace curtains; somewhere a man was sawing wood, somewhere a hen was clucking over an egg—but here, on rubber soles, was war. And

118

what did it mean? And how could he find out? And how, having found out, could Schröder be extracted?

Obviously the first thing to do was to engineer a talk with Frau Lantz, but not here and now—by darkness preferably because there was little doubt that she was virtually a prisoner.

He stood up with his mug of coffee and stretched; then he gazed ruminatively out of the window. The man stared at him suspiciously. He smiled back. "Looks as though we're in for a fine spell, eh?"

The man grunted and returned to his paper.

Alan studied the sky—pale blue with great blocks of grey-white cloud. At the end of the backyard was a wall with a door in it. Presumably a lane ran behind the houses. He then noticed that the yard wall was broken on the left-hand side, and surely . . . ? Yes, the house to the left was not occupied; it looked as though a shell had hit it.

Frau Lantz was watching him intently, trying to understand his thoughts, in which some sort of plan was germinating. He could only rely on her intelligence now. Once the man suspected him—or suspected him more than he did already—it would queer the pitch entirely. If, however, he could get behind that broken wall this evening, if he could then attract the old woman's attention, if she could make some excuse for going into the yard . . . if, if, if. But it was possible, and he did not think that she would be deterred—except by brute force.

He said, "Thank you very much for an excellent meal. I'm sorry I troubled you." He glanced at the yard. "Perhaps I could do something in return. Maybe you have wood to be chopped, or . . ."

He could see, in her clear eyes, how she was striving to follow the line of thought which was far from clear in his own mind.

119

"The meal is nothing," she said. It was pathetic to witness her desire to speak. "Particularly after you have come so far," she added meaningly.

Behind him the man folded up the paper and said, "You should find it easy to get a lift from here to . . . to Bremen, did you say?"

"Yes, Bremen."

Frau Lantz rubbed her roughened hands together. It was a telling gesture—all impotence and anxiety were in the bent fingers. "The young man has been so kind as to offer . . ." she began.

"Wood," said the man. "Your shed out there's full of wood."

Her eyes clung to his as if she were drowning. "Yes—" she was in an agony of indecision—"yes, to be sure, we have plenty of wood. I just thought . . . ."

"I'll walk along with you, and put you on the right road," the man said. He was implacable. The eyes were quite blank, and there was something . . . something—but what?—about his features. He walked over to the door and waited.

There was no alternative. Alan smiled at the woman and followed him. At the door he turned and looked back, then he winked at her—a slow, deliberate wink. He saw the strain lift from her face momentarily; it was not much but it was a promise. A peculiar promise, he thought as he followed the man to the door, because neither he nor she knew what it meant.

They walked in silence up the prim, ugly street; at the end of it another, even more ugly, ran at right angles. The man pointed to the left.

"Along there," he said, "until you reach the main road. You shouldn't find it difficult to get a lift." He stared up at the tall young man, his boot-button eyes twisted against the glare of the sky. "I hope you find your uncle," he added, and there might, conceivably might, have been faint sarcasm in his voice.

Alan conquered a natural inclination to reply in a like manner and turned away, walking quickly. He did not risk a backward glance, not even when he came to the road, turned to the right and so was lost to view. Once round the corner, however, he slowed down. He was seized with the sudden, terrifying idea that even now a car might be drawing up before the house in the Ludwigstrasse; he saw, in his mind's eye, how the door opened, how three men hurried down the yellow steps escorting another, a middle-aged man, how they bundled him into the car and drove quickly away, leaving a small woman with grey hair wringing her hands on the doorstep. It was all so real and so possible that he came to a dead stop staring at the dusty road. He knew at once that it was inconceivable that his mind should be at rest unless he could keep an eye on the house. He turned, looking back towards the town, his forehead wrinkled in concentration. In full sunshine it was indeed hideous—raw red brick, yellow stucco, grey slate with the stumpy church spire like a . . . The church! Of course.

He crossed the road and hurried towards it, remembering how the weeds and the grass had turned the once orderly graveyard into a miniature jungle. He was now in the main street of Neulingen, and here the battle had raged strongly, leaving only the shells of houses and a few patched up shops. He realised that it was a town without a centre, which explained the silence and the emptiness; it was hardly a town at all, in fact—merely a few rows of genteel semidetached houses absurdly surrounding a battlefield.

He entered the churchyard, which was deserted, circled the hideous edifice itself and walked with caution down an overgrown avenue of young cypresses. The number of graves surprised him until, kneeling in the long grass to peer under

121

the sweeping branches of a chestnut, he saw a rusted helmet, looked further and found a plain cross: Hans Untermayer, Private, 614 Regt. Neulingen's tasteless architect had supplied the ground; a later generation had filled it.

He was now hidden from view among grass and weeds. To his left the cemetery ended in a high, grey wall beyond which were roofs; to the right were the church and countless rows of graves overgrown and forgotten; ahead, over a rough wooden fence, was the Ludwigstrasse. He wriggled forward to the cover of another mournful cypress and raised his head. Immediately in front of him was a house with blank, uncurtained windows and sagging roof. With any luck . . . . Yes, it was Number eighteen, the back of which he had seen from Frau Lantz' kitchen. He crept forward again, making for an unusually luxuriant clump of willow-herb which grew round a small yew. As he had hoped, this position gave him an excellent view of the house. He eased the haversack off his shoulder, settled down, and began to study the upstairs windows. No movement, no sign of life. Around him was the buzz and murmur of a myriad bees and insects on a warm afternoon in early summer. He stared at Number seventeen Ludwigstrasse, which returned the stare without interest.

A breath of wind sighed in the grasses, and with it came melancholy, inescapable, heavy-fingered—a sense of waste and futility. He did not have to look far for the reason; graveyards were not conducive to gaiety at the best of times. A tingle ran down his spine; he stiffened. Somebody moved behind the left-hand upstairs window, somebody lifted the sash and leaned out; it was the man who had pretended to be Schröder. He looked up and down the street, resting his arms on the windowsill. The windowsill was dirty, and he frowned, rubbing the dust off his cuff, then spoke to someone over his shoulder and turned back into the room.

Alan took the plain white envelope out of his pocket and looked at it, pursing his lips. After a moment he put it away again. He had no wish to open it for a variety of reasons, and none of them the one which Kellandale would have supposed. In the first place he wanted to bring this off by himself—a matter of professional pride, perhaps; secondly, he did not relish the inevitable publicity incumbent on aid from "official" quarters . . . . And yet how long could he afford to wait? What exactly were those men doing in the house across the road? And who—for on this, he suspected, it all hinged—who and what was Schröder?

The afternoon dragged on.

At three-fifteen the man in the blue suit came out of the front door and hurried away up the street. At five minutes to four he returned carrying two bottles roughly wrapped in brown paper.

The breeze stirred in the trees and the grasses shivered.

At four-ten a face, possibly Frau Lantz, moved up to the window of the dining room and receded, pale, obscure, like a fish in a tank. At twenty-five minutes to five somebody shut the window, cutting off the drone of voices which had been going on all afternoon. At five-thirty Alan fell asleep, head pillowed on the haversack, midges wavering over him.

He awoke with a jolt at seven, stiff and cold and momentarily panic-stricken. The house looked neither more nor less empty than before; he wondered for a moment whether they had gone. Then he saw a man walking to and fro in the upstairs room; the sun was low in the west and the rich gold light shone in at the window catching his coat as he moved —to and fro, to and fro.

Alan opened a tin of sardines and ate them with dry biscuits. He was extremely thirsty and the midges were biting him, but having waited so long he refused to move now. At half-past eight he promised himself that he would

123

go round to the back of the house, but not before. In the meantime he scratched and mused.

The sky had clouded over and by eight-thirty a satisfactory between-light, more confusing to a watcher than darkness, had settled on the tangled graves and the street beyond. He was not sorry when the time came to leave; imagination and dusk lent an unutterably forlorn atmosphere to Neulingen churchyard.

At the foot of a headless angel which stood over the last resting place of an ex-mayor, he hid the haversack among weeds and dead leaves. Then, taking only the Lüger, he set out for the lane which he knew must lie behind the back doors of the Ludwigstrasse. It was not difficult to find, but instead of the waste ground he had expected to see beyond it, there was a murky canal, the water covered with nauseous green slime. In view of the fate which had overtaken the greater part of the town, he trembled to think what lay beneath. Moreover, the lane, bounded on both sides as it was, gave him an unpleasant sense of captivity, but it was too late now for a change of plan.

He kept close to the wall and walked quickly, glad of the dusty surface which deadened the sound of his feet.

In a sense it seemed absurd to be walking into danger like this without any purpose, but long ago during the war he had learned the folly of making plans before you had seen the lie of the land. No amount of Intelligence data could ever make up your mind for you: they had moved the flak ship, they were holding an anti-invasion exercise, or had altered the times of their E-Boat patrols.

The first setback was that someone, a landlord presumably, had nailed up the back door of the ruined house. This had a contrary effect on his spirits; he smiled almost happily. The nails were five- or six-inch at least, judging by the size of their heads.

124

He remembered that the walls dividing the backyards were high—a good ten feet—and he did not relish the idea of climbing them; it was bound to be a noisy procedure, it made sudden escapes difficult, and it would leave him, for a second or two at least, a clear target against the sky. There was only one alternative.

He moved on slowly towards the door of Number seventeen and examined it. In one place the frame had warped and he caught a glint of light between it and the brick; there was a crack of sorts, but plaster and cobwebs obscured it. With the blade of his knife he probed gently; a little cement pittered onto the concrete paving beyond the wall. He paused listening. There was no sound. He brought his eye up to the crack and looked through. The view was curtailed but clear. Frau Lantz was in the kitchen, ironing a sheet, which was a hopeful sign; he could just glimpse the flight of iron steps leading up to the door (the yard was below the level of the ground floor), the edge of a water tank, the centre post of a clothesline.

He did not for a moment suppose that the old woman was alone, but on the other hand it seemed doubtful that any of the men would be out in the yard; the night was showing every sign of being chilly and wet.

He gently lifted the latch of the door. If it was locked.... No. He felt it give imperceptibly. That might or might not be a good sign; it could mean unpreparedness or a trap, with equal likelihood. There might—a shiver flickered in the small of his back—there might easily be a man, the stocky man with black-button eyes, waiting for him on the other side. With the fear came, as always, swift exhilaration. *Insh-Allah after all*, he thought. A bullet had once nicked his ear; for that matter he had been torpedoed twice. If the man was waiting . . . . Well, he was waiting and that was the end of it.

He gripped the latch firmly and pushed the door open. It squeaked faintly, protestingly. For a moment he stayed thus, listening, not showing his body. There was still no sound. He stepped into the yard and closed it behind him. His heart was pounding furiously. He half-drew the Lüger from his pocket and held it there, not wanting the light from the kitchen window to glint on its barrel. He felt entirely exposed standing by the door, and moved into the oblique shadow of the woodshed.

Somehow he must now attract the woman's attention, and it was certain that he could not do so from where he stood. He must get nearer. For a minute or two he studied the house, paying particular attention to the darkened upstairs windows. They were shrouded in lace curtains and therefore quite blank, dangerous. He did not like those windows. The back door, of course, would be locked, but if she could make an excuse to fetch wood for the stove, or to bolt the yard gate, or to put the cat out . . . anything, anything. Or, if that failed, a message dropped from the kitchen.

But first things first. He must attract her attention. He moved stealthily towards the house, leaving the shadow with reluctance; the glow from the window seemed glaring, a searchlight on his face. He made for the next shadow—an irregular patch by the water tank. This stood near to a ragged gap in the side wall caused by the shell which had demolished Number eighteen. He crouched, listening and watching. Frau Lantz carried the freshly ironed sheet out of his range of vision and returned with something else over her arm. By the ironing board she paused, staring out of the window; her lined, fragile face seemed to be listening anxiously. He felt that she was waiting for him and his spirits rose at the thought. He could now see that there was a door under the iron stairway—a cellar, perhaps, at any rate a room of some kind.

And then, just as he was tensing himself to move, he saw something which turned him to stone; again that prickle of terror ran over his back and up the nape of his neck. The darkened upstairs window had moved. Between the bottom of the sash and the sill there had appeared a line of blackness. As he watched, the line broadened. Gently, very gently, somebody was opening the window.

For one moment he thought, *Schröder. Can it be Schröder?* He saw something dark creep over the sill—dark, gleaming—and he knew that it was the barrel of a rifle. His throat went dry suddenly and his brain refused to function; for an eternity he was blank, mindless. Then he turned and ran, and in that instant a picture flashed across his mind of the yard as it must look from the window, bare and softly lit from the light in the kitchen. He flung himself sideways and rolled through the gap in the wall, sprawling among rubble; it was a peculiar balletic leap and it saved his life. The rifle spoke—*psst*, like an angry snake—and he found himself thinking as he fell, *Oh the fools, the bloody fools.* Didn't they know better than to use a silencer which muffled not only the sound but the aim?

He picked himself up and dodged across the yard. Mercifully (God bless suburbia) it was identical to the one he had just left—same water tank, thrown on its side and gashed by the shell, same woodshed in the angle of the wall. He raced towards the latter, jumped for its sloping roof, and dragged himself onto it, almost winded by the force of impact. The rifle spoke again and the bullet ricocheted skywards, singing angrily.

He found himself thinking, *One's for a miss, Two's for a kiss, Three's for something better* . . . . Then he grabbed the top of the wall and scrambled up it, throwing a leg across and balancing for the jump.

Again the rifle flashed, and he fell.

127

For an instant he lay still in the dust, wondering whether this was the end; he could feel blood sticky against his body, and his face had hit a stone on landing.

Then a voice shouted. Two voices. Someone was running down the iron stairs. A door banged.

Somehow he stood up. Somehow he began to run down the lane, the wall mocking him on one side and the canal on the other. He kept his right arm tight to his side, unsure whether it or his body had taken the bullet. The lane was a hundred miles long and it seemed that he was moving infinitely slowly, if at all. It felt so much like a nightmare that he thought, *Perhaps this is a nightmare.* An instant later there was a sharp report behind him—a revolver this time, and further away than he had dared hope.

He found suddenly that he was running easily and fast, that the precious Lüger was still in his pocket, that the end of the stretch was only a few yards away. He tensed himself, flung out his left arm so that it smacked the wall and levered him round the corner. He could not aim but fired blindly towards the bobbing shape of his pursuer. It would serve as a check, perhaps. Then he turned and ran once more—ran and ran, turned right, turned left, across rubble, across grass, and into a quiet street.

His side—it was not the arm then—was hurting abominably, and he could feel the warm flow of blood down his thigh. It nauseated him and for a second the world reeled giddily. He leaned against an iron railing, the breath catching at his dry throat. In the silence he could hear voices, footsteps; the beam of a powerful torch flickered onto the houses across the way. They were hunting him.

He ran on, blindly now and in great pain, his whole body seeming to be coated with blood.

The voices, the voices, he thought. *Oh God, let me hang onto that.*

128

He stumbled across another heap of rubble towards the dark façade of a shattered building. *Shadow,* he thought, *keep to the shadow, and don't forget the voices. Don't forget....*

And suddenly the ground dropped from under him and he was falling. He was falling, falling, falling from a great height like a steeplejack he had once seen in Leeds—a tiny, cart-wheeling figure drifting lazily down from the top of a chimney.

But he clung to his Lüger and to the voices. Tenaciously, in midair, he held to the memory of what he had heard as he lay inert, shattered in the dusty lane: someone running down the iron stairs from Frau Lantz' kitchen, and a man shouting—a man shouting in Russian.

Then he hit the ground and was at peace.

4 – OFFICER, GENTLEMAN . . . AND FOX

ALAN HEARD A GIRL'S VOICE. "KEEP STILL," IT SAID. "THIS WILL hurt but keep still. Hold something. Otto, give him something to hold."

He tried to sit up but she restrained him firmly.

The boy came solemnly to the table on which Alan was lying and handed him a piece of wood which he took between his two hands. He could not see the girl's face, but her forearm moved above his eyes from time to time, golden and smooth.

"Now," she said.

The pain came upon him like a crushing weight; it was as if she had flung a rock at the side of his waist. His knuckles showed white against the brown wood and he shut his eyes.

"Again," she said, and again it fell upon him.

129

The boy—he couldn't have been more than fourteen—stood watching, round-eyed, as if the man's pain fascinated him.

"Again," she said.

He didn't think he'd be able to stand much more, and as if to reassure him or to answer a question he had not asked she said, "This will be the last. It must be cleaned, you see."

He did not answer because once more the rock fell, crushing him.

"Thank God, you're not a Frenchman anyway," she said. "The English have guts."

He was taken by surprise. "Not . . . English," he said, but she did not reply. "And anyway the . . . French are as brave as anyone."

She laughed gently. "They are your traditional allies, are they not? You must stick up for them."

The agony was over. He raised his head and glanced at her. She had two safety-pins in her mouth and her short, boy's hair fell forward, hiding her face.

"Lie down," she said. "Possibly you're right about the French. What does it matter, anyway? We're each as bad as the other."

"Are you a nurse?" he enquired.

"Why? Aren't you satisfied?" She pushed him down again. "How do you feel?"

"Much better."

"You're lucky. It's not deep. It grazed a rib."

"Bloody painful."

She laughed again. "You speak good German for an Englishman—it's all right, we shan't say anything. God knows, we're used to minding our own business in this country." She pinned the bandage. "But you're lucky, all right. Lucky not to be dead, lucky that you fell where you did too, lucky that we had the bandages—they're hard to get these days . . . like anything else. Is that too tight?"

130

"No, it's fine."

The boy, very brown, very fair, had not moved all this time. Alan handed him back the piece of wood, and winked. The boy smiled.

"Is he your brother?"

"Otto? No. I have no brothers. We don't have neat little families here like you do in England—not unless we're very lucky."

He lay back on the table and she stood arms akimbo, staring down at him. With the lamp shining full on her she was all one colour, all a soft brownish-gold—hair, skin, even the faded khaki shirt and trousers.

"Yes," she said, following his eyes. "They are British made."

"I wasn't thinking that."

She brushed back the fair curls from her forehead and regarded him calmly. The eyes were gold too—deep amber. She might once have been beautiful, he thought; not that she was old now, merely weary, sad, perhaps hungry. He was glad that he had the coffee in his pack, and a few tins of meat, and the cigarettes.

She said, "How fat you are!"

"Fat!" He laughed, but knew that it was no laughing matter that to her his lean body should seem well-covered.

"You can dress now. I'll mend your shirt when it's dry. In the meantime these will fit you." She threw him a bundle of clothing, and sat down.

"I've got to go out," he said.

She shook her head.

"But I've got to. I may even have to go to Hannover."

"Tonight?"

"Yes." He was excited now, light-headed, and yet his head throbbed angrily. He dressed in silence.

"You're not going out again tonight," she said after a while.

131

"Where are my things?"

She nodded towards a rickety stove before which his shirt and trousers were steaming. "Your gun and papers and so on are on the chest."

The room was warm and friendly, but ramshackle. He walked stiffly to the battered chest of drawers, propped up on four bricks in the corner. The white envelope looked less innocent now than when Kellandale had handed it to him— it had a smear of blood on it. With a twinge of regret he slit it open and drew out a thin slip of paper. The name was more or less what he had expected, "Lt. Colonel B. J. Hanson, D.S.O." but the address took him by surprise: "No. 3 G.E.S.P.O., Neulingen, Hannover. Give your name as Emil Werther." What G.E.S.P.O. meant he had no idea, but it was typical of Kellandale to have his "official assistance" so near at hand. Again Alan wondered how much of what had happened that bland, heavy man had expected; again faint anger stirred inside him that there had been no warning when a warning would have saved so much trouble.

He was on the point of asking the girl whether she knew where No. 3 G.E.S.P.O. had their headquarters when a memory flitted across his mind. What . . . ? Someone had said . . . ? He fought with it for a moment, very much aware of her eyes on him and the throbbing in his head. Then, suddenly, it came—the corporal in the truck. "You'll hear us called the Gestapo, cock." G.E.S.P.O. Of course. The usual consummate tact in high places; they couldn't have chosen more unfortunate initials. He said, "Is there a British Headquarters in the town?"

A flicker of malice crossed her face. "Yes. I thought you might be something to do with them." She was faintly contemptuous.

"Well, I'm not," he snapped. "If you knew how little I had to do with them you might be surprised."

132

She raised her eyebrows at the quiet anger in his tone and pointed at a chair. "Sit down. You look terrible."

He felt terrible and obeyed unsteadily. "I must go there," he said. "Tonight."

She shrugged. "Just as you wish. As I say, we don't ask questions."

He felt that her friendliness had gone and was surprised to find that he minded.

"I . . . I have nowhere to sleep," he said. "May I come back here?"

She stared curiously. "Why don't you stay there—with your own people?"

He grinned wanly. "Because I don't like the Army. Because the less they know about one the better. Because I'm in your blasted country under false pretences."

She remained impassive, her arm round the small boy's shoulder. The two of them stared at him steadily. Finally she said, "I don't believe you. There are lots of funny stories going round about the Gestapo. That's what we call them, or the William Tell Boys. . . ."

He remembered their sign—the arrow piercing the red circle.

"No." She was firm. "I don't believe you. You can sleep there."

"Listen." He stood up again. "I *can't* sleep there. They might. . . . No, it's out of the question. But, of course, if you won't let me come back here, I suppose I can find somewhere else."

Her eyes wavered. Plainly she didn't know whether to believe him or not.

He said, "I hope to God I don't run into those damned Russians again, because . . ."

"Russians!"

He glanced up, amazed. The amber eyes flared in the bony

133

face; she looked suddenly astonishingly beautiful. "Then they *were* Russians."

He was bewildered by her passion. "Why, yes . . ."

"Otto said he thought so—he heard them talking—but I wouldn't believe him. What are they doing here?"

"I wish I knew."

She was trembling now, biting her lip, and the eyes were frightening in their intensity.

For what seemed a long time they stared at each other, and there was silence. The boy glanced from one rigid face to the other. The logs in the stove settled noisily. Somewhere outside, rain was pattering on corrugated iron.

At last she said, "It is because of them that you must go to the . . . to your Army?"

"Yes."

She turned suddenly and caught her coat off the table. "Come, I will take you."

He moved over to her. His side was very stiff now. At the touch of his hand on her shoulder she became still, half-turning.

"Will you let me come back here?" he said. "I promise you on . . . on my honour—" he said it wryly, thinking of Patchway suddenly—"that I am nothing to do with the Army, or the police, or . . . anything."

She faced him frowning. After a moment she smiled. "God, what children you English are. Honour! As if we knew of such a thing."

"You don't believe me?"

She sighed. "Yes, I believe you—that's what is so amusing. Anyway, we have nothing to hide—nothing out of the usual. Everyone is a criminal these days. Put on this cape."

"I have one of my own." He explained how he had hidden his things in the churchyard. She called the boy to her and told him to go and fetch them. Then she helped Alan into the cape and led him out into darkness and rain.

He was astonished to find that the room had been underground. Sensing this the girl said, "It is a cellar, or it was a cellar."

"You've . . . lived there long?"

She did not answer at once. They were picking their way across more rubble.

"I was born there," she said finally. "Not in the cellar, of course."

"And you came back?" He was surprised. Neulingen did not seem the sort of town one would return to.

"Yes. Why not? One had to go somewhere. I thought that perhaps. . . . There *are* still one or two of the old people left here."

They had reached a street now. Somewhere, in a house, a small clock was striking.

"Is that midnight?"

"Yes."

He had not realised it was so late. Colonel Hanson would not be pleased, if he had retired to bed.

"You must have been very fond of the place," he said, "to come back."

"I hated it."

He stumbled and she supported him. He was feeling very weak about the knees and his chest hurt him.

"Are you all right?" She peered closely in the darkness.

"Perfectly."

"I hated it," she repeated. "I wouldn't stay here in the old days, you know. I thought it dull, provincial."

"I dare say it was."

"Yes. But we have found that there are worse things than dullness, haven't we?"

"That's why you came back?"

"Yes."

He was moved by this picture of the callous, carefree girl craving for excitement, for escape . . . of the war-torn, weary woman craving for dullness, for safety.

She led him across a small square, past the church, down an alleyway and into another road. There were fields on one side of it, and ahead in the darkness, he saw lights among trees.

"The Gertlers used to live there," she said. "They thought no end of themselves, and their tennis parties were longer and larger and duller than anyone else's. No one knows what became of them."

What an epitaph, he thought.

She said, "I shan't come in. I will wait here."

"No. No, you must come with me."

"Why?"

"Because I want you to. It will look better. I don't want them to know that I'm English. Only one of them must know."

She stared at him in the darkness. He could see the light, wavering between moving branches, on her face.

"All right then. I'll come. But they . . ." She shrugged wearily. "It's not their fault, they're men and away from their women."

"You'll be left alone, I promise."

She laughed.

"Oh yes, you will. Come on."

They approached the gate. The sentry eyed them suspiciously.

Alan said in German, "I wish to see your guard commander."

The sentry said, "Oh cripes. Don't you speak blinkin' English? *Sprechen* English?"

"No. I wish to see your sergeant."

"He'll be bloody mad," said the sentry, grasping the word *sergeant*. "Can't you come back . . . ? Oh hell." He waved his arm towards the town and said, "*Morgen, morgen*."

"No." Alan stood firm.

The soldier sighed resignedly and blew three blasts on a whistle. After a moment he repeated them, the call wailing mournfully among the dripping plane trees.

"He'll be fair bloody ravin'," he said sadly.

Eventually, just as he raised the whistle again, the sound of boots crunching on gravel accompanied by lurid swearing materialised out of the darkness. The sergeant was small and wiry with a sallow, bad-tempered face.

"I thought I told you . . ." he began, but Alan said, still in German, "I wish to see Colonel Hanson."

"Oh Gawd." The sergeant stared.

"Hanson," repeated Alan.

"*Morgen*," said the sergeant.

"No. At once. Urgent."

They argued for a little while. At length the sergeant agreed to ring the Mess and find out if the Colonel had gone to bed. They trooped to the guard hut. The Colonel had not gone to bed. He was playing bridge.

"Look here," said the sergeant. "Got a couple of 'em down here say they've got to see him. They say it's urgent." He glared. "God knows. I can't speak the bloody lingo. Well, he gave orders last week that if . . ."

Alan wondered whether those orders had anything to do with Kellandale and thought that they probably had.

The sergeant was fast losing his temper. "He won't know their bloody names, will he? Of course, they aren't. If they were, they'd know the routine, wouldn't they? Oh, all right." He turned from the telephone. "What name? *Name?*"

Alan said, "Emil Werther," and thought, *That ought to get the old boy moving*.

137

"How spelled?"

Alan spelled it. The sergeant relayed the information and there was a momentary pause. It was like the lull while a fuse is burning. Alan smiled at the girl. The amber eyes were withdrawn, guarded.

The telephone cackled.

"Gawd," said the sergeant. "Well, how the hell was I supposed to know?" He slammed down the receiver and shouted, "Corny. Corny. Come here."

Muffled cursing arose from an inner room where the guard was sleeping. A dishevelled figure appeared, struggling with its belt.

"Take these two up to the old man's office, and get a move on. He's waiting."

Alan wondered a little at the long arm of Kellandale, wondered also exactly what relationship existed between him and the commanding officer of No. 3 G.E.S.P.O.

The soldier led them up a drive bordered with plane trees and into a side door of the house. They were met by an extremely smart and efficient corporal who said in faultless German, "Are you both seeing the Colonel?"

"No," Alan replied. "This lady will wait for me. I don't want anyone to worry her either."

The corporal looked aggrieved. "Of course not. Please step in here, Fräulein." He opened the door of a small bare room furnished with a stove and four leather armchairs. Then he ushered Alan along a short passage at the end of which was another door labelled "C.O."

Alan had expected Colonel Hanson to be old, but the man standing by the fire was not more than forty—clean-shaven and elegant. As soon as the door had shut he said, "Trouble, I take it?"

In English now, Alan said, "Yes."

Hanson moved forward. His face was clean-cut, decisive,

and his eyes surprisingly merry. As he passed under the light his hair glinted red. He gave an impression of polished acuteness; it was easy to see that Kellandale would be taken with this quality. He stared intently at the younger man and said, "What's the matter? You look ill."

"I've just missed being killed." He described the wound.

Hanson became a trifle more serious, waved at a chair and sat down on the edge of his desk.

"I want the piece of paper with my name on it," he said abruptly.

Alan produced it from his pocket and handed it over. Hanson held it up to the light, nodded, and rolled it into a ball which he flicked into the fire. "You're Morgan," he said. "No, don't frown. After all, you know who I am! Fair exchange, eh?" He rang a bell on the desk. "Our . . . mutual friend is a very remarkable man, don't you think? I imagine . . ." The door opened. "Brandy, corporal, and two glasses. I imagine he found you very much to his taste."

Alan smiled. "Why?"

The other stared at the fire. "Action," he said finally. "Men of action. They'll be the death of him finally. Why? Because one day he'll hit on one that'll act for himself, overreach himself. I might. You might. Unless, of course, we're careful." He smiled charmingly. "Are you careful?"

"No."

"Of course not. It's a paradox."

"He said that too."

"Oh, yes, he realises it all right."

The corporal returned with the brandy, then withdrew. Hanson poured two large glasses. "Your health. Did someone dress your wound properly?"

"I think so."

"My doctor'll look at it in the morning if you like." He

still perched on the edge of his desk. "Now tell me. What's happened?"

Alan looked into the brandy. "How much do you know already?" he said.

The other laughed. "Excellent, excellent." Then he was serious again. "I know a great deal more than you do; put it that way."

Alan told him of his arrival at Number seventeen, Ludwigstrasse, of his vigil in the graveyard, of his return visit via the backyard, and of his escape. When he had finished there was a long silence.

Hanson stared at the fire, biting his lower lip. "Russians, eh?" he said at last. "Greedy devils." Then he was silent again for a long time. "Of course, they've no right to be there. They'll be masquerading as Germans just as you are." He stood up and began to walk up and down the room. "The point is," he said, "one has to be careful when it comes to the international stock-pot."

Watching him, Alan realised that the man was ruthless—ruthless and ambitious; he would presumably need to be ambitious to achieve his rank so young. Again he wondered what sort of game he was playing with Kellandale—the power game, presumably, and very dangerous too. Dangerous, and thus useful: the longer the lever, the greater the purchase.

After a time Alan said, "Who *is* Schröder, by the way?"

Hanson stared absently, then smiled. "A friend of Lord K's as far as I know. Why?"

"He must be a friend of the Kremlin's too."

The other gesticulated. "It would seem like it." He was blank, granite-hard.

"I'm sorry. I shouldn't have asked."

"No harm in asking, my dear chap—as long as you don't expect a truthful answer. I agree it's very galling to the

140

intelligence, but then. . . ." He came to rest once more on his perch. "You'll be needing all the intelligence you can muster to get this lad back to England." He stared, smiling. "I rather admire you. What were you in? Navy?"

"Yes."

"I thought so." He seemed perfectly calm; it was evident that he had made up his mind.

"Well?" said Alan.

"Yes." He sipped a little brandy. "Yes, it's my move now, isn't it? I'll tell you what I'm going to do. I'm going to arrest the whole bloody lot of them."

Alan was startled. "Frau Lantz too?"

"Yes. Frau Lantz, the Russkies, the whole caboodle." He laughed boyishly. "The Gespo strikes. What a name, eh? And what a stink there'll be."

"What does it mean, by the way?"

"Gespo? Oh, Whitehall, where is thy sting? It means 'General Enquiry Section, Political Organisations'. Can you beat it?" His eyes were dancing with merriment now. "If what's going on at Number seventeen, Ludwigstrasse, isn't a political organisation, then it looks enough like one to let me out."

"What do you mean there'll be a stink? The Russians?"

Hanson looked at the fire through his brandy glass. "I don't know about them. They'll be on thin ice, won't they? Their three bravoes will need a little explaining away." He mused. "No, I think the Russkies may keep relatively quiet."

"Who then?"

"Ah." The eyes glittered. "You had better watch your newspaper, as they say. I'm a damn clever chap, you know. It may all go off without a hitch, particularly if you go to bed—where you ought to be, by the way—and stay there until I send for you."

"Don't you want me to identify Schröder?"

141

Hanson smiled. "I think I can manage that. The main thing is that my actions should not have any . . . any provable connection with yours. I take it that you're staying with your Samaritans?"

"Yes."

"You don't know the address?"

"No."

"When you go to see my doc in the morning, give it to him in an envelope. I'll send for you when I need you."

"All right."

He lifted a field telephone from the desk and pressed the buzzer. "Duty officer? Who is it? Oh yes, Newman. I want you to call out the duty escort section. Yes, and I want them fully armed. As soon as you're ready, report to me here. Jeeps and motorcycles, my staff car and the Maria. Yes. At once."

He replaced the hand set and smiled placidly at Alan.

"We will now," he said, "do a little General Enquiry into Political Organisations—just to prove that it's a free country."

He sat on the wall with his legs dangling and watched the children working in the garden. Beyond, were three Nissen huts, humped among a tangle of trees and bushes like monstrous beetles; but in the garden itself all was in regimental order—beans, cabbages, lettuces, potatoes, neatly ruled lines of green on the dark earth.

The girl came towards him down a cinder path between the bean rows. She walked with an easy stride like a man, and yet there was nothing masculine about her, in spite of trousers and shirt and her curly, short hair.

She paused beside him, looking at the children bent industriously over their vegetables. He saw that she was smiling.

142

"Good work," he said.

She nodded. "The Sisters are wonderful. Nothing deters them—absolutely nothing." She leaned back, against the wall beside him. "It is the least one can do, don't you think? For the children there's a chance."

"And for . . . us."

"For us?" She laughed. "What do we deserve? We're the guilty ones."

"And you think these youngsters will grow up wiser?"

"Wiser!" She stared at him. "Of course not. But perhaps they will have a little happiness. Children can be happy under strange circumstances—they're spared comparisons."

He said, "You sound as though you'd ceased living. Don't you want happiness too?"

She did not answer at once. Then, "You're a child yourself. I don't look forward to anything. There will always be the memory of what I have seen. And done. Don't look so serious."

"Isn't this a serious conversation?"

"No." They strolled in silence. "What is there serious about us? If anything, we're contemptible."

The hopelessness in her voice touched him. He took her arm on an impulse. Half-mocking, he said, "Is there no hope for us, please?"

"Of course. We want faith of some sort. It doesn't matter what we have faith in—in God, like the Sisters, or . . ." She turned the amber eyes on him. ". . . or in oneself, like you."

"So you think I have faith in myself?"

"Yes, I do."

"Isn't that selfishness?"

"Of course. But you are selfish."

This touched him. He felt a momentary twinge of anger, but he knew immediately that she had spoken the truth, and he thought of Linda waiting in Antwerp. Between these two women there seemed to be a kind of link. Or was it that he was a man, and that all women were therefore linked against him?

As if to underline his thoughts, she said, "I don't know what you're up to here, but obviously it's something outside the law."

He nodded.

"You're a child," she said for the second time, "and, what's more, you're a fool. We *have* to live like this." She indicated the wrecked town. "You don't."

"What do you mean?"

"I mean that you have no reason to be doing what you are doing. You should go home, and get married and have children of your own."

"How do you know I have no reason?"

She laughed. "Because of your eyes, and the way you talk and smile."

They had arrived at the broken steps which led down to the heap of rubble that had once been her father's house and garden. She paused at the top staring at him. "What was it you told me you were when I asked last night? 'An adventurer,' you said, and I said, 'What's that?' and you said, 'Oh, a little boy who can't sit still'!"

"I was being funny."

"Were you? It's true all the same." She waved absent-mindedly to Otto, who had just come out of the cellar. "And when you were coming round after your fall you kept saying the same word, you know."

"I did? What word?"

"Dispossessed."

He started.

"Why?" she continued. "You're not dispossessed."

"I've had my troubles," he said, pompously.

"Have you?"

144

Her cool voice made no comparisons, and yet the comparisons were there. And what were his "troubles" compared with hers? What indeed?

"I don't know why," she said, gazing down at the little boy standing among the rubble, watching them, "but I get a feeling that you don't really like what you're doing. I get a feeling that you're straight-forward and simple at heart. That's why I call you a child." She stared at him again. "You need a woman—not a woman like me, not a cynic—but an ordinary decent woman, someone to keep you in order."

It was his turn to laugh then, but again he thought of Linda and the danger into which she had meandered, merely in order to be at his side. His own selfishness seemed very real at that moment.

"I've got a woman," he said, and even to himself he sounded surprised.

"Then what in Heaven's name are you playing at crime for?"

Their eyes met and held, and hers were so full of the misery and suffering which they had seen that he was ashamed of himself.

"I don't know," he said. And meant it.

Otto was calling out now—he seldom spoke except to the girl—and came running to meet her. She turned and went down the steps, but Alan remained at the top staring after her, and only pulled himself together and followed when she shouted from the bottom, "What's the matter? Have you seen a ghost?"

Otto was full of the town's gossip: how the "William Tell Boys" had descended upon the Ludwigstrasse and arrested Frau Lantz and no less than four men, in the middle of the night.

The girl glanced at Alan but he avoided her eyes.

What everyone wanted to know, Otto continued, was

145

what Frau Lantz was doing with four men in her house anyway, let alone at that hour.

Alan said, "What else are they saying, Otto?"

"Some Americans arrived this afternoon."

"Where?"

"Here, in Neulingen. Men in white helmets and a general in a car."

"A general?"

"That's what Frau Unsbach said."

As if to help him, the girl added, "Frau Unsbach is apt to exaggerate a little."

Alan nodded to her. "What else, Otto?"

"Nothing else. They all went up to the Gespo place, and Frau Unsbach said . . ."

"Yes."

"That Bertha told her that there was some sort of trouble up there."

The girl, busy at the stove, said, "Bertha goes there to help with the cleaning. She . . . knows one or two of the soldiers fairly well."

Alan said, "What else, Otto?"

The boy shook his head. "Only this. One of your people brought it just after you'd gone."

He opened the envelope and read:

"Please come to my office immediately." It was signed "Hanson."

The girl was watching him.

He said, "I've got to go up there at once."

She shrugged. "There'll be something to eat when you come back."

This time there was no trouble with the sentry. It seemed that orders had been given to admit him as soon as he arrived.

146

Hanson was as courteous as before, but not quite so self-assured beneath the façade.

"I thought something had happened," he said. "I sent the note an hour ago."

"I was out."

"By the way, may I have it, please?"

Alan handed it over and watched the long nervous fingers tear it across and across. "You don't take any risks," he said.

"Do you?" The quick eyes were almost venomous. "And in any case this is not a moment for taking risks."

"I gather you have visitors—if town gossip can be relied upon."

"It can indeed be relied upon." Once again he perched on the edge of his desk. "Yes, I have visitors." He ran a hand over his smooth, foxy hair. He was, now Alan came to think of it, entirely foxlike: elegant, sly, bright-eyed, handsome.

"Yes," he repeated. "Visitors. I suppose you're thoroughly suspicious by this time."

Alan shook his head. "I think I realised long ago that there was something fishy about it. Kellandale lied to me, of course."

"What did you expect?"

"I'm not sure."

Hanson laughed suddenly. "Look here," he said. "Let's simply say that you're being paid to get Schröder to England and no questions asked."

"That's reasonable, so long as I'm treated fairly."

"Haven't you been?"

"A little truth would have saved a lot of trouble. Couldn't he have said, 'This chap Schröder is an important man, very important, and you may find yourself up against other people with the same idea as yourself'?"

Hanson nodded. "He could have said that, I suppose."

147

Alan lay back in his chair. "Now, I take it, your 'stink' has come to pass."

"Yes. Yes, indeed." He mused for a moment. "All right, I'll play fair. Schröder *is* an important man—one in whom the, er . . . the Allies, shall we say, have a certain interest. It was hoped that when he left Berlin for a destination unknown, he would not be . . . well, noticed. Unfortunately we underestimated the interest which was being taken in him."

"Why," said Alan, "hasn't officialdom made use of him if they're so interested?"

Hanson stared. "Isn't that obvious? From what you've seen here in Neulingen?"

"International hocus-pocus."

"Yes, as you succinctly put it, international hocus-pocus. If one country . . . appropriates something of value, another promptly raises an outcry. Schröder is 'something of value.'"

This had the same honest ring to it as much that Kellandale had said. Now, instinctively, Alan mistrusted it.

Hanson went on, "It was Kellandale's idea—a rather brilliant idea, I must own—to steal the bone while the dogs were . . . well, stalking round each other, shall we say?"

"And now, complications."

"Exactly. And the, er . . . the dogs have bounced out of their kennels in the usual order: your friends at the Ludwigstrasse, my visitors of today, and—lastly, with magnificent hauteur—our own compatriots."

Alan nodded. "You're playing a risky game, aren't you?"

Hanson smiled and the eyes were merry for an instant. "In that respect, Mr. Morgan, the clue is very simple: my mother was Irish."

They both laughed, but the Colonel was serious again at once. "I tell you this because I admire you and because I don't think the Boss played quite fair with you. The situa-

148

tion is now as follows: I have, in my lockup, Herr Paul Schröder and three dubious fellows calling themselves Prei-stadt, Muller and Kraft—very fishy . . ."

"And Frau Lantz?"

"She was taken home at once with instructions to stay put for a day or two. All right." He tapped his forehead with long fingers. "This morning I am visited by my American opposite number from Berlin, charming fellow but cagy. This afternoon I receive a call from my own immediate chief. Neither of these gentlemen mentions Schröder by name; both think that my action of last night was concerned with his disappearance from Berlin, but . . ." He pointed. "*But* they don't know that I know anything about the man —except, of course, the usual official dope which means nothing. They think that I simply arrested three Russians who had no business to be in my area. They have their own ideas about what these gentlemen were up to, but they aren't letting me in on them. See?"

Alan said, "Whew. Is this representative of a day's co-operation among Allies?"

"This," replied Hanson, "is child's play compared with some of the tangles. But you understand?"

"Perfectly."

"Good. Now, this evening I get information—from what might be called 'reliable sources in high places'—that an official complaint is to be lodged by the Russkies against my conduct."

"But . . ."

"But they have no business to be here, you are going to say. Correct. What do we infer? We infer, my friend, that the case of Herr Schröder is very soon going to emerge from suggestive twilight into the very revealing glare of midday." He stood up and went over to the window. When he spoke again his voice was calmer, more reflective.

"I like danger," he said. "I believe you do, too."

"Up to a point."

"Of course, up to the point where it gets the better of one. I also like Kellandale. But I happen to know that he might not be so friendly towards me if anything went wrong in this particular little goose chase. And I need him to remain friendly. He's useful."

"Will anything go wrong?"

"I don't think so. But you see how closely our two lives —should I say fates?—are linked in this matter. That is why I have been so frank. It means a good deal to both of us that Schröder should reach England intact."

"I see."

Hanson glanced at him over his shoulder. "I'm glad you see."

"And now what?"

"Ah, that's the point. We are distressingly much the focus of interest, aren't we? But we still have the great military advantage of surprise in our favour. Nobody knows, yet, what we are up to." He turned back into the room. "But we've got to act at once."

He returned to his perch on the desk.

"For once," he said, "the official passion for keeping facts to themselves, and expecting junior officers to do their jobs without proper information, is going to boomerang on them."

Alan frowned.

"You would not be expected to understand, because you do not labour as I do in the toils of bureaucracy." He leaned forward, bringing his bright, brown eyes close to his visitor's grey ones. "The salient point in all this is that no one has let me into the secret of Schröder—not officially."

Alan saw light suddenly. He sat up.

"Precisely," said Hanson. "I don't know Schröder, so how the hell can I know that I've got him in my cell?"

"You'll release him."

"I'll do more than that, my lad. How do you cross the frontier? I don't want details or names. Where's the rendezvous?"

"A small farm the other side of Mülheim."

"Have you arranged it?"

"No. It's short notice for that. I have to write."

Hanson swore. "You won't have any time for writing. You'll have to make your contact some other way. Can you?"

Alan remembered the address in Mülheim, Frau Straus, Weserstrasse. He remembered also the confident, comfortable voice of the blue-chinned driver: "I make the journey most days."

"It should be possible," he said. "It might mean a delay, all the same."

Hanson said, "Better a delay at Mülheim than here."

"Of course, I'll manage it somehow."

"Good." He walked back to the window, nervously, excitedly. "Can you drive?"

"Yes."

"All right. Then you'll drive tonight, and you'd better drive like hell. I'll have a van waiting for you a mile down the Hannover Road at eleven. Schröder will be in it." He was serious suddenly. "You must realise that this is all the help I can give you. You're safe until the balloon goes up —that's to say until somebody accuses somebody else of hiding Schröder. Then everyone'll have it in for you, but I hope for your sake you're out of Germany by then."

Alan stood up and they faced each other.

Hanson said, "How's the wound? Can you make it, do you think?"

"Certainly I can make it." He was excited too—glad to be moving again.

The Colonel laughed. "Lucky blighter. I wish I was going with you. I'll have a map marked for your best route." He paused, eying the young man critically. "You know what the incalculable factor in this little drama is, don't you?"

Alan shook his head.

"The Russians, my lad. As ever, the Russkies. You don't imagine they aren't watching, do you? The arrest of their three bears in the Ludwigstrasse came as a nasty shock, I've no doubt. So far there haven't been any official repercussions. Why? Because the bears had no right to be there. But—" he waved a long finger—"that won't stop them monkeying about with you if they once suspect that you're holding the honey pot."

"I see."

"That's why we've got to get moving. The sooner you're in dear old England the better for all of us."

"In fact," said Alan, "the sooner you see the last of me, the happier you'll be."

Hanson laughed. "That's just about it. Have you got a gun?"

"Certainly I have."

"Good." Once again he dropped from laughter to sudden seriousness. "You'll probably need it before you've finished."

5 – ILLEGAL EXIT

THE GIRL WALKED WITH HIM TO THE EDGE OF NEULINGEN. IT was a still, close night, moist with the smell of rain and the promise of more rain. After her moment of extrovert criticism when she had told him, so casually, about himself, she seemed to have retired into the high tower of her own loneliness—retired and locked the door.

She said, "Are you doing . . . what you are doing for money?"

"For what else?"

At this she laughed gently, sadly. "Ah yes, for what else?" He could barely see her in the warm darkness. "People used to do things because they felt they had to . . . once."

Alan held her arm. "If you mean, 'Am I risking my life for King and Country?' the answer's 'No'."

"And yet," she said, "you are not really a crook—not like others I've known."

"And you've known a lot of course," he mocked her.

"Yes, many." The flat acceptance of her tone made him ashamed of his mockery.

"Our life here," she added, "makes us like that. When people have nothing particular to hope for, they don't much mind what they do or how they do it."

"The dispossessed," he said gently.

"Yes, and you are not one of us. Go back to your girl. She loves you."

"I've got work to do."

"Is it so important?"

"To me, yes." He could feel her peering at him but would not turn to meet her eyes.

"Because you think you have a grudge against society, I suppose."

"Not necessarily." Again he was surprised by her perspicacity.

She said, "We have too many young men like you—I know the symptoms. I wouldn't have thought you so weak."

"Am I weak?"

"Yes." She laughed once more—a cold, almost contemp-

153

tuous laugh. "I'm arguing for your girl now. Doesn't she say this sort of thing?"

"No."

"That's because she loves you, but she thinks as I do all the same."

He was beginning to realise how little he knew about Linda, beginning to see himself as he might appear to her. It was a disturbing picture.

Suddenly, out of the night, the girl said, "I shall say good-bye here."

He turned, aware that already she had left his side. Dimly he could see her standing in the road. He went back to her. "You've been very kind."

"Only human."

"Both are rare."

She shrugged. "You must grow up, my friend. You live in a schoolboy's story book."

"You're very critical."

"Children must be criticised if they are ever to learn anything. Good-bye."

He made a move to kiss her, but she evaded him. "Sentimentalist," she said.

"That too?"

"Oh yes. That and much more. All the usual male tricks. I could love you, though you might not think it."

He felt great pity for her suddenly.

"Go," she said. "Go, go, go before I start to tell you my life story. Good-bye and good luck. Thank you for the coffee and things."

And she turned and walked away, a tall, pale figure in the darkness.

For a moment he stood alone looking after her, his heart heavy because of her vast aloneness. Then, somewhere, a clock struck the three-quarters and he remembered where he was.

After he had walked for ten minutes he caught the glimmer of a red light in the darkness ahead, and a moment later saw the shape of a small van silhouetted against the sky. It seemed strange that now, after so long, he was to meet Schröder face to face.

A man was standing in the road and greeted him in German; he was a civilian. He flashed a torch in Alan's eyes and seemed satisfied with what he saw. Then he said, "Open your coat and shirt."

Alan revealed the dressing over his wound.

The man grunted. "And the name of your passenger is . . . ?"

"Schröder."

"Good." He smelled of garlic. "Follow, please." He led the way round to the side of the van, and flashed the torch through the window.

Alan looked into startled blue eyes, glimpsed the haphazard features which he seemed to know so well, the high forehead, long chin, very fair hair merging to grey at the temples. It seemed that already he knew the man well.

"All right," he said. "That's him."

Out of the darkness came a grubby hand holding some papers. "Instructions," said the voice. "From the small firm of Karl Traube at Freibach; they deal in agricultural machinery. This authorises Werner Sagan to take their van to the Strelitz people at Mülheim . . ."

He remembered Hagenaux' mentioning this factory. "Strelitz and Sonneberg?" he said.

"That's them—to collect spare parts. All right?"

"Fine."

"Don't use the papers unless you have to. The other chap

155

has a map with a suggested route marked out for you. That's all. Good luck and don't stop this side of Hannover."

The torch flicked off and the man turned away. Alan stuffed the papers in his pocket and clambered into the van beside Schröder. He was relieved to find that there was nothing unusual about the gears, and a moment later they moved off.

He said, "So we start at last."

The other grunted. "There is a map here if you should need it." His voice was precise, dry, over-educated—it reminded Alan of his tutor at Cambridge. "I may as well say at the outset that I have instructions not to discuss anything with you."

His primness irritated the young man. He said, "Believe me, the last thing I want to do is talk about it. I'm fed up with the whole business."

There followed an astonished silence.

"In fact," he continued, "the less we talk the happier I shall be. We may as well conserve our energies for saving our skins. Have you got a gun?"

"No." The voice was less sure now.

Alan swore. "Well, keep your eyes open."

"What for?"

"For anything in uniform, anything suspicious out of it, anything following us. In fact, anything. And wake me up if I seem to be going to sleep."

They drove in silence after this.

He was irritated—unreasonably so, he realised. His personal feelings or opinions had never been part of the bargain, and the instinctive dislike which he felt was therefore nothing whatever to do with the matter in hand. To him Schröder should be merely a valuable parcel which had to be delivered. Unfortunately, however, the parcel lived and breathed;

it was a man. Moreover it was a man without a gun. The irritation remained.

God, he thought, *who am I to start developing scruples? A petty criminal, a mercenary adventurer.*

He said, "You have the map there?"

"Yes."

He switched on the dashboard light and was pleased and surprised to find that it worked. "The route is marked, I believe?"

"Yes."

"Does it go through Hannover?"

"Yes. Then to Hameln."

He struggled to remember his own map which he had studied so carefully in Antwerp. "Then?"

"Paderborn. Arnsberg. They estimate the distance from Neulingen to Mülheim as two hundred and ninety kilometres."

Alan calculated. A hundred and eighty miles—and they might average thirty, or thirty-five if they were lucky. Say thirty. That meant six hours, allow seven for losing the way and bad roads. Given anything like a fair break they should reach Mülheim by six o'clock the following morning. Then . . . His mind was not at all clear as to what should follow. As ever, he declined to plan too far ahead. If possible he would like to contact the driver of "Souchon" at once—either via Frau Straus or by waylaying him on the road to the frontier. Although he was fairly sure that Colonel Hanson had not been entirely frank with him, he knew enough now to make him uneasy. Speed was the essential factor because counteraction when it came would be swift. His body tingled with excitement at the thought. A slip, a false step or a betrayal, and the dogs of three countries might be snapping at his heels.

He was struck suddenly by the enormity of what he was

157

doing and glanced sideways at the man upon whom all this pivoted. He was studying the map still, and his profile was curiously wooden—the long face, the small, pointed nose, the delicate mouth, the fair hair: wooden and ageless.

What are you? Alan wondered, *and what do you think about all this?*

The body, he saw now, was big-boned, loosely built; he was probably a big man when he stood upright. The hands, holding the map, were long but surprisingly ugly with broad, knobbled fingers.

He felt less personal about the man now he had looked at him. He seemed, at any rate, to be fairly placid, which was a good thing. The idea of transporting a bundle of nerves over a frontier was not exhilarating.

Alan thought, *I'll get you to England somehow, you lump. You're valuable to me. I shall cherish you, Paul Weibach Schröder, as I would cherish a bag with two thousand pounds in it.* He said, "Can you drive, Herr Schröder?"

"I would prefer not to."

"But you can?"

"Yes, I can."

"Then if I tell you to drive, you will do so."

The man glanced at him and he thought he caught a momentary glint of anger in the eyes.

"Is that clear?"

"Yes. I will drive if it is necessary."

They were approaching Hannover. Alan remembered the road. He saw in his mind's eye the open squares, the deserted streets, the patrolling police, both British and German. No, there was something unhealthy about all that. He slowed down and drew up at the side of the road.

With the aid of the map he worked out a rough bypass of the centre of the city. Whether the streets which they travelled were the ones he supposed them to be was neither

158

here nor there. By luck, he felt, rather than good judgment the plan worked. It did him a power of good and restored his confidence.

Once they were on the Hameln Road things became easier. Occasionally they passed other commercial transport, once a convoy of army trucks. The road surfaces were generally bad, but not having any great turn of speed at his disposal, he was glad of this. It helped to keep him awake.

Beyond Hameln there was slight fog, but once they had crossed the Weser it dwindled away to nothing. The sky cleared slightly and there were moments of scurrying moonlight. Then the clouds closed in once more and a thin warm rain began to fall gently.

It was all so ordinary, so calm, so like any night drive in any country that Alan soon found himself lulled into complacency. Schröder had fallen asleep, his big head lolling forward, knees drawn up, lumpy hands folded on them. It seemed incredible that Neulingen had ever existed, and Hanson was like a figure in a dream. Only the ache in Alan's side told him that it was not a dream, told him that here now, behind that hedge perhaps or in this approaching lorry, men were on the lookout for . . . for what? Hanson had said, "We still have the great military advantage of surprise in our favour." That was true—as yet. On the other hand it was known to the Russians at least that Schröder had been in Neulingen. Supposing it was also known that he was now in a small van being driven westward by a man called Werner Sagan, supposing . . . But what was the point in supposing anything? The main thing to do was to cross the frontier into Belgium before anyone knew anything for certain. Then, if all that Hanson had suggested was true, it seemed likely that there might be serious trouble indeed. Surely, until that moment, there was little need to worry.

A grey featureless dawn found them at Iserlohn, and an

159

hour and a half later—at five-thirty to be precise—they entered Mülheim. Nothing had happened; no one had waylaid them, demanding their authority to travel; no high-powered car had edged them off the road in a deserted place. Without melodrama, suffering only from stiffness and hunger and, on Alan's part, sleeplessness, they had finished the first stage of their journey.

How much of this untrammelled state was due to luck, and how much to the route which Hanson had directed, there could be no saying. It hardly mattered. At five minutes to six, having left Schröder and the van a hundred yards down the road, Alan found himself standing outside a grubby little shop in a grubby side street. It was perhaps fortunate that the Weserstrasse was not in a more genteel part of the town because already, so early, a light showed behind the shutters of Frau Straus's establishment. The grey pavements under the grey sky were loud with a clatter of boots. The Weserstrasse was going to work.

An alley ran down one side of the shop, and in it, punctuating the otherwise blank wall, was a door. Listening outside it, he heard the unmistakable sound of ashes being raked in a boiler. He knocked. The sound ceased and there was absolute stillness. He knocked again. No answer. He said, "Open, please. This is urgent."

After a pause, a woman's voice, breathy and anxious, replied. "Who is it? What do you want?"

Grasping at the only possible link between himself and the unknown, he said, "Souchon."

"What?"

"Souchon," he said louder.

Indeed the word might have been abracadabra because the door moved at once and a thin, grey face peered out.

"Who are you?" said the voice. An eye surveyed him suspiciously.

160

"Are you Frau Straus?"

"I am."

"Is the driver here?"

"What driver?"

"The driver of 'Souchon'."

For an instant longer she regarded him. Then the door opened properly and she said, "Come inside."

She was scraggy and pathetic in a dirty, rose-pink garment of indeterminate function. Her hair was tied up in a twist of yellow cotton. Between these two colours the haggard face was ghastly. She coughed. "Are you the chap he brought in the other day?"

"Yes."

"He was expecting you to write."

"I know. Is he here?"

She shook her head. "There's trouble," she said.

For a moment his heart faltered. "Trouble?"

"Yes. You'd better go. He hasn't been for two days. I knew something would go wrong. I warned him." Her lower jaw was quivering now, and it seemed she might either scream or weep or even throw a fit at any moment.

Fiercely he said, "What sort of trouble? Tell me. What do you mean?"

But she only continued to tremble; it was a pathetic and a nauseating performance. Suddenly she screamed, "Jan, Jan," in stifled, strangled terror. "Jan. Come here." And she ran out of the room.

A moment later a man appeared. Evidently he was in the process of dressing; a shirt and a pair of trousers hung awkwardly on his meagre body. The face was pinched and sallow but not underfed. He said, "Good morning. Oh shut up, Else. You're the chap that Pierre brought in—last Saturday, it would have been?"

"Yes."

161

The woman leaned against the door breathing heavily. "Why don't you all go?" she said. "I never liked it. I always said . . ."

"*Shut up.*" The little man turned on her with surprising ferocity. She gave a screech and subsided.

Alan said, "What does she mean 'trouble'?"

"They caught Pierre."

"At the frontier?"

"Yes." He produced a packet of cigarettes and offered them. They both smoked.

"Then . . . I can't get back that way."

"Certainly you can't. The whole place is swarming."

"How did it happen?"

The man shrugged. "That's what we'd like to know. They didn't even search the lorry; as soon as he stopped, up went the ladder."

"Then. . . ." Across the writhing smoke their eyes met.

"Yes. Somebody betrayed him."

A terrible knowledge—terrible, instinctive and absolutely certain—overwhelmed Alan: he knew without a shadow of doubt that in some devious way this was connected with himself.

He said, "And Monsieur . . .? I mean . . ."

"Monsieur?" suggested the man, making an abrupt Gallic gesture indicating Hagenaux' stomach.

"Yes."

"He is very angry." He smiled. "I pity the man who did it. Monsieur is not a nice one to have as an enemy."

"You have seen him. I mean since . . ."

"Yes. I saw him last night. He said that if it had been you who had been caught he would never have forgiven himself."

Alan smiled. It was strangely comforting at that moment to think of Hagenaux, but inside him doubt stirred—doubt

162

and a tremor of fear. He said, "I *must* get across the frontier either today or tonight."

The little man shrugged again. "You will have to run for it then."

"Run?"

"They all do, you know, the children. . . ."

He remembered his fellow traveller with the battered suitcase—adult eyes in a boy's face.

"No one will take you over any other way—not after this."

The woman burst out again. "You must go. You can't stay here. If they catch one they'll catch the rest, you see—and mine's a respectable house. . . ."

The man nodded towards her and raised his eyes to Heaven.

Alan, weary now after his night of driving, said, "Well, I can't just walk into Belgium. Where can I find someone to show me the way?" He remembered how the driver, Pierre, had greeted the boy with the suitcase as if they were old friends. "That kid," he said. "The one who came in with me last Saturday—do you know him?"

"Where did he get off?"

"Two or three kilometres this side of the frontier."

The man smiled. "Fair, about fourteen with an old, brown suitcase?"

"Yes."

"You must go," cried the old woman suddenly, like a parrot. The man turned on her with a raised fist and she fled to the passage, stood there watching them.

"Old witch," he said. "Yes, I know the kid. They call him Rikki."

"Would he take me across? He must know the way."

"Oh yes, he knows the way all right. Can you pay?"

"Yes."

"Then he'll take you. He'll do anything for money."

163

"How do I find him?"

The man rubbed his chin. "Look here," he said. "If I tell you where he lives, don't let on how you found out. He's a devil. All right?"

"I shan't say a word."

"It's a little village . . . well, a cluster of houses really, called Rudolsbach. How are you getting there?"

"By car."

"Take you about an hour and a half." He produced a grimy map from his trouser pocket. "His old man used to be a farmer in a small way; it's the only farm in the place so you can't miss it. Lies about a hundred yards off the road on the right-hand side with some pine trees round it."

Together they pored over the map while the old woman hovered in the background muttering to herself. The route was perfectly clear. Alan thanked him, laid a note on the table and returned to the van, glad to be rid of Frau Straus and her keening.

Schröder looked up nervously as he opened the door and said, "I'm hungry."

Alan did not reply, but started the engine and slipped into gear.

Schröder said, "I'm hungry. We must stop for a meal."

Alan glanced at him then, disliking the grey face intensely. "You'll do as I say, Herr Schröder. Our first job is to get where no one'll find us."

The man flashed him a look almost of fear. "You have reason to believe they know where we are?"

"It's always possible."

Schröder spread out his big hands and looked at them. "How are we going to cross the frontier?"

Turning out of the Weserstrasse Alan replied, "We're going to run, as far as I know."

Herr Schröder looked extremely doubtful at this intelli-

164

gence. Alan reflected that he was probably considering the inane sense of humour of the English race.

The boy studied them critically, his grey eyes half-closed, an unruly lock of fair hair falling forward over his forehead. Then he said, "You'd better come into the barn. Bring the van too."

He held open the wide door so that Alan could drive into the earth-smelling darkness. Schröder—sleepy, hungry and bad-tempered—stood to one side with his large hands thrust into his pockets.

The boy said, "Who sent you here?"

"A friend of yours."

He snorted at this. "And how much will you pay? I'm not doing it for nothing, and I'm not taking marks. Francs, dollars or pounds—or nothing doing." He wiped his nose on his sleeve with the practised air of one dismissing a subject.

"What do you usually charge?" Alan asked.

The boy grinned. "What do you usually pay?"

Schröder burst in suddenly. "Oh for God's sake. Pay whatever the urchin asks."

Alan ignored him. "We want food too," he said. "We want it now."

The boy nodded towards Schröder. "Who's the old geezer?"

This game might have gone on indefinitely had not a girl appeared suddenly in the door of the farmhouse and shouted something which Alan did not catch. At once the boy, Rikki, dropped his tone of good-humoured bartering. He said, "Get inside, quick. Get in the loft. There's the ladder."

They stumbled up into an even thicker darkness and felt their way cautiously to a wall, where they stood panting and listening. Schröder said, "Is nothing arranged? Is nothing planned? We shall never reach England if . . ."

165

Alan snapped, "Keep quiet." He had heard the throb of an approaching engine—a jeep, judging by the deep tone of it.

Below, in the barn, the boy was shouting at somebody. "Anything, anything . . . those'll do." There followed a thudding and thumping, and suddenly the motor of the van sputtered into life.

Now that he had grown accustomed to the darkness, Alan saw that there were chinks of light where the beams had warped. Gently, because the floor was none too secure, he tiptoed towards them, selected a large one and pressed his eye to it. He was in time to see the van shoot out into the yard and lurch away towards the main road. At the same moment the other vehicle—yes, it was a jeep, all right—swung into the lane which led to the farm. He could make out the dung-coloured blur of khaki and caught the glint of gun metal. His heart beat a little faster.

For some reason he had supposed that the boy was driving the van, but in this he was wrong; the slight figure now strolled into his line of vision. In the centre of the yard he stopped, staring towards the two cars which had met and stopped. One of the khaki-clad figures got out gesticulating, then turned down the lane towards the farm. The boy went to meet him. He shouted, "Good morning, sergeant."

The sergeant, in excruciating German, replied, "Rikki, you devil, where did you get that truck?"

The boy shrugged. "It's not mine. I'm only using it. Ernst left it here last night."

The sergeant said, "I'm going to check up anyway. It looks fishy to me, and if anybody's lost one it'll be the jug for Ernst. And you can tell him so."

In equally excruciating English Rikki said, "O.K., Sarge."

The sergeant swore good-naturedly. "Got anything else

166

tucked away?" He strolled across the yard to a ramshackle shed, pushed open the door and looked in.

Schröder, from the darkness, said, "What is it? What's going on?"

Alan, his spine prickling, said, "It's a search. Don't talk."

The sergeant had moved out of view now, but by watching the boy it was possible to tell where he was. His boots rang on the rough stones of the yard, and suddenly the barn door beneath them was flung open. Instinctively Alan felt for his revolver, but knew that he could not use it—except perhaps as a cosh. For eternity there was silence. Then the sergeant grunted, seeming almost to be in the loft, so thin was the floor. A moment later he reappeared in Alan's line of vision, cuffed the boy, who parried neatly, laughed, and made off towards the jeep, which was now backing onto the main road. He paused to inspect the van in passing; it appeared to be full of sacks, flung in, no doubt, in the few seconds that followed the girl's warning. Then he climbed into the jeep and drove away. The boy, still standing in the middle of the yard, said, "All right. You can come down now."

"Was that a routine inspection?"

Rikki shook his head and eyed them wonderingly. "No. They came only the day before yesterday."

Alan said, "When will you see us over the frontier?"

Strangely the boy did not now prevaricate. "This evening. We start from here at a quarter to five. Come." He led them towards the farm and into a low-ceilinged kitchen. The girl glanced up from the stove and stared.

"Food," said the boy. "Now."

"It'll be dinner in only two hours." She came forward and Alan saw that she limped; her face was sallow, bad-tempered, and her hair dirty.

"Now," the boy repeated and she merely shrugged. "My

167

sister," he explained and turned away. It was evident that his word was law.

Schröder sat down in a rickety chair and disassociated himself from the proceedings. Alan took the boy's arm and led him back into the yard. "Let's talk business," he said. "First of all, I want to telephone."

The boy indicated the huddle of cottages which was Rudolsbach. "You'll have to do it from the shop. Everybody'll listen."

"That can't be helped. Come on."

Together they walked down the short drive which joined village and farm. As they went, Alan attempted to talk to this child in whose grubby hands his safety lay; but he received no response. There was, in that fourteen-year-old heart, no trust, little humour, and a self-reliance which bordered on mania.

He was perfectly correct, however, in his estimation of the village shop. As soon as Alan lifted the telephone receiver a silence fell; the few customers, the proprietors, indeed it seemed the whole village listened unashamedly.

He gave the number of the hotel in Antwerp, and suddenly, at the thought of hearing Linda's cool voice, all his weariness and his irritation dropped away from him.

But, instead of Linda, a man said, "Hullo, this is the hotel manager. Are you enquiring for Mrs. Linda Hamilton of Room 137?"

Alan said, "Yes." A cold fear started up inside him, so that he could almost anticipate what was to come next.

"Mrs. Hamilton is not here. Her bed was not slept in last night, her room has been ransacked. Would you be kind enough to give me your name . . ."

He held the cackling receiver away from his ear while wave after wave of fear poured over him. For what seemed an eternity he could only stand like a fool while the absurd

168

microscopic voice went on with its agitated plaint. Then action returned to him. He snapped, "Don't worry. Your bill will be paid," and slammed down the receiver. A moment later he was asking for Hagenaux' number.

Now the waiting was interminable, and he could have screamed at the polite exchanges of repartee between the different switchboards. At first he was assured that the number did not exist, then that it did exist but was disconnected, then that it was not disconnected but engaged. Finally a voice which was definitely not Hagenaux' said, "Hullo." Alan recognized it as Josef, the little manservant.

"I must speak to Monsieur Hagenaux."

"Monsier is not at home."

"Where is he?"

"Perhaps if the gentleman will leave his name . . ."

Alan was beside himself. Manifestly he could not speak his name with Rudolsbach village listening to every word. In that case, said Josef, he was afraid . . .

Alan called him back imploringly. "Has a lady visited Monsieur Hagenaux? An English lady?"

Josef replied that many ladies visited Monsieur Hagenaux, but that it was not his place . . . etc., etc. He added that if the gentleman would leave a message. . . .

This Alan did. "Send car to Bonneville's at nine o'clock tonight."

Josef said that he would relay this to Monsieur as soon as he came in. No, he had no idea when Monsieur might be expected.

Alan could only hope that Hagenaux would remember Bonneville's factory, opposite which the lorry had waited. He asked again whether Josef had any idea when Monsieur would return. No, Josef had no idea.

Alan swore, knowing absolute discretion when he met it.

169

Josef, again requesting a name and not receiving one, rang off apologetically.

Alan strode through the shop, aware of goggling eyes (they probably understood French too, being so near the Belgian frontier) and out into the road. The boy was waiting. They walked in silence back to the farm.

Alan told himself that there was no need to worry, that Linda would have got in touch with Hagenaux at the least sign of trouble. And yet the precise voice of the Hotel Manager—"Her room has been ransacked"—rang and rang in his brain. On the other hand, he had also said, "Her bed was not slept in last night." At least she had not been taken by surprise. Obviously, Alan insisted to himself, she came back, found that somebody had searched her room and went straight away to get in touch with Hagenaux. However he might insist, it was cold comfort all the same.

And who, in the name of Heaven, could have searched her room? And for what?

When they got back to the farm a meal was waiting. Schröder sat, still in unrelenting silence, by the fire.

Alan was beginning to hate him, and to hate all the endless complications in which he was involved. He found, perhaps to his surprise, that this affair, which had at first seemed so exciting and vital, had lost its glamour.

"Her room has been ransacked, her room has been ransacked." It had a hideous final ring, and the echo of it in his own heart told him, more plainly than he cared to admit, that whatever he had felt about her before, he cared desperately for her safety now. He was sick with a fear which was new to him: the fear, not for his own skin, but for somebody else's. And there was Rocky to consider also. Supposing. . . . A cold sweat crept on his back.

After the meal Rikki escorted them up to an attic in which were two camp beds made up with palliasses and Army blankets. Schröder, who had not spoken during the meal, now said, "Is it arranged? Is the boy reliable? I expected something better organized than this."

Alan lay down and closed his eyes. "Go to sleep," he said. "You're going to need it."

The German, however, had dozed during the previous night; now, with his hunger assuaged, he felt fresher and apparently more timorous. "I don't trust the boy, and that's a fact. What's to stop him betraying us to the English?"

"Nothing."

"We're near the frontier here. We could cross it ourselves. If these children do it, so can we."

Alan rolled over and looked at him. He sat morosely on the edge of the bed, his hands dangling limply between his knees. They regarded one another with guarded dislike. "Listen," he said eventually. "I don't know who you are or what you're up to, but I'm being paid to get you to England. I'll do it too, but only if you shut up and do as I say."

"But . . ."

"Otherwise . . ." His anger against Kellandale rose up and became identified with this lumpy stranger. "Otherwise it'll give me great pleasure to hand you over to the English myself."

Schröder's jaw dropped.

"I've no intention of risking my own skin to save yours. And right now I'm going to sleep."

He turned over again but it was a long time before he could sleep—a long time before the attic, the smelly blankets, the hovering danger and the valuable but irritating burden he must carry, all dropped away into merciful oblivion.

He awoke only when the boy shook him back to consciousness. The sky outside the tiny window had deepened to a flat grey-blue twilight, and he felt eager and vital once more.

171

Schröder, on the other hand, looked even greyer, more shambling. Presumably he had lain awake all afternoon worrying about the journey before him. Alan thought, as he pulled on his shoes, *I wonder what you've got on your mind, my lad? Whatever it is, I'm glad it's not on mine.*

Downstairs in the kitchen the girl had prepared a meal of soup and potatoes. Again Schröder ate hugely, but Alan, as always before a journey, even a minor one on a comfortable train, could stomach very little.

There was another boy there, tiny and wizened, and a youth, of perhaps eighteen, who showed every sign of being cretinous. Rikki explained their presence. "That's Pauli," he said, pointing at the youth, who grinned vacantly. "He can't help the way he looks and we find it useful, don't we, Pauli?"

He was answered by another grin.

"The other's Zut." The wizened child nodded over his soup. "He's so small that they never even see him."

Alan said, "And what's your specialty?"

Rikki smiled and pushed back his hair. "Oh, I look innocent," he said. "The frontier guards make friends with me, and give me chocolate. I'm like their little brother at home, you see. For me it is easy."

So much, thought Alan, *for childhood.*

When they had finished eating, Rikki led them into the yard and gave Alan an axe, Schröder a sack. The others watched in silence from the door, and their good-byes were suddenly bored, disinterested. To them, it was all ordinary: men came, men went; some were caught, some got through; some were shot, some went to prison, a few simply vanished. In a world where there were no values, no roots, no future, what of that? They turned back into the kitchen.

Rikki led Alan and Schröder up a steep lane between pine trees. "There are woods here," he explained, "and they are cutting them down to make props for the mines. Each day

172

the men come up from the villages and from the camp over there beyond the road; each evening they go back along the edge of the wood. "Look." He pointed, and they saw a ragged procession moving along the top of the rise in two's and three's, singly or in groups. "On the other side of the trees," he said, "is the frontier. Now, we will join them."

It was a dark, overcast evening, poised on the edge of rain. A mist lay among the trees and the light was hazy, indeterminate and confusing. The line of men moving along the edge of the wood was indistinct at times, merging into damp shadow. An axe blade winked, a red shirt glowed, a man sang roughly in the distance.

The boy and the two men were indistinguishable from the others. They dawdled along until a group had passed them, then fell into place in a wide gap. Behind were a couple engaged in earnest conversation, then another long space and another noisy group.

The path twisted and dipped into a small valley. The boy spoke again. "There is wire along some of the frontier, but it has been so often cut and patched and even carried away completely that you will find big gaps. We shall go to a gap, but mind how you step in case there are bits of it left in the grass."

He was less like a child now than Alan had yet seen him. He wondered a little what sort of young man this boy—and thousands like him all across Europe—would grow into.

"Soon we shall come to a cottage on the right. It is empty —all falling to bits—and the path turns away from it. We shall move up to the men in front—I'll tell you how near— and when they are out of view round the corner we shall run to the right behind the cottage."

Schröder glanced over his shoulder apprehensively.

The boy said, "There is a long bend, and the ones behind should be out of sight too, with luck."

173

Schröder muttered, "If not . . ."

"If not," said the boy, "they will say nothing. They see many things up here which they don't mention. There—" he pointed—"that's the cottage." The path began to curve round towards it and they quickened their pace. When there remained about twelve yards between them and the men in front the boy said, "That's enough."

Alan looked back and saw that a good fifty yards now separated them from the pair behind, who were still talking vociferously.

Just as Rikki had said, the road twisted, the trees fell back, and suddenly the cottage was on top of them. The group in front swung round the corner and dropped down out of view.

They turned and ran, the boy first, then Schröder, lumbering, then Alan. In a few seconds they leaned panting against the rough stone wall and heard the two men go by on the other side of it.

Rikki indicated that they should crouch down. Then he led them swiftly into a narrow gully, a stream bed, no doubt, because it was still soggy from recent rain. They flung themselves down beside him and listened. An owl, out hunting early, cried somewhere beyond the trees.

The boy pointed again. "There is a clearing down there, about a hundred metres from that big, red tree trunk. You will see the frontier line away to your left but you must run straight or you will hit the wire. Get your breath first." He glanced apprehensively at Schröder. "There might be a patrol there; you will be able to see from the edge of the trees. Leave the axe and the sack here. Also . . ." He grinned, holding out his hand and scratching the palm with a grubby forefinger. Alan gave him the money in Belgian francs and he counted it laboriously, then buttoned it into his pocket. "Good," he said. "Remember the red tree trunk,

174

then the clearing. You will see the fence away to your left —about fifty metres. Make sure there is no patrol and then run. Or . . ." He glanced at Schröder. "You can walk. It's very easy. Give me two minutes to get back to the path. I don't want to be around if you're caught."

Schröder caught his breath and the boy grinned, winking at Alan. Then he gathered up the heavy axe, whispered, "Good luck," and was gone, moving swiftly among the tree trunks.

When the two minutes had passed Alan said, "Follow me. Don't hang back and tell me if I go too fast." He felt almost lonely without the boy for company; there was something helpless and unreliable about this German which he did not like.

They moved as quickly and as quietly as possible down to the tree with the reddish trunk. The mist seemed to be thickening with the advent of evening, and it was suddenly cold. Soon the trees grew thinner and the clearing of which Rikki had spoken lay before them. It was unpleasantly open and the half-light made it difficult to distinguish a broken stump from a waiting man. The owl called again, suddenly near to them. Alan saw his companion start and look round nervously. He thought, *Well, in a couple of minutes I'll have you out of Germany with any luck.* But again he could not help wondering what lay behind the nervousness.

They crouched, for a time, under a half-fallen pine watching the clearing. The ground was damp and Schröder kept muttering to himself, shuddering, glancing over his shoulder. A faint silvery light lay over the open ground, and beyond it the woods began again, no longer dark and unfriendly, however, because they were in Belgium.

Alan listened and watched until he was sure that no person or thing moved as far as his eyes could see. Away to the left a meagre barbed-wire fence ended in a torn spiral and coiled away into the long grass.

"All right," he said. "There's no sense in waiting. When I give the word, stand up and run. Don't go too fast to begin with." He looked at the colourless, impassive face and wanted suddenly to slap it into some kind of animation. Instead he felt for his revolver and said, "Come on."

They began to run slowly—oh, infinitely slowly—out of the trees and into the open. Alan felt as if a dozen machine-guns were being aimed at the small of his back, but he would not (or could not) increase his speed lest Schröder—lest those comfortable two thousand pounds—should be left behind. So, like city men chasing a bus, they lolloped forward into the clear twilight.

Nothing happened. The owl hooted again, and somewhere far away, as if in imitation, a train whistled forlornly.

Then something caught at Alan's ankle. He lurched and called out, "Wire. Be careful."

At the same moment Schröder gave a yelp and swerved to the left. They continued thus, hopping and swearing in the half-light with a kind of desperate intensity. Alan found himself laughing though he could feel the blood on his ankle.

A second later he was free; the trees of Belgium came out to greet him. But his companion gave one despairing leap, tripped and fell.

Thus—on his face—did Paul Weibach Schröder leave his Fatherland.

They sat on a bank and inspected their wounds. The owl flapped lazily overhead, dipped across the clearing and wavered away into Germany.

IT WAS NINE-THIRTY. THEY HAD BEEN STANDING IN A SHADOWY
doorway of Monsieur Bonneville's factory for three-quarters
of an hour, and Alan was beginning to doubt whether Josef
had given Hagenaux his message—or, indeed, whether he had
found an opportunity to do so. Five times since they had
stumbled across the frontier he had telephoned that number, and four times he had received no answer—not even
the blunt obstinacy of Josef's discretion. Either there was
nobody in the flat, or orders had been given for the telephone to remain unanswered. The fifth call, however, was
perhaps the most terrifying of all. A sharp voice, belonging
to neither Hagenaux nor his servant, said, "Who is that?"
Alan replied, "I wish to speak to Monsieur Hagenaux."
"Your name, please."
"My business is with Monsieur . . ."
He then heard the rattle of the receiver being jerked up
and down and the voice cut short a genteel enquiry from
the lady at the exchange: "Trace this call at once, miss. I am
Inspector Parmière, City Police."
Alan dropped his instrument as if it were red-hot, slammed
out of the kiosk and was dragging an astonished Schröder
down the road—all in the space of a few seconds. A local
bus swiftly put five miles between themselves and that particular telephone. But the fact, the uneasy fact, remained:
there were police in Hagenaux' flat.
Schröder had lapsed into gloom. The rigours of their journey from the frontier—on foot, by bus, by farm cart and
milk van—had worn down his obstinate garrulity. He no
longer asked questions as to how, where and why.
Now, huddling miserably into their doorway from the
searching rain, they were both silent. Even the urgent ques-

tions in Alan's own mind had tired of their endless pacing
—up and down, round and round, like caged tigers. He
could no longer cope with their demands; he had no answers
to throw to them, and, wearily, they lay down. He only
knew that if anything had happened to his three friends—to
Linda, or to Rocky, or to Hagenaux, that diverse trio—then,
by God, someone should pay for it . . . and that someone
would be Lord Kellandale.

He was musing thus, furiously, impotently, foolishly, when
the car drew up on the far side of the road. For a moment,
because he had expected a lorry or at least a van, he did not
recognise the opulent black shape of Hagenaux' own limousine. Then, joyfully, he seized Schröder's arm and hurried
him through the blinding rain towards it.

A pallid moon-face peered at the back window and Hagenaux said, "Put the Boche in front. Hurry. We mustn't
hang about."

In a moment the warm interior of the car had enfolded
Alan. As it glided away he fell back into soft upholstery,
and the rich smells of leather and cigar and Hagenaux' expensive perfume wrapped him in a sudden childish relief;
they seemed so secure.

"Heavens above," said the fat voice, "you look half-dead
—from what I can see of you. Here."

In the half-darkness a flask was thrust towards him.
Brandy was fierce in his throat, fiery in his empty stomach.
He choked and said, "Linda? Where's Linda?"

Hagenaux chuckled. "She's safe. Now sit back. Breathe.
Relax."

"And Rocky?"

"Rocky is magnificent. They are both magnificent." He
frowned. "My dear young friend, will you please relax.
Here, eat."

178

Alan took the sandwiches, and gestured towards Schröder, silent and hunched into his coat collar.

"The chauffeur will feed him." Hagenaux leaned forward and closed the glass partition. Then he switched on the radio so that soft dance music cut off the sound of their voices from the front seat.

Alan gripped his arm. "Emile, the police are in your flat. I rang up . . ."

"Yes." Again the fat chuckle. "That dense fellow, Parmière. We know each other well." His solidity was soothing —but, to the young man's taut nerves, irritating also.

"Well, *some*thing must have happened," he snapped, resenting the other's complacency.

"Indeed yes. You forget, my friend, that I am at my best in an emergency. I may be getting old but I still like action. Because I am calm, it does not mean that nothing has happened."

"Tell me, for Heaven's sake."

"It's hard to know where to start."

Alan pointed at Schröder's back. "Start there. Who's he?"

Hagenaux shrugged. "My dear boy, that is your problem; one I don't envy you either. All I can do is to tell you what has occurred in your absence; I can give no explanations because I know none. First of all the frontier was closed and extra guards were mounted. Every person and every vehicle was searched from top to bottom. Why? I don't know. But I can guess." He switched on the light and placed an evening paper in the young man's hand.

Reading where the stubby finger pointed, Alan saw: "Russians Arrested In British Zone. It is understood that three Russians were arrested late last night at Neulingen near Hannover. The men were masquerading as Germans, though for what purpose is unknown. Information from reliable sources reveals that a fourth man escaped arrest and is be-

179

lieved to be in hiding in the zone. This might account for the recent tightening of frontier control. It is understood that representations have been made by the British and American Military Governors, and that an explanation has been demanded from the Russians."

Hagenaux switched off the light. "So. I ask no questions. I know too much already. But I agree with the paper; I connect the Russians with the frontier. I go further since I know more. I connect *him*—" he pointed—"with the fourth man, who escaped arrest. I tremble . . ." He chuckled hugely. "I tremble to be in the same vehicle with you both. But there, it is a risk I must run in the name of friendship—and so far they think you are still in Germany."

"Go on. What about the Hotel?"

Hagenaux held up a fat hand.

"To me, now that I add two and two, the Russians, bless them, are the clue. In Antwerp, as you maybe know, we have a strong Communist cell. Indeed it is so in all the big ports. So that when your beautiful Mrs. Hamilton rings me up and says, 'My room has been searched,' I add two and two and again two. There are many watchers on the docks, and, believe me, Papa Poiret's is not the least observed corner of them. I think, in short, that somebody has a very good idea of where your friend in the front seat is heading. No doubt all airports as well as all seaports have been warned. . . ." He held up a restraining hand. "Fantastic? Not at all. One should not underestimate the Russians: they are efficient, my friend—more efficient than the English, who do not know the meaning of the word."

"Then?"

"Then they began sifting detailed information, and they found that you arrived from England, quietly, in a fast motor-boat with a crew of one and a lady passenger. You are

180

not unknown on the dockside, you know that. You *and* your . . . history."

"True."

Hagenaux chuckled. "You like Emile's jigsaw? What a loss I am to the police, eh?"

"Go on. What next?"

"The lady passenger is traced to the Hotel des Trois Couronnes; her room is searched. They find nothing, I think. But the lady is frightened; she runs to me, and I . . ." He slapped a plump knee in merriment. "I am *always* suspect by *everyone*. They conclude at once that something fishy is in the air. But. . . . Ah, Emile is also no fool. He also concludes that something is in the air. I send, very quickly, to Poiret's, and your fine boat, with its fine crew, sails quietly downriver in the mist." He chuckled again. "Two hours later, a bad fire breaks out at Papa Poiret's. The boats in Berths Number 10, 11, 12, and 13 are destroyed."

"The *Bonny* was in 12."

"I know. Precisely." He leaned forward, all merriment evaporated. "We have escaped, my friend, but we have also given them a valuable lead; we have virtually incriminated ourselves. They feel they are onto a hot scent."

"And they're damn well right."

Hagenaux was serious now. "As you say, they are damn well right."

"And how about the police in your flat? How did they get there? And where are Linda and Rocky?"

"Gently, gently. Don't rush me." He heaved a ponderous sigh. "I am out concluding a little business deal when Josef rings me to say that the police are at the door. Why are they there? Obviously because someone, in order to put me out of action, had told them that I knew something about the missing Russian at Neulingen." He waved a fat hand. "You see, my friend, you have raised a wasps' nest. However, I

181

tell Josef to say nothing and to do nothing—to lie upon his bed, and, if they break in, to say that he sleeps soundly."

"That's why nobody answered when I telephoned."

Hagenaux nodded gravely, but his gravity broke into a rumble of subterranean mirth. "I do hope Parmière is treating little Josef nicely. They are not the best of friends."

"And Linda?"

"Ah, she is good, that one. She is—" he waved fat hands—"*sympatique*. One could love her." He searched the young man's face in the gloom. "Perhaps you do?"

Alan did not reply.

"At all events, she and the admirable Rocky—and the *Bonaventure*—are all waiting for you together."

"Where? Is it safe?"

"Entirely. If they do as they are told, and stay in the boathouse."

"Boathouse?"

"Yes. One of the foreign consuls—and I shall not commit myself by saying which—is a great friend of mine. He has a delightful villa at Zeemar . . . You don't know Zeemar? Oh, it's a charming little place on the right bank of the Scheldt, a few miles out of Antwerp. Deserted at this time of year, of course. The consul has a magnificent boathouse."

"We're going there now?"

"As fast as we are allowed. Not as fast as we *can,* because the police might stop us for speeding." Again the rumble of mirth. "And one does not go near the fire when one is carrying high explosive." After a moment, his tone serious once more, he added, "I do not like this business, my friend. In all the years that I have been, as it were, outside the confines of the law I have never come upon a case which I liked less."

Alan nodded. He was beginning to feel the same way.

"You see," said Hagenaux, "not only have the frontier

182

officials—German, Belgian and British—combined against you, but the American Military Governor, as well as your own, has demanded an explanation from the Russians. And the Russians, as we know all too well, are not disinterested themselves." He held up a fat hand. "I ask no questions—I don't want to know any more than I do already."

Alan glanced at him. "What are you trying to say?"

Hagenaux's moon-face was anxious in the pale, reflected light from the dashboard. "I am trying to say, my friend, 'Hand him over to the authorities.' It could be arranged, and I don't doubt that they'd pay well."

Alan shook his head. "I was commissioned to get this fellow safely to England, and I'll do it."

"Idiot! Complacent, quixotic, stubborn idiot!"

"Possibly. It's a personal matter, Emile. Pride, if you like."

"Oh, the devil take pride. It's dangerous." But, seeing the obstinacy in the other's weary profile, he shrugged. "One has to admire you—even if you are a fool."

Alan jabbed a finger towards Schröder's back. "Emile, who *is* he? *What* is he? Make a guess."

Hagenaux chuckled. "My dear boy, if this were a detective story he would be the proposed founder of a Fourth Reich, heir-presumptive to Hitler—or he would carry in his head the formula for producing atomic power from sea water. As things are . . ." Again he shrugged, and a plump hand waved irritably. "Oh, don't ask me. I shall be glad to see the last of him, that's all I know."

The great car swung round a wide bend in the road and settled down once more to its smooth, steady destruction of the miles.

Hagenaux said, "Another half-hour should see you off Belgian soil." He glanced sharply. "Why did you bring the girl? It was wrong of you."

183

The force of this criticism took the young man by surprise. He was constantly surprised by the strong moral sense, in certain unexpected directions, of those—as Hagenaux himself put it—"outside the confines of the law."

"She had ideas about me," he said. "If the police had started asking questions in Wainport. . . . Besides, she wanted to come."

"Of course. She loves you. That would seem to me to make it more despicable that you apparently thought nothing of bringing her into this danger."

"I don't intend to discuss it, Emile."

"Excellent. That means, I imagine, that you are ashamed of yourself. Excellent."

They did not speak again for what seemed a long time.

The road was lined, for some miles, with small suburban houses, and the sky to their left was lit by the lurid glow of a city's lights. Evidently it was the outskirts of Antwerp. Presently the houses grew larger and more widely spaced. There were fields, and then expanses of sand and the gleam of water. The road ran along a causeway, over innumerable bridges.

Hagenaux said, "We're nearly there. On arrival we will act quickly. Georges will stay with the car; you and the Boche follow me. Your little *matelot* has instructions to keep the engines warm; he will start them up as soon as he sees us. We will throw open the doors of the boathouse and you will be gone before any watchers can act."

"You expect . . . watchers?"

"Certainly. Not here at Zeemar, I don't think. We moved with speed and under cover of yesterday's fog. Besides, the house of a consul is not suspect by such people." He pointed. "Now. Get ready."

The car swung off the road, between rustic gates and into a sandy drive. Damp bushes flickered in the glare of the

184

lights, and the red trunks of fir trees. Alan caught a glimpse of a trim, white house with wide verandahs before the chauffeur flicked off the headlamps. The car jolted to a standstill. He was reaching for the door handle when suddenly, vice-like, Hagenaux' hand gripped his arm.

"Listen!"

Through the open window he heard the faint sigh of wind in the firs, the murmur of water, the drip of moisture.

"I don't . . ." he began. And then—oh then, never to forget —he heard it: a wail of broken agony and the words, "Oh, for chrissake . . . for chrissake. . . ."

It was Rocky's voice.

He flung off the restraining hand and leapt out of the car, his scalp tingling with horror. Hagenaux, with the astonishing agility of fat people, was out before him and lumbering down a sandy path between the trees.

Somewhere ahead a man shouted, a wooden door slammed. Hagenaux stopped dead, raised his arm and fired. Behind him Alan caught a glimpse of a dodging figure between the pines; he swung the Lüger upward, took brief aim, and stroked the trigger. The running man jerked his arms out sideways, took a few more drunken steps and fell.

As if in answer, another gun spoke from somewhere among the trees, and he was aware, horribly aware, that Rocky had stopped screaming. He ran forward, trying not to think what might be happening, trying not to see Linda's face in his mind's eye.

The path twisted and revealed the boathouse, a white, prim toy with windowboxes. A door, gaping blackly, was suddenly streaked with fire; the bullet sang past his head. Hagenaux shouted and flung himself off the path. At the same moment another figure shot out of the door and dodged away into the trees, firing blindly over his shoulder. Hagenaux fired and fired again. The figure vanished surprisingly and completely. There was an explanatory splash.

Alan, not heeding the Frenchman's shouted warnings, ran to the black doorway. He heard his own voice, as if he listened to it from a long way off. "Linda. Rocky. Linda. Rocky," it was calling.

The half-expected bullet did not whine out of the door to meet him, but he peered into impenetrable darkness, thick with the smell of tar and paint and sea water. There was silence, the silence of nightmare.

He felt rather than saw Hagenaux materialise at his shoulder. The light of a small torch flickered over the trim shape of the *Bonaventure* and came to rest on Rocky. He had not fallen to the ground because a knife, rammed through his arm and into the wooden wall, held him upright. His shirt hung open and his body was a mess of blood. He was dead.

Alan lost control of all his faculties; for an eternity he was witless, dumb, blind—but not so blind as he could have wished.

Hagenaux said, "They tortured him."

Water lapped softly. The fir trees sighed as if impatient of so much waste.

Alan finally found speech. "Linda," he said. Then, as Hagenaux' torch found another body crumpled on the landing stage, he nearly cried out in fear. But it was a man, a stranger. He also was dead. Presumably Rocky had killed him first.

"Linda," said Alan again, hoarsely.

They turned out of the boathouse.

"Linda," he called—an agonised voice.

The firs sighed.

Then, quite near to them, she stepped out from behind a tree, her face blank, ravaged by horror.

186

"I heard," she said. "I had to listen. They *hurt* him."
Then her knees gave way and she crumpled up on the sand.

Alan could not comprehend the helplessness which had
seized him. Action generally found him alive and vital, but
this time, all life, all vitality, seemed to have seeped out of
the soles of his feet. And nausea, a vile stranglehold of
nausea, cramped his stomach. He watched while Hagenaux
knelt and pressed his brandy flask to the girl's lips. He
merely stood and watched—helpless, hopeless, a weak child
without guts, without strength, without courage.

Linda opened her eyes and said, "Sorry. I . . . They surprised us. I got away through the other door."

Her eyes found Alan's and they stared at each other. He
saw pity there, and horror: pity, horror, relief, anger . . .
and, yes, recrimination.

He could not bear that. He turned and stumbled away
into the trees. He mumbled something about fetching
Schröder, but in his head a shrill voice had suddenly started
to scream, *Your fault, your fault.*

Hagenaux called after him. "You must hurry. No time
to waste. Quick."

Your fault, screamed the inward voice. *Your fault, your
fault, your fault. . . .*

SECOND SEASCAPE

SEA AND SKY WERE COLD, GREY, EMPTY. BETWEEN THEM THE grey, lean shape of the boat seemed suspended and helpless. Sometimes a bitter spurt of spray would lift from the bows and patter across the cabin top. Otherwise there was no sense of movement; it was credible that no land existed on all the globe—only grey sea.

Linda knew that she had dozed into restless sleep when something jolted her back to consciousness. Schröder on the other bunk was snoring lightly. She swung her legs to the deck and watched Alan at the wheel; from the darkness of the cabin she could study him without his being aware of it.

Dawn seemed to be breaking, for he was lit with a cold unearthly radiance which made his face all stone. She had never in her life seen a face so rigid; only the eyes were alive, glancing to right and left, reading the messages of sea or sky.

For a long time she sat there, watching. She wanted to talk to him, to make him talk to her, but she was afraid. It seemed just then that between his sex and hers was fixed a vast gulf, and that she would never in a thousand years understand the complexities of his taut, bitter silence. Yes, she was afraid to approach him, and yet there was inside her a deeper force than fear; because she loved him, her

188

whole being ached for his misery. Anger in such a predicament was possibly a male emotion—she did not know about that; she only knew that she felt none of it. But unhappiness she did feel—a deep, desperate sense of waste and of loss. Though she was perhaps in a position to judge, she did not do so. How could she judge, when she knew so agonisingly that he, standing up there at the wheel, was judging and condemning himself—over and over again.

Whatever he was suffering, and however much she feared to break in on that awful isolation, she knew that it was in some devious way her duty to go to him. She found the thermos, poured out a mugful of coffee, laced it with rum, and joined him at the wheel.

The sight of her seemed to hurt him; he flinched. But immediately, as if she represented some other reality that had to be faced, he pulled himself together, took the mug which she held out and drank eagerly.

"You haven't slept. Why don't you get forty winks?"

He pointed ahead. "Can't now. Landfall any minute." After a time he added, "Thanks for the coffee. Did you have some?"

"Not yet."

"Well, go on then." When she turned away he said, "You'll come back."

Her heart leapt. "Yes. In a minute."

When she rejoined him she thought that some of the rigidity had left his face, but she could not be sure.

Away to port a white light blinked at them. The sky had grown appreciably brighter. She watched him alter course. When the compass had settled, he said, "Take over a minute, will you?"

She took the wheel.

"Steer two-nine-five."

She nodded, concentrating on the compass.

189

It was then that the meaning of the bearing struck her. Two-nine-five—almost due north. She glanced at him apprehensively. He was studying a chart.

"You're right," he said. "You don't imagine I'm putting back into Wainport, do you? There'd be a reception committee by this time."

The grimness of his voice brought a crowd of questions clawing at the barricades of her brain. He must have seen this in her puzzled eyes, for he said, "Don't ask me. I don't know any better than you do." He glared for a moment at the cabin whence came, softly, the sound of Schröder's snore. "But I'm going to find out," he added savagely. "By God, I'm going to find out."

The savagery, and the sudden abysmal misery of his expression, goaded her into speech. "Please trust me," she cried. "I can't bear to see you like this. You can't go on keeping it to yourself."

He stared at her as if puzzled.

"There's nothing to tell that you don't know already—nothing that matters now, I mean." The pulse in his temple began to throb again. He flung the chart away convulsively and took the wheel from her, and, in that moment of proximity, the blazing unhappiness of his face was too much for her.

"Work it off," she cried suddenly. "Smash something. Get mad at *me* if you like."

"Oh that." He seemed to understand her at last, but he did not look at her. "Why should I get mad at you?"

"You can't go on bottling up anger indefinitely. Something'll break."

"I'm keeping it," he said quietly. "I'm going to need it quite soon now."

The pulse at his temple continued to throb. She watched it, fascinated.

PART III

Full Circle

1 – WHIP HAND

LORD KELLANDALE LIKED HIS BREAKFAST RITUAL AS WELL AS any of the rituals with which he surrounded himself. He had long ago discovered that after juggling all day with the destiny of millions of people and pounds, he needed a home life of unparalleled quiet and efficiency; everybody had to relax at some time or other, and since he could never be sure whether his working day would last for two hours or for twenty-two, of one thing he made abundantly certain: that his leisure (which occupied the remaining two or twenty-two hours) should be absolute. Hence the many ceremonies, each one a granite block to his house of quietness. In business anything extraordinary might happen; at Number one, Park Place West, he could be sure that nothing extraordinary ever would.

So, on this bright spring morning, he was awakened as usual at eight o'clock exactly. He sipped his grapefruit juice and admired the sunshine across the fresh green of trees in the Park. At eight-twenty he went to his bath. At eight thirty-five he returned from it and dressed himself carefully in the underclothes, socks, shirt, tie, suit and shoes which his almost invisible valet had put out for him.

At nine he went downstairs to the morning room, where

breakfast was waiting at a small table in the window. It was his favourite meal.

In fact, on this fine spring morning as he opened his own newspaper and shared his own editorial with his five million readers, Lord Kellandale was in his heaven, and all, therefore, was right with the world. Just.

For at that moment the door opened; a silent-footed butler materialised and placed a grubby envelope on a silver salver near, but not too near, his lordship's right hand.

Kellandale stared at this offensive thing, took it, opened it, read a crumpled sheet of notepaper, and stared again.

"The gentleman," said the butler, who had been reluctantly forced to admit that the untidy young man *was* a gentleman, "is in the kitchen."

"The kitchen!" Kellandale choked, controlled himself and crunched both note and envelope in a big hand. "Send him up."

"You'll . . . see him, sir?"

"Damn it, did I or did I not say send him up?"

"Yes, milord." The butler withdrew.

Kellandale jerked convulsively to his feet and exploded into profanity. The ritual tottered and fell; the acolytes of quietness, propriety and order fled trembling to the corners of the room.

He did not immediately recognise the young man, but he saw at once why he had been wise enough not to try and gain admittance by the front door, for he would never have succeeded. Number one, Park Place West, was famous for its inaccessibility.

Alan, in jeans and reefer jacket, with a day's stubble on his chin, looked completely authentic to Kellendale; he had hired a buccaneer, and here, facing him, stood a buccaneer.

The butler withdrew, goggle-eyed.

Kellendale said, "I thought I told you . . ."

"You told me a lot of damn lies."

The whip in that young voice took the older man by surprise, though he did not show it, of course. "How dare you come here?" he said angrily.

The other did not answer, but stared with such a bright, intelligent hatred that his eyes were difficult to meet.

"If I make a contract," continued Kellandale, "I keep it. I expect the other party to do so too."

"Then why," enquired Alan quietly, "did you agree to see me?"

The question was startling, unexpected.

"Because . . ." he began, and hesitated, hesitated and was lost.

"Because," said the young man, "you're frightened. Aren't you frightened, Lord Kellandale?"

"Don't talk nonsense. What do you want?"

"Various things."

There was, Kellandale noticed, a dangerous little throb just under the dark hair at the young man's temple.

"Well?" he said defiantly, though he did not feel exactly defiant.

"Well," echoed Alan, never removing that mad stare. "How much is this man you call Schröder worth to you?"

Kellendale stiffened. There was what seemed a long silence.

"My dear young man," he replied finally, tightly, "you aren't by any absurd chance trying to threaten me, are you?" But a black doubt had seeded itself in his mind. It struck him suddenly that Hobart had been right about two things —he should never have revealed his identity in this matter, and he should certainly have made arrangements to meet the boat and to remove the German at once.

Alan watched him. "I asked a question," he said. "Since

195

when have questions been threats? How much will you pay me for Schröder?"

"I'm paying you for your journey. That was understood."

"Oh no, you're not. You're paying me for your honourable German boy friend, who once did you a good turn." The sarcasm bit deep. "And you never forget a good turn."

Kellandale's eyes narrowed. "I have only to lift that 'phone . . ." he began, but the whip-lash voice sliced his sentence in half. The young man shouted suddenly—yes, *shouted* in Number one, Park Place West, "Can't you see when you're beaten, you fool?" The sacrilege stood fierce and naked between them, desecrating the shrine. Kellandale began to tremble with rage; he had not trembled for years—with rage or any other passion.

"I've got the upper hand," went on that young, merciless voice out of the haze of blood which troubled Kellandale's sight. "If you don't play, I shall wring the fellow's neck. If you have me arrested he'll die of starvation; I shan't ever say where he is, **and** no one will ever find him, I can assure you of that—not until it's too late."

He watched while with a tremendous or truly epic effort of will, Kellandale controlled his temper; the process took a full two minutes. He waited until he saw him draw breath to speak, and added, "Please don't say, 'You'll regret this,' because I shan't."

Kellandale had been going to say just that. He felt, suddenly and for the first time, the hand of age laid heavily on his shoulder. There was something overpowering about so much merciless hatred so early in the morning.

Alan went on: "I shan't regret it for one instant. If I die tonight I shall be glad I got the better of *you* before it happened. It may teach you not to tell lies when you say you trust people."

Kellandale brooded. "There was trouble then?"

196

"There was killing." He almost choked. "My God, how I despise you."

The fine head—head of an Emperor—jerked up. "Don't dramatise yourself. I hired you for a job, didn't I? You're a crook."

"Yes, but you disregarded rule number one." Alan laughed without any mirth. "Honour among thieves. You forgot that."

"My dear young man." Kellandale moved away, as if he found the conversation tedious, and spoke looking out of the window. "My dear young man, you don't honestly suppose that you can adopt this attitude towards me and get away with it, do you?" He gestured. "I've destroyed men for less than this."

"I think," said Alan evenly, "that Schröder means a great deal to you. I think he means enough to keep me out of danger for the time being."

Kellandale gazed up at the clear sky. "Has it ever struck you that I am every bit as ruthless as you are? Suppose for a moment that this German is as important to me as you seem to think." He turned, and his eyes now were quite cold and impassive; it was hard to imagine that they actually belonged to a human being at all. "If that were the case, do you imagine that I'd let you get out of this house until I knew where he was?"

The young man, in his weariness, felt suddenly insecure before the impersonal malevolence of those eyes.

"Just suppose," Kellandale continued, "that Schröder *is* so vitally important to me. What on earth makes you think that I should let you . . ." The eyes flickered like a snake's. "That I should let *you* stand between him and me."

Alan realised, in a flash of intuition, that power—the kind of power with which he was faced—was as much a matter of complete self-assurance as of fact. Absolute egotism, in

197

the hands of such a man, became a battering ram—an almost physical assault on an opponent's courage. Victory, for Kellandale, was the inevitable outcome of any battle in which he cared to take part. His colossal confidence staggered the younger man, a fact which Kellandale was swift to notice. "You," he said, "would appear to be the fool—if your suppositions about Schröder were true. In point of fact they aren't. He matters to me only slightly. As a twinge of conscience, if you like."

It was necessary, Alan knew, to resist this overwhelming personality with all the strength at his disposal. And he knew the way to summon up that strength, too: he forced himself to remember something he had no wish to remember, the picture of Rocky as he had last seen him—the thin arm with the knife impaling it to the wall, the sagging head, the mess of blood. It was horrible, but it broke the Kellandale spell.

"All right," he shouted. "If Schröder's so unimportant you can do without him. I'll . . . By God, I'll hand him over to the police." He turned towards the door.

"You'll find," said Lord Kellandale gently, "that it will be impossible for you to leave the house.

"Until," he added, "you see fit to deliver this man into my safekeeping."

Alan looked back. His blood was up now, and he felt unreasonably sure of himself again.

"I thought I made myself clear," he said. "I don't intend to let you know where he is, let alone deliver him to you, until you pay me what he's worth. I'm thinking in terms of five figures, by the way."

Kellandale nodded. His absolute stillness of body was in itself unnerving. "I think you will, if necessary, tell me where he is."

A cold shiver ran up Alan's spine, but, as always in times

of danger, a kind of crazy exhilaration had seized him. He returned slowly into the room; forced himself to advance step by step until only a yard separated him from that motionless body, from that face hewn in granite, with eyes of cold steel. He knew that now, or never, he must make the final effort of will.

He said, "You underestimate me, Lord Kellandale. I come of fighting stock. One of Drake's captains was a Morgan, and so was one of Marlborough's generals. I'm no jumped-up pit boy."

He thought for an instant that the man would strike him; he saw the big hands twitch violently, and then lie still.

"You could tear me limb from limb," he went on, grinning. "You could rip off my toenails one by one—that's what the Spaniards did to my ancestor. But whatever you did, it would give me pleasure *not* to tell you where I've hidden that German runt." Somehow he contrived a laugh. "Why, you want him so badly you can't even bluff properly."

He was exhausted. He knew that he had shot his bolt, and that there was neither the strength nor the invention inside him to go any further. Yet for a little longer he must steel himself to meet those cruel eyes, and not allow his own to waver.

In the silence he could hear a barrel-organ playing in the far distance. He could hear birds in the Park, the whistle of an errand boy, the overall rumble of London traffic. It was the endless silence of eternity, so charged with emotion that it actually hurt his head with a physical pain.

At last—at long, long last—Kellandale nodded to himself, turned abruptly, and went back to the window. That bored note had returned to his voice when finally he spoke again. "Well," he said, "how much do I have to pay for my own carelessness on this occasion?"

"Carelessness, my foot! You're paying for not being able

199

to trust other people to give orders, for being a liar, for causing the death of as decent a little man as ever lived, for the upkeep of his mother, and for my passage out of this country to a place where you won't find me."

"And how much is this hotch-potch going to cost me?"

"The value of Herr Schröder. No more. No less."

Kellandale nodded. "It's a pity, from your point of view, that you don't know just a little more, isn't it?"

The young man smiled a slow grim smile.

"I know quite enough. I know where Schröder is, and I know that he'll stay there, if you're not feeling generous."

Kellandale nodded again.

"Now," said the young man, his face grey from fatigue in the bright morning light. "Make an offer. I'll double it."

"You're very sure, aren't you, that Schröder is more to me than simply a friend." He seemed to have found, hanging in some inner cell of the mind, a cloak of calm. He turned back into the room, and even his eyes revealed nothing.

But the young man who faced him was equally calm. "Yes, I'm very sure," he said. "Go on. Make an offer."

Farquarson faced Colonel Patchway across the latter's massive desk.

"Of course," he said, "it's only guesswork, but the facts hang together, such as they are."

"Let's have them."

Farquarson produced a note book from his pocket and opened it. In his unshapely tweed suit and with his ruffled sandy hair and mournful expression, he looked more than ever like a not particularly successful schoolmaster.

He said, "A week ago yesterday—that's Tuesday—Alan Morgan was in London. I saw him, you saw him."

Patchway nodded grimly. "I did."

"The following Saturday one of my fellows went down to

this place, Wainport, where Morgan's been living for the past two years. He wasn't there. He'd sailed the previous evening—Friday. According to the locals, he went in a big launch. I'd say it was the one he and MacBride used last year." He glanced up. The Colonel nodded.

"Again according to the Wainport people, his crew consisted of one small man, a Londoner with a mop of hair."

"Rockingham?"

"Looks like it. He was one of the old gang anyway."

Patchway sighed. "Go on."

"Now there's a gap until Sunday evening. . . . Then we get an official chit, 'Most Immediate', 'Top Secret' and all the rest of it, saying that Heinrich Meister, who was being 'observed' (whatever that means) in Berlin, has vanished; believed smuggled out of the country on his way to England." He scratched his head. "And I'll confess I'm flummoxed. I thought Meister was dead anyway."

"Everybody thought he was dead until a couple of months ago; he was *proved* dead. Then some French bigwig who'd known him before the War turned up in a lather and announced that he'd seen him on the street in Berlin."

"So we aren't sure if it *is* Meister."

"Oh yes, it's Meister all right, no doubt about it. He was pulled in for questioning—by our people. Then the Americans got wind of it and so did the Russians, and the French were in it from the start, of course."

Farquarson grunted in impatience.

"A muddle, yes." Patchway smiled faintly. "Then, while they were sitting round like four big dogs all after the same bone—eying each other, you know—weighing each other up . . . while they were dithering, Meister vanished again."

"And that's as much as we know."

"Yes. Except that it may have been him who put in a brief appearance at this place, Neulingen, where the three

201

Russians were arrested. If it *was* him, and if you're right in thinking Morgan was after him, that's probably where they met. Now you know as much as I do."

Farquarson studied his notebook. "Well, it fits. It's still guesswork, but it fits."

"Go on then. Let's have the rest of it."

"Early this morning, old Poinier comes through from Brussels saying that there's been a bust-up at a villa outside Antwerp. Four bodies. Three of them well-known Communist thugs, and the fourth . . ."

"Rockingham."

"Yes."

Patchway gazed meditatively out of the window. After a while he said, "Yes, as you say, it fits. It's the sort of job Morgan would go for." He cocked an eye at Farquarson. "Any idea who might be behind him?"

"None at all. But if this chap *is* Heinrich Meister. . . ." He waved his hands hopelessly.

Patchway sighed again. "Yes, you're right. If it is Meister, anyone might be after him."

"The papers haven't got it yet."

"They won't be long now. They've got the scent and it'll be a first-rate scandal when it breaks. We'd better get hold of Morgan quick, and ask him a few questions. Circulate a description and all the rest of it."

Farquarson grinned. "I've done that already."

"Good. If Meister gets into this country, it won't be for a long stay. He'll be on his way somewhere else—somewhere we shan't be able to touch him."

They regarded each other steadily.

"It's going to be a big job then?"

Patchway nodded grimly. "It's going to be a battle. I've had Scotland Yard on the wire three times this morning, and the Home Office twice. If young Mr. Morgan's holding

Heinrich Meister, he's holding a stick of dynamite. Whether he knows it or not is another matter."

Men are always advising each other not to trust women; this is probably the reason why women become doubly irritated when men do not trust them. Linda was no exception. She had found herself, in the very early dawn, standing on a derelict wooden pier amid what appeared to be a no-man's-land of misty marsh. It was cold and her dress was made of thin cotton. In one hand she held a pound note and a florin—the latter in case she might wish to catch a bus!—and in the other a piece of paper on which was written the name of a London public house and the street in which it stood, where she was led to believe she would be met by Alan Morgan at eleven-thirty that same morning.

The main road, he had told her, was "a couple of hundred yards" up the lane at the end of the rotting pier, and there she would "easily get a lift" because it was "a busy spot." After she had watched the *Bonaventure* chug away upstream, after she had walked a good mile to find a perfectly deserted secondary road, and after she had wandered there for half-an-hour and had been ignored by the driver of a large, comfortable car, she could willingly have seen Alan Morgan to damnation.

His further instructions, or suggestions, were more fortunate, however. She came at length, by courtesy of a milk van, to the small market town of Leddenbury, where The George supplied her with a bath and breakfast, just as he had predicted, without flinching at her sudden appearance, unattended and with a handbag for luggage, at six a.m. on a summer morning. A fatherly night porter conducted her to the bathroom, provided towels, soap and a mysterious box of toilet powder which could only have belonged to some lady guest or to the manager's wife. He personally served

203

her with a bountiful meal, and looked up a suitable train to London.

She found herself, after all this, lapped about by a not entirely justified sense of well-being. Indeed she even had time during the two-hour train journey to analyse this false mood and mock herself because of it. A woman in love, she thought wryly, might apparently spend four days of grave danger in a foreign city, might escape possible death by hiding behind a tree, might act as accomplice in what was rapidly revealing itself as serious criminal activity . . . might do all this and yet be cosily contented.

She could only surmise that here was the reason why women never had, and never would, become superior in action and intellect to men; they could be content with too little.

In vain she repeated the frightening circumstances in which, as far as she knew, she was involved; but the harsh facts were continually swept aside by a host of merry, intimate details—the way his eyes closed slightly when he smiled, the hard security of his arm around her, the adult manner in which he had left that first decision, whether or not she should accompany him, to her.

Only when it came to Rocky, to that vitality and courage and high good humour stilled forever by a mean and unnecessary death, did the bright sky darken and the light lie heavily on fields and woods beside the railway line; joy went out of the day, and she remembered Alan's anger, a driving fury, and what was it driving him? She was assailed then by a host of creeping doubts; she knew so little of what was happening. Questions began to plague her once again: who, why, when and what next?

Thus, when eleven-thirty found her sitting quietly in a corner of The Three Kings, Grahame Street, West one, her mind was fixed in a juxtaposition of fearful anticipation because of all the future might hold, and careless joy because she loved a man and would see him presently.

When he came in—at ease, despite the fact that his blue jeans and reefer jacket attracted every eye in the room—all fear left her and she was simply (and foolishly, she told herself) happy. He had shaved, or been shaved; and although his face was lined with weariness, some of the tension seemed to have faded. Superficially he was in high spirits. He brought two drinks over to her table and said, "It makes me feel cool, calm and collected just to look at you."

"Goodness. Why?"

The dark eyes flashed; he smiled. "Because you're beautiful. Obviously. Why else?"

This took her breath away. She said, "Is . . . is everything all right?"

At this, something of the old haunted look moved over his face. "Things are improving," he said. Then, as if suddenly embarrassed, he glanced away and added, "It strikes me suddenly that I had no right to expect you to meet me here. You ought to be back in Wainport, telling everybody that you've been spending a few days with your aunt in Wolverhampton."

"Not Wolverhampton, please."

He gesticulated. "You know what I mean."

"Why bring this up now?" she asked.

"Why? Because. . . . Because I've just seen you for the first time, and realised what sort of mess I'm getting you into."

They were both silent.

"Also," he added hesitantly, "I . . . I've been worrying all morning about you."

"About *me!* Why?"

"Oh damn it," he said, quietly intense. "Do I have to tell

205

you any more than you know already to make you see that this business with Schröder is lethal?"

"Who is he?"

"I don't know yet. But he's extremely valuable to certain people, I can assure you. Extremely valuable." He smiled abstractedly, and then frowned. "That's neither here nor there. You'd better go back to Wainport."

His face was alternately so secret and assured, and then so boyish and uncertain that she was moved to put her hand over his.

"You know as well as I do that nothing short of a strait jacket would make me leave you at this juncture."

He flashed her then a look of such pure gratitude that it transformed his whole expression. "Really?" he said.

"Yes, really."

"I was worried about you, all the same."

"Keep me in view," she suggested, "and then you won't be worried any more."

At this he beat his fists together. "But don't you see we *must* keep apart now? It's the only hope."

The only hope! Something mournful and frightened echoed that phrase in her heart. He saw this presumably, because he removed his hand from beneath hers and laid it on top. Strangely, absurdly, she was reassured.

"All right," he said. "Listen. I was commissioned to fetch Schröder by a rich and powerful Englishman; he promised me that Schröder was nothing but a chum of his. In fact he lied. I don't know yet *who* that long-faced runt really is, but I do know that he's somebody pretty considerable. Questions are being asked—international questions. So far there's nothing much in the papers, but they don't get hold of that sort of thing until the Nabobs want them to. When it breaks, believe me, it'll be news." He glanced at her, and she nodded.

"In a few minutes I'm going to an office round the corner here, and I'm going to collect a lot of money: the money I'm being paid for Herr Blasted Schröder—for keeping quiet about him."

"You . . ." Her stare wavered. "You . . ."

"Yes. I'm the only person who knows where Schröder is. I'm doing a little quiet blackmail." He was savage on the word.

"No." She looked away. "No, you shouldn't . . ."

"And why not? Did he respect me? Did he do anything for Rocky?"

"Oh no." Linda shuddered. "You mustn't go on. Wrong upon wrong upon wrong."

He gripped her hand, crushing it. "You'd better face reality," he said, fiercely but quietly. "If I'm a crook, what is he, that fine, rich, powerful old hypocrite? And what is Rocky's mother going to live on for the next twenty or thirty years?"

She stared.

"You see," he insisted, "there are realities."

He saw in her eyes exactly what she was thinking. He released her hand and looked at it as it lay limply in his —a crushed, pink flower. "You asked for all this," he said. "You knew what I was. You had to start uncovering things. Old Hobart's gun set you off and you haven't looked back."

Linda said nothing.

"Go home to Wainport."

"No."

"If you don't go," he said, making each word clear, "I shall use you. I shall drag you further into this mess."

"All right."

"It'll be far from all right."

"Don't go on," she said faintly. "You know perfectly well why I'm here."

He stared intently into her eyes. "You won't reform me," he said. "You haven't a hope in hell."

Staring back, just as intently, she found words on her tongue which were hardly of her own thinking. Before she realised their meaning, she said, "That's all right. You'll reform yourself in the end."

She knew as soon as she had spoken that some instinct, some wisdom she could not claim as her own, had touched on the very heart of his problem. It was true; she knew now whither that fury drove him, and the knowledge was infinitely sweet.

But he did not evidently see it in quite this light. He stood up abruptly and went over to the bar, his face very hard suddenly.

Watching his back and seeing how smoothly the dark hair curved behind his ears she thought, "Yes, that's it; that's what this anger really means. It's not society he hates, not civilization, not what he calls the antheap, not even this rich and powerful man who lied to him. He hates himself; he hates the bitterness and smallness of cheating and swindling."

Sitting in a corner of a drab saloon bar, Linda prayed fiercely, earnestly, clenching her fists, that his fury and disgust would drive him to salvation before it destroyed him. She knew, instinctively, that there was little she could do except watch the spell working itself out, and be near to him when he might need her.

Thus, when he came back from the bar, eyes impersonal and blank, voice hard, face fixed in a mask of alert wariness, she could find it within herself not to be hurt or disappointed. Strangely—and all along there had been a strangeness in her feeling for him—she felt calm and assured now that a course lay open to her. She had clung to him, or to the idea of him, blindly through those days of danger, and

208

now there was light and she was no longer blind. Hope had come to her, and hope was sweet.

"You can drive," he said. A statement.

"Yes."

"Listen then." He no longer questioned her, but simply gave orders. "If you go out of this door and turn left, you find yourself in Grahame Street. The second turning on the right—that's on the other side—is Buckingham Mews. I'll say it again: Turn left, second street on right, Buckingham Mews. You'll find a car there. I don't know what it looks like, but the number's ZLP-072. Got that?"

"ZLP-072."

"The ignition key will be in the right-hand pocket of the back seat. Repeat all that."

She repeated it, pleased to surprise him with her quick memory.

"Good." He grinned, but automatically, without the old warmth. She could almost respect the catlike integrity which trusted only itself. He went on: "Under the floor covering of the driver's seat you'll find a licence and all the other papers—in case you happen to be stopped by the police. You won't be, but just in case." His eyes were quite cold and analytical—it seemed that the only interest she held for him now lay in her ability to do as he instructed.

"Get into the car and drive as though you owned it. If there's a man sitting in it, just ask him the way to Piccadilly Circus, and ask loud, because it'll mean the police are watching you. Then come back here—via Piccadilly Circus, of course." Again he grinned, but Linda's heart was beginning to pound nervously.

"Do you think you can find your way to Leddenbury, where you were this morning?"

"Yes, of course. How long can I take?"

"I shan't get there until—" he calculated—". . . until about

209

half past three. You'll be leaving here at twelve and it's only fifty or so miles."

"You're meeting me in Leddenbury?"

"No. When you get there ask someone to put you on the road to Godswater. It's a tiny village about three miles out of the town. Directly opposite the church, you'll find a pub called The Fox. Drive into the yard at the back. The landlord's an old pal of mine called Fred Butcher. Tell him whom you're acting for and he'll put the car out of sight for you, and give you a meal. He's a good fellow; you'll like him. Is it all quite clear?"

"Quite." She would not allow herself to show any misgiving, or for that matter any other personal emotion. She said, "I suppose there's a river at Godswater."

"There is."

"The river we were sailing up this morning when you pushed me ashore."

"Yes."

"And that's where you've hidden the German?"

He did not answer this directly. "The less you know about that," he said, "the better."

"Don't you think that since I'm now an accomplice or an accessory or whatever they call it . . ."

"For that very reason," he interrupted her. "If you're pulled in by the police, you'll find it more convenient not to know anything."

She had never been an expert liar, and could not, therefore, deny that he was right.

"Then what do I do, after Mr. Butcher has hidden the car and fed me?"

"Well, it's a pretty little village, and parts of the church are pre-Norman. There's a rather attractive house there too. It's empty, so if you care for elegant ruination you might like to explore it. You'll find the front door open and

210

a very fine Grinling Gibbons ceiling in the dining-room. And there's an early Adam staircase."

"You seem well up in facts."

"Why not? I was born there."

This really did take her by surprise, but she was quick to notice, and take warning, from the bitterness of his voice.

"You might," he added, "be interested to see the splendour into which you might have married had things been . . . otherwise." He looked away from her, and she sensed for the first time how days of strain and sleepless nights were beginning to tell on his nerves. He went on speaking, however.

"The galloping major and I will be arriving—at the house, I mean—somewhere between half-past three and four."

She realised that in his own strange way he had let her know where he had hidden Schröder.

He glanced at his watch and added, "It's twelve now. You'd better get moving. If anything goes wrong, come back here at one o'clock. I'll wait from ten to until ten past." His tone was so abrupt that she could not help saying, "I hope you aren't going to worry about me this time." She stood up, but he remained seated, not looking at her.

Finally he said, "You know I shall worry. I shall worry like hell, the more fool me." But still he stared at his drink. "Go on. What are you waiting for?"

"You're hating yourself for this, aren't you?" she said.

"We won't get analytical over it, at all events. I've told you again and again that it doesn't matter to you *what* I feel."

"On the contrary," she replied sweetly. "I'm delighted that you're hating yourself. Continue the good work."

And, when he did look up, she had gone.

The telephone on the left side of Farquarson's desk was

on a direct line to Colonel Patchway; he picked it up now and pressed the buzzer.

"Yes, Farquarson."

"I thought you might like to know, sir. . . ."

He spoke ponderously on the 'phone, so that the Colonel frequently found himself longing to shout, "Get on with it, man." He said, however, "To know what?"

"We've found Morgan."

"Good. Have you pulled him in?"

"No, sir."

"Then do so."

Farquarson coughed. "I think we'll learn more by leaving him alone."

"Morgan's a slippery character."

"I know."

"Might get away."

"I don't think he'll do that. He's having lunch at the moment. I'm going after him myself. You see, sir," he added quickly, hearing his chief draw breath. "You see we've nothing against him at the moment except guesswork."

"And?"

"And if he *did* bring this German over, and if the German *is* Meister . . ."

"You think he'll give himself away."

"Yes, I do."

"It's Morgan you're dealing with, remember."

"I know him pretty well, sir. Judging from what my man tells me, he's on edge; he looks dead-tired and he's wearing the sort of clothes he'd go to sea in. Now Morgan's not a fellow to do that in London—a bit of a dandy, if you know what I mean."

"I see." Colonel Patchway knew that this was the kind of reasoning which made Farquarson so deadly; he worked,

212

it was often said, inside the heads of the men he was after. "I see," the Colonel said again.

"We could probably pull him in for questioning right now, sir, and we *might* get some information out of him; then again we might not. Either way he'd be out of here within an hour, we couldn't hold him, and on top of that he'd be warned."

"All right," said Patchway. "But if he's up to anything which might connect with this German business, don't for Heaven's sake lose him. Things are brewing up. The Home Office have been at me again—that makes four times."

Reproachfully Farquarson said, "I don't lose people, sir."

"No. No, of course, you don't. But this young man's devilishly unprofessional. He's surprised us before, you know."

"He's an adventurer, sir—more than a crook. But I think he's had his last adventure."

"I hope you're right." There was a pause. Then: "Has he got anyone working with him?"

"No, sir. He's alone in this one."

Which shows that though he may have been right about many things, Farquarson was not infallible.

He replaced the receiver, put on his hat and went down to the mews behind the offices. There, he selected a most unlikely-looking car, a dusty and bruised shooting brake which nevertheless had an unusually powerful engine. His driver, who had a sad predilection for immaculate city suitings, he thrust into an ancient tweed overcoat of his own, and they set out for the back streets of Mayfair.

He found his subordinate in a milk bar, gloomily sucking a milk shake, with one eye on a shabby Italian restaurant across the street.

"Where is he? In there?"

213

The subordinate nodded. "Yes, sir. And there's no back way out. Not unless he gets up on the roof."

Farquarson smiled sleepily. "He won't. He's not that sort. Still dressed up as a sailor?"

"Yes, sir." The subordinate thought privately that Alan Morgan in his sailing kit looked a lot more presentable than his superior officer in that disgraceful tweed suit with bags at the knees. Also he was tired of milk shakes; this was his third.

Farquarson said, "All right. I'll take over. You go and join Munnings in the car. It's just round the corner in Hartney Street, next to the telephone box. When I want you again I'll give you a ring, and for Heaven's sake get moving when I do."

"Yes, sir."

Farquarson settled himself on the vacated stool and ordered a peach Melba, a concoction to which he was much addicted. Unfortunately it had no sooner been placed beneath his nose by the bored blonde behind the counter than Alan emerged from the Italian restaurant and set off quickly towards Bond Street.

Farquarson was after him like a fox terrier, leaving a less bored blonde with open mouth and hand outstretched for payment. It was not difficult to keep that distinctively dressed figure in sight. They turned right, and left, and right again, and, just when Farquarson was beginning to perspire freely (the weather was much too hot for baggy tweeds) his quarry vanished into the back entrance of St. Clair House.

Farquarson, after the requisite pause, followed him and arrived at the bottom of the lift shaft as the lift itself returned to ground level. The information which he presently elicited—namely, that the weirdly-dressed gentleman had gone up to Gage and Mountview, Electrical Engineers, on

214

the third floor—was not very helpful. However, Farquarson had been in his particular profession for too long to expect any *one* piece of information to be of much use on its own. He possessed abundant, uncanny patience. So, patiently, he went back to the street, enlisted a constable to watch the front entrance of St. Clair House in Piccadilly, called up his dusty shooting brake to a more convenient hiding place . . . and waited.

Major Hobart had evidently prepared himself for assault both physical and ethical. He barely raised those bushy red eyebrows when he saw his visitor's uncouth appearance. Alan decided immediately that Kellandale had confided little in his henchman; it was obvious that the major had been given instructions to do as he was told but to watch out for trickery, and equally obvious that he did not like the situation at all. A good clear order, a "do this" or a "do that," was more to the regular soldier's taste. Neither his taciturn hauteur nor his air of knowing a thing or two rang in the least true.

Alan, finding himself treated like a junior officer under close arrest—a sensation about which he knew too much already—went into the attack at once. He said, "What did Kellandale tell you?"

Hobart winced at this harsh use of the name, turned agitatedly to his secretary, a tall stringy spinster with a profusion of unbecoming auburn curls, and said, "Miss Spooner, if you wouldn't mind. . . ."

The lady arose, clutching files, a handbag and a cup of tea, and retired sinuously to an outer office, where she could be seen through the glass partition coiling herself behind an alien desk like an eel in an aquarium.

Hobart said, "I am to do as you say. When you hand Schröder over to me, I am instructed . . . that is to say. I

215

have a package which I shall pass to you." He picked a brief case off his desk and tapped it knowingly.

Alan nodded. "We're driving out into the country."

"I was prepared for that." The slight glance which he directed at his overcoat seemed to indicate that the gun might have returned to its old hiding place.

Alan said, "I'm ready if you are."

They went down by the back stairs (the major, it seemed, was not prepared to be seen in the company of this disreputable person) and out of the back entrance into Paton Street.

Hobart's car stood not far from the door and Alan climbed, without question, into the driving seat. The major stifled whatever he had been going to say and sat decorously beside him, arranging the overcoat on his knees, pocket uppermost. The brief case he tucked between himself and the door of the car—as far away as possible from the driver.

They moved off, swung left into Bond Street and left again into Piccadilly.

Behind them trailed a dusty shooting brake.

The major said, "I wouldn't advise you to try any tricks, young feller-me-lad."

"You can relax," Alan replied, "and you can put your gun away. It might go off."

Behind them Farquarson said to his driver, "If you lose that car, Munnings, you're going to wish you'd never been born."

The driver laughed in a subordinate sort of way—and then decided, on second thoughts, that there hadn't been anything very funny about his chief's tone of voice.

2 – DUEL IN A DEAD HOUSE

I F THIS IS CRIME, LINDA THOUGHT, NO WONDER IT'S SO *popular*.

Except for a few anxious minutes as she walked up to the car in the mews, climbed in and drove away, the whole of her first premeditated criminal action had been as pleasant and as simple as any other summer car ride into the country. She found Godswater without difficulty, and The Fox, contrary to all her expectations, really couldn't be missed; it stood facing a small, triangular village green. She drove into the backyard, was met by a smiling Fred Butcher, who had been warned by telephone of her pending arrival, and was ushered into a back parlour where awaited her a royal repast of ham, hard-boiled eggs, salad, homemade bread and the most delicious butter she had ever tasted.

No questions were asked and no money accepted.

When she had finished eating, Mr. Butcher, still smiling, showed her the shed where he had put the car and instructed her in the art of opening the doors quickly and quietly. "In case," he added, twinkling, "you might want to get away quick and quiet, like."

Linda dearly wanted to know the why's and wherefore's of his accepting such underhand preparation as part of his day's work; she did not, however, see her way to asking him and presently he returned to the house, chuckling and shaking his head.

It was now three o'clock, which left her half-an-hour before she might expect Alan to arrive. There was no need to ask the way to the house; it could only be in one direction because the village lay upon the north side of the river and she, approaching from the west, had passed nothing larger than the vicarage. She strolled eastwards along the lane and

217

came at length to a long, crumbling wall beyond which lay a belt of beeches. Between the slender trunks she caught a glimpse of undulating parkland and a grey stable surmounted by a white cupola.

She climbed the wall and set off between the beeches, hoping that it was not going to be a long walk. The afternoon had grown very hot; giant towers of misty, white cloud had reared themselves along the horizon and, pausing, she sensed rather than heard the far-distant grumble of thunder.

Ladeleigh took her by surprise in more senses than one. She glanced up and it was suddenly there, where a moment before had been nothing but trees. What had appeared to be a wood revealed itself as a great wide avenue made up of clumps of beeches. At the end of it, pale grey against the woods and against the lowering sky beyond, every pediment and cornice clear-cut in the slanting sunlight, the house itself lay brooding with blank windows. There was something a little menacing about the elegant Georgian façade: a dreary emptiness, hopelessness in the blind stare of the windows and the overdramatised posturing of the many statues which gazed back at them. The grass grew rank on what had been spacious lawns, and only a tumble of roses, a drift of sweet syringa or a bowed lavender bush remained of all the neat flowerbeds which must have delighted Alan as a boy.

Linda found that her mood of excitement had vanished. Empty houses always saddened her, but none that she could remember had ever affected her quite so personally. She had not, in any case, expected it to be so very large.

Again, but seeming yet more distant, thunder rumbled along the horizon like a barrel rolling across cobblestones.

She remembered suddenly that somewhere in that grey tombstone of a house was an imprisoned man. The thought made her shudder, but she approached it nonetheless—slowly, because the heat was all-enveloping.

Steps led down from the columned portico to a paved terrace. She mounted them and peered in through one of a line of tall windows. The room beyond, the saloon, she judged, was sliced by thin swords of sunlight so that the corners were dark by comparison. Gold glinted from the walls, and muscular mythical legs writhed about the ceiling.

She wandered idly round to the front entrance: another, smaller portico with a covered carriage-way so that the ladies might alight from their coaches and remain dry. The front door was unlocked, as Alan had said; she tried the handle, felt the door give, and hesitated. But the fascination of the unknown—of an unknown which was so personally connected with the man she loved—triumphed over her more conventional fears. She stepped into the hall, musty-smelling and elegant with pilasters, and listened. If she had expected to hear a distant voice calling for help, or the beating of fists against a wooden door, she was disappointed. There was absolute stillness. A moth fluttered through a bar of sunlight, and, in the dead house, each tiny sound of nature was clear and magnified from the garden outside: coo of a distant pigeon, drone of a bee, flutter of leaves, creak of grasshopper. Then, impinging on the natural chorus, the approaching throb of a car's engine. Turning, she saw through the slightly open door a long vista of driveway and the car itself at the end of it. She glanced at her watch and found that it was indeed a quarter to four; she had idled far longer than had seemed possible.

The car swung round in front of the house and crunched to a standstill. Alan climbed out, waved the major back with a curt word, and came towards her. She stood immediately facing the door so that her presence in some shadowy corner should not alarm him. As soon as he saw her, his face relaxed; from tense pre-occupation, he smiled.

"All right?"

"Perfectly."

He glanced back at the car and Major Hobart. His expression was anxious again. "I think we were followed," he said. "I'm not sure. We lost them in Leddenbury." He took her arm and drew her into the heart of that dark, desolate house; the sound of their feet echoed disconsolately down the long corridor. Finally they came to a back staircase, older than the Georgian hall, relic presumably of some earlier building, round which later generations had spread. Under it, in a small alcove, he caught at the panel moulding and pushed with all his strength. It slid aside.

"No." He grinned. "Not a secret monk's hole, I'm afraid. Just the old cellar. My great-great-grandfather didn't like it—not enough room for the copious masses of wine he used to drink. So he built a new one, and used this for cockfighting."

He had led her, by the light of his torch, down a flight of stone steps. The cellar was large.

Linda said, "He must have been some drinker."

"He was."

"I don't envy your prisoner."

"Oh, he's all right. The Army had this place during the war. They built a nice little underground H.Q. down here —one of the invasion precautions."

He unlocked a door on the far side of the cellar, and bare stone gave way to match-boarding; there were trestle tables against the wall, severed ends of telephone wire, a litter of paper. Light glimmered beneath yet another door, and this one he unlocked also and kicked open savagely.

The scene was grotesque. Lit, half by candlelight, half by a cold gleam of day from the high, barred grating, Schröder stood facing the door, hair on end and terror in the long face. One hand was held to his mouth and in it there glinted something apparently metallic. As soon as he saw who it was, he tottered and nearly fell. It did not occur to Linda that he had been expecting the police; but Alan darted forward, seized the big hand and forced it open. There was a brief scuffle and the German fell back against the wall. In his own language he said, "Give it to me. Please."

Alan held it up so that Linda might see.

"What is it?"

He grinned. "Compound Angel of Death."

She stepped closer, and saw a narrow capsule.

"Many the good German," said Alan, "who has saved himself trial and execution with one of these." He stared curiously from the tiny lethal thing to the man, sweat beading his forehead. In German, he said, "I'm glad I haven't your secrets, my friend—nor your conscience. I am only a simple crook."

"What's in it?" Linda enquired, peering cautiously.

"Prussic acid, I expect." He held the capsule out and Schröder took it, pocketed it quickly. "You may need it yet, Mein Herr. But I've finished with you, thank God. Come."

He snuffed out the candle and pushed the man towards the cellar. They made their way back to the daylight and fresh air—a curious procession.

At the front door Alan gestured to Linda, indicating that she should not show herself. Standing back in the shadows of the hall, she saw him lead Schröder to the car, saw Hobart pull a photograph from his pocket and compare it with the man's face. A few words were exchanged and the brief case changed hands. Alan looked inside it, and appeared satisfied. A moment later, the car was moving away down the avenue. Soon it vanished from view, and the country sounds of wood pigeon, bee and grasshopper again held sway.

Alan came back to her. He looked suddenly younger, less weary. From his face, her gaze moved to the palatial hall-way, the wide staircase sweeping up to a circular domed gallery.

He followed the direction of her interest and laughed. "I sense questions."

She did not reply at once. Then, "You were happy here." It was a statement rather than a question.

"Was I?"

"Yes, I think so. What happened?"

He took her arm and led her towards the stairs. "Nothing very extraordinary. I was born, I was a little boy, I went to school, I came home for the holidays, I took everything for granted—in that mindless way children do. I went to a uni-versity, I came home for the vac. . . ."

"And then?"

"Then there was a war." He paused, drawing her to a standstill on the staircase. "Are you looking for drama? There is none."

"For explanation, rather."

"There's no explanation either. What I . . . What I am, has no root here—just as this—" he waved a hand at the gracious magnificence—"has no place in our shoddy world today. I was a fool; I did something that almost everyone in the Navy did at one time or another: I smuggled. I brought home presents for a few friends. Wine for my father—he was alive then—nylons for a girl friend, a watch for my cousin." He laughed drily. "I was caught—that was the difference between me and the next man. I was held up as an example, court-martialled, chucked out, branded. . . ."

"Oh no."

"Oh yes." He was savage. "They called it 'wholesale smuggling on a commercial basis.'"

"Was it?"

"Ha! I found the girl friend had let me down, so I sold the nylons to a man in a bar. I was drunk. People do get drunk when they've been let down by girl friends." He stared at her angrily. "Go on, call me weak. I'm not."

"No, you're not."

"I just got to loathe society. I found that people wouldn't speak to me because of the court martial. *My* sort of people, you see—the sort of people that a house like this and a private income and a University education collect round them."

"Aren't you generalising a bit?"

"Maybe. But they didn't even pause to ask what I was court-martialled *for*. Why should they? I've no doubt the story improved in the telling."

She was overwhelmed suddenly by the passion of his bitterness. It was in some way childish, as well as tragic. She sensed through it—through this particular crook, whom she loved—a compassion for every other inhabitant of that dim nether-world of crime.

"I got to loathe them," he said again. "I got to loathe the sniveling little world of permits and forms and official bric-a-brac which they all put up with. I saw them as dead, finished. Sans guts, sans faith, sans everything."

"Yes, I see," she said.

"Oddly enough, I believe you do."

"But I wouldn't call it exactly reasonable, all the same."

"Reason!" He snorted. "There's too much reason about, these days. And don't," he said, swinging round, "don't think I'm asking for sympathy. I'm not." He walked away from her round the gallery. Below them the well of the hall was slatted with bars of sunlight from chinks in the shuttered windows.

Linda was afraid suddenly—afraid that all her grandiose ideas of salvation for this bitter young man had been mere imagination. His fury and his misery seemed to have evap-

223

orated. Could it be that, having revenged himself on whomever it was he felt to be responsible for Rocky's death, he considered that he was now free once more? Free to go on with the pursuit of lawlessness; piling, as she had said in the pub that morning, wrong upon wrong upon wrong?

For the first time she doubted herself; she wondered whether he really was irreclaimable. In adversity she had seemed to touch his inmost heart; but now adversity retreated, and he was hard again. Confident. Metallic. Secret. Intent on his own devious plans. Intent, she feared, on his own destruction.

At the far side of the gallery he threw back one of the shutters, and light streamed in. They stared at each other, separated by the chasm of the well—she felt it to be almost symbolic—and his next words only strengthened the feeling.

"Don't you want to go back to Wainport?" he said. "Aren't you tired of melodrama?" His voice was cold, distant. She could find nothing to say.

Looking at her, Alan saw her indecision. The sympathy he felt for her only goaded him on to further brutality. It was not so much that he didn't love her as that he couldn't bear to see her suffering in her love for him; he couldn't bear the sight of her weary face and the way she leaned on the balustrade as if too weak, suddenly, to stand. Her trust and her loyalty rose to shame him—rose like the cobra preparing to strike—rose up and up and up so that he could see nothing but her face, suffering for him. And he thought, in panic, *Dear God, can it be that I do love her?*

And at that same moment a sound caught his ear. He spun round to the window, his heart pounding.

Below him, in the circular sweep of the drive, stood a large shooting brake. Farquarson and three other men were climbing out of it.

While he stood, shocked into indecision, Farquarson

224

glanced up and saw him; then he waved a white hand—the most casual salute, as if he were a guest arriving for a week-end. At the same time the other men made off in different directions round the house. Farquarson advanced on the front door.

Linda, seeing only his tense horror, said, "What is it? I thought I heard . . ."

He silenced her; ran round the gallery, seized her arm, thrust her towards the dark mouth of a long corridor.

"It's the police," he said. "Do exactly as I say. Quick. And take this." He gave her the brief case which contained the money.

She stumbled in the sudden gloom, but he held her up.

"At the far end of this passage there's a door on the right. It's a big cupboard. Go inside and wait. Quick."

He pressed his torch into her hand, and watched the beam of it wavering away into the distance. Already, behind him, Farquarson's footsteps rang in the empty hall. His precise voice, with its seemingly false Scottish accent, said, "Alan Morgan, will you come down a while? I want a wee word wi' ye."

Then, since he received no answer, "Reeves, get along there and see if you can find the back stairs. Wait at the bottom. Don't on any account go up. He might . . ." The voice was raised for Alan's benefit. "He might get panicky and shoot."

In all this he remained easily conversational. Farquarson never shouted, never became excited.

Alan, his heart pounding like a pile-driver, backed along the corridor until he came to the place where another crossed it. Thus, he stood at the centre of the house. He could see, framed in the dark square of the passage, part of the brightly lit gallery and the head of the staircase. His hand, holding the Lüger, trembled; he was afraid, and he knew that there

225

had always been this fear of Farquarson lurking at the back of his mind—that there had, perhaps, always been this moment when that fear would manifest itself.

Farquarson's voice said, "Morgan, you'll save us both a lot of trouble if you'd come out and talk."

He bit his lip to still that agony of fear, but kept quiet.

"After all," continued the voice, "we've got nothing on you just yet—certainly nothing as bad as attempted shooting of a policeman."

Alan, trusting his hand no longer, slipped the Lüger into his pocket. At the same moment, Farquarson—Farquarson's head smiling, almost as though he sensed the young man's fear—appeared on the top step of the stairs. Slowly he mounted into view.

Alan said, "You make a fine target."

Farquarson did not pause. It had never struck Alan that he was a brave man, but it did now.

"You have," the precise voice said, "too much intelligence to shoot, Al my boy." At the mouth of the passage he halted —a dark shape against the bright gallery beyond. Alan stepped aside into the crossing corridor, so that he could just see the other's figure. He brushed the dark hair down over his forehead and held an arm over the lower part of his face so that there should be no whiteness showing in the gloom. Farquarson might be confident that his adversary wouldn't shoot; the compliment was not returned. There were stories about this schoolmasterly policeman—stories of "accidents," stories of "shooting in self-defense," stories of information elicited by means that were not in the regulations. So Alan Morgan covered his face with a dark-clothed arm, showed only his eyes. Waited.

Farquarson, hand in overcoat pocket, leaned against the wall.

"Where's your German chum?" he enquired, conversationally.

"Not here, at all events."

"If," said Farquarson, "you felt disposed to tell me where he is, and who commissioned you to get him, I might see my way to going home quietly. I might call off my men."

"And arrest me later for complicity?"

Farquarson chuckled. After a pause he said, "You know who the fellow is, of course?"

Was there, Alan wondered, *a trap in this too?* Curiosity warred with caution. He did not answer.

"Meister." Farquarson answered his own question. "Heinrich Meister. You've heard of him, no doubt?"

Memory stirred. Standing in the ominous gloom, in this dead house of his childhood happiness, the young man frowned, searching the name for its meaning.

"Heinrich Meister," repeated the voice, rolling the *r* with pleasure. "I suppose you could say he's the world's leading authority on artificial fuels. Until atomic power becomes a workable reality—which won't be yet awhile—whoever holds Meister may very well hold the reins."

Alan remembered now, remembered reading of the man's research, so nearly completed, which might have turned the course of the War—of many wars. Kellandale, he thought drily, had good reason to be worried—good reason to pay well for the safety of a man whose brain might make oil-wells unnecessary—who, with a formula, might alter the balance of world power, economic and otherwise.

He remembered, too, all that he had heard of Kellandale's oil interests in South America: of the virtual fuel monopoly he already held in certain quarters there. The last pieces of that edifice of lies which Kellandale had built at their first meeting fell away now, and he saw the truth. Once the German reached South America he was safe, no matter what

227

crimes he had committed; and the formulae, which at present were all that existed, would turn to gold—would turn to power. There was no telling just how much power the production of artificial fuel on a commercial basis would place in Kellandale's hands.

Anger turned over in Alan's stomach, blurred his vision, pounded in his head.

Farquarson took a pace or two towards him. He stiffened, touching the Lüger. It gave him a sort of reassurance, and he found words.

"I know nothing about it," he said, "but wouldn't you do better to get going after this superman? I tell you he's not here and I'm speaking the truth."

"Where is he then?"

"I don't know—or care."

Farquarson assimilated this. "The trouble is," he said finally, "that we have very few clues to go on. It would take us a long time to find out for ourselves as much as you already know."

The menace in that voice did not escape the young man. He shuddered. He knew, with terrible certainty, that if he let himself be caught, he would be forced to speak; and if rumour could be trusted, Farquarson's ways of forcing people to speak were not pretty. He saw himself suddenly as one, tiny, insignificant link in a chain of very great importance. If Heinrich Meister was the stake, then he, Alan Morgan, would be torn limb from living limb without compunction in order to get the necessary information. And there was Linda, too. Furiously his brain began to work.

Farquarson took another few steps down the passage. "There are," he said, "various other reasons why a young man like yourself might feel it his . . . yes, his *duty* to tell us what you know."

Silence.

"Meister is a wanted man—not because of his research, but because he is a murderer."

Alan stiffened.

"Exactly how many men he has killed in his time is uncertain; there is proof for the death of sixty-seven. Don't think I'm appealing to your charity, or your patriotism; I wouldn't resort to that. You yourself would know, better than any other man in England, whether you think he is guilty or not."

Alan remembered the prussic acid raised to a mouth slack with terror. He clenched his fists.

"It became necessary," went on that voice, "to find out what the effects of his synthetic fuel would be on the men who used it. There were various elements. . . . However, I needn't go into that." He came a pace nearer, nonchalant to the point of nightmare. "And so guinea pigs were supplied for tests. Of the sixty-seven I mentioned, twenty were Jews, and the rest were young men much like yourself: air-crew, sailors, soldiers—British, Colonial, French, American . . ."

Horror crept on Alan's back. He knew suddenly, blindingly, that all this was true; it supplied a piece of the German's character that had been missing.

"It seems probable," said Farquarson, "though it remains unproven, that some two hundred men were . . . *used* in various experiments—many as targets for a certain flame-throwing sideline which Meister wished to perfect."

Sweat trickled down Alan's spine.

"It seems," said Farquarson, "rather, shall we say, ironic that you, an ex-service man with a fine service record, should have gone to all that trouble merely to rescue such a creature. And then, of course, there was Rockingham . . ." He must have heard Alan groan, very softly, in the darkness because he left the sentence, artistically, in midair. "A decent little fellow."

The young man thought he had known fury before; thought that he despised Kellandale as much as it was possible for one human being to despise another. It had not been so. He knew an anger now which was so cruel that it gnawed at his vitals like the rat in the Chinese torture; he felt that he would burst if he could not give it expression.

Farquarson was dangerously near; a mere six or seven yards separated them. He could smell the tweed of the policeman's coat.

"It seems to me," the merciless voice went on, "that whoever enlisted you for this job is not only dangerous but entirely without moral sense. But then, there are men to whom the death of ten thousand youngsters, let alone a mere hundred or so, means nothing."

Kellandale, Alan remembered, had made most of his fortune from munitions of war. He was trembling helplessly.

"Couldn't you," added Farquarson, "simply tell me the name of this employer of yours?"

Yes, yes, by God he could. And would. *Kellandale:* it was poised on his lips. But he didn't speak. Mere speaking would never be enough now; the why's and wherefore's were obscure—he had no time to consider them in any case—but he knew with absolute certainty that in this he must act alone, or go down forever into the mud of self-hatred. If it was the last thing he did on this earth, he would see the end of what he had started. And he knew that not only Rocky's tortured flesh, but also Linda's face, weary with love for him, would drive him to that end.

In a moment his anger crystallised; the trembling ceased; indecision fled. He felt for the Lüger with his right hand; his left slid gently into his trouser pocket and closed round the first coin it touched.

"Morgan," said Farquarson, very near now, "come out. This thing's bigger than you are, can't you see that?"

Alan drew back into darkness. Waited. He heard another soft footfall, and another. Slowly, infinitely slowly, he raised the Lüger—raised it high above his head. All the time he watched, with catlike fixity, for that blurring of the clean line of the wall which would mean that Farquarson was upon him.

A board creaked. The precise voice said, in his ear it seemed, "Morgan, come out."

Then he flicked the coin; it spun across the passage and rapped the opposite wall. He saw Farquarson start and twist. Then he struck.

It was a good, true blow. The man fell with hardly a sound, and lay still.

Alan stepped over the inert body and moved quickly, quietly, down the long corridor. It was unlikely, he knew, that this Reeves, who was waiting at the bottom of the back stairs, would have heard a sound; two, solid, green-baize doors separated him from the upper landing.

Linda gave a small gasp of relief to see him. "I heard," she whispered. "I thought he'd hit *you*."

Alan took her hand. "We've got to be clever," he said. "There are three more of them. And don't for Heaven's sake drop that."

She clutched the brief case more firmly and followed him down the corridor. They came to a swing door, beyond which were maids' bedrooms. He gestured to her to walk quietly. Together they tiptoed past the head of the back staircase.

The corridor twisted to the left and went on; it seemed interminable. Another swing door gave onto an enclosed bridge; she glimpsed, through a small window, the white cupola of the stables. At the end of the bridge they came to a long, bare hall.

"The playroom," he whispered. "We're over the stables now. Careful."

He led her round the edge of the big room, to avoid squeaking boards, and into what was either a tiny closet or a large cupboard.

"Now," he whispered, "the fun begins."

She noticed at once a narrow, roughly made door in the wall. He was clearing away rubbish from around it.

"Grandfather had this made so that he could visit his precious horses without going out of the house."

The door squeaked agonisingly as he prised it open. They paused, listening, eyes wide. There was no answering sound.

With infinite care he continued to open it, pressing a handkerchief over the rusty hinge. A breath of stable loft came out to meet them, warm and friendly. A rat scampered across bare boards.

"Go slow," Alan said. "The wood always was rotten."

He led her slowly into the gloom, keeping once more to the utmost edge of the floor. Three times they stepped over strong, old crossbeams.

Linda realised that they must have come well over two hundred yards from her hiding place in the cupboard.

At last, he drew her to a standstill. They had reached a small hatch—used, evidently, for the hauling up of sacks.

"Now," said Alan, "get ready to run. It's daylight from here on." He peered at her. "Are you all right?"

"Yes."

"Where's the car?"

"In a shed at the Inn."

"Good." He slid the bolts with some difficulty, and pushed. Nothing happened. She saw his hands, light against the dark wood.

"Damn."

"What is it?"

232

"Nailed up."

Strangely this nearly made her laugh, but his fingers, vice-like over her arm, put an end to that.

A man's voice, seeming to be in the loft with them, said, "No doors this end, Reg."

"Where's the Guv?"

"Inside."

"Is he all right?"

"Dunno. He said don't go upstairs. Better get back to the house anyway. Reeves is in there with him." Footsteps on cobblestones receded, and gradually Alan released his grip on her arm. Again he pushed the door. It groaned gently but did not budge.

"Listen," he whispered, "this is our only chance. We've got to take it."

"What'll you do?"

"I think this thing'll open if I give it a real hiding. There's a wall just under it and to the right. I'll go first; you give me the brief case; then I'll help you down. We'll have to run along the top of the wall for about a dozen feet—it's quite broad, so don't worry—then jump to the right into the orchard. If they don't see us, we're free. All right?"

She nodded.

"Good girl."

He lay down on his back, head away from the hatch, then drew up his knees until they touched his chin, paused, and drove forward with all the power of his legs. The sound of the impact was deafening. A slit of daylight appeared along the top of the frame. Swiftly he drew his legs back and rammed again. The hatch flew open in a flurry of dust, and hung from one hinge. In a moment they were on the wall, and never in her life had Linda felt so conspicuous. Somewhere behind them a man shouted, another answered.

Then they jumped. A stray twig slapped her face, and she fell, rolling, in long sweet-scented grass.

"Run," he was hissing at her. "Come on, run."

Across the orchard, through a tangle of hedge, into a mercifully dry ditch, along it. Breathless, she followed him, thorns tearing at her legs, nettle stings smarting on her bare arms.

The ditch ended at a small wicket gate in a wall. Beyond it was a dusty lane, and, miraculously, another gate leading into the backyard of The Fox.

"Did they see us?" she panted.

"No. They heard." He vaulted the second gate, dragged her over it somehow.

"There." She pointed to the shed which held the car.

"You drive," he shouted.

The doors crashed back, and the engine started to her first touch. Alan, by this time, was under a rug on the floor of the back seat.

"Drive like hell," came his voice. "Left out of the yard. They won't know you or the car."

More by luck than good judgment she did not carry the gate post with her, did not kill an enquiring Fred Butcher, who leapt aside just in time, still, she noticed, with a smile on his face.

Suddenly, and without hindrance, the open road was before her.

"Left again at the crossroads," came the voice from the floor.

"Where are we going?" she asked, as lightly as she could.

"That's the hell of it." His voice was calm but deadly. "I don't know yet, but I'm going to find out, if it's the last thing I do."

She wanted to ask him what he was planning, but the words would not form themselves. In some strange way

234

she could no longer care; the emergency had flung them together, and she knew that she would do as he wished now, without question, without criticism. It was as if the common danger had stripped her of all the conventions which he disliked so much. She loved him and would stand by him. And that was that.

Presently the muffled voice from below and behind her said, "I'm sorry about this. You wouldn't get out of it when I told you to. Now you're stuck."

"You needn't be sorry."

After a pause he said, "Well, I am. I . . . I feel bloody about it. But there's no backing out now. I'm going to finish this dirty business."

Her brain, weary and resigned and yet strangely at peace, would not question him.

"I said I'd use you, didn't I?"

"You've no alternative."

"When you come to the main road," he said, "turn right."

"And then?"

"You'll come to a village called Marling. Just by the church there's a telephone box. Stop there."

"Won't they be following?"

"Not this way. I don't suppose Farquarson's come round yet in any case; they won't know what to do without him. Tell me when you see the village."

She told him, and he came up off the floor. In the driving mirror she saw how set and rigid his face was once more: the face she had seen—oh, long, long ago—at dawn that morning, coldly lit by the first light at sea.

He jumped out as soon as she drew the car to a standstill, and slammed into the kiosk. His brain was clear now; it would need to be clear if he was to succeed in what he intended to do.

The trim voice of the operator chirped into his ear. He

gave the number and, while he was waiting, wrapped his handkerchief round the receiver. Presently another voice said, "Gage and Mountview at your service."

Alan took a deep breath, and assuming, as nearly as he knew how, the accents of the senior officers' mess, replied, "Major Hobart here. Give me my secretary, will you?"

"I can hardly hear you, Major Hobart. The line's very bad."

"Give me my secretary," said Alan, more loudly, unwrapping the handkerchief slightly.

"Very good." A pause, and "You're through."

"Helloo," fluted a genteel voice.

"Miss Spooner?" enquired Alan, thanking his lucky stars that Hobart had used the unforgettable name in his presence.

"Yes, Major."

Good. The exchange had announced him.

"Suddenly struck me," he said. "Might have to stay down here a day or two . . ."

"The connection," said Miss Spooner, "is fraitefully indistinct."

"Shockin'."

"You did say you might have to stay, Major, before you left."

"Yes, yes. Question of any important letters. Forward them, won't you?"

"Oh yes, Major."

"Got the address all right?" He held his breath. This was the testing moment. On this it all hung suspended—on this infinitesimal thread of a secretary's pride.

"Of *course*," said Miss Spooner.

Oh, would she, he thought, *could she resist this implied slur on her efficiency?*

No, she could not.

"I have it here on my desk," said Miss Spooner, smugly. "Hurst View Hotel, Poole, Dorset."

Alan sighed.

"I beg yours, Major?"

"Nothin'. Capital. Excellent. Good-bye."

"I can *hardly* hear you, Major. The line's very bad."

"Good-bye."

"Oh, good-bai, Major." Miss Spooner simpered, and rang off.

Poole, Alan was thinking. They were proposing to send Meister by flying boat then.

He glanced at his watch—a quarter past five. Then he looked at Linda waiting so patiently in the car. At the sight of her, he was filled with a terrible sense of insufficiency, of helplessness; there was something about her loyalty and her determination which made him feel small, mean and despicable.

But, in spite of this, in spite of all she stood for—or perhaps because of it—he intended to go through with his plan.

He stepped out of the telephone box and went back to the car.

"Poole," he said. "Straight through the village and turn left onto the Oxford Road."

3 – THE BREAK IN THE CIRCLE

THE HURST VIEW HOTEL STOOD AT THE EDGE OF POOLE HARbour. It was a tall, flat building, constructed so that the maximum number of rooms might have the much-desired view of the sea.

By the time Linda brought the car to a standstill on the road outside, it was quite dark. The windows of the hotel gleamed, tier upon tier, between the straight, dark trunks of pine trees. There was a pleasant fresh smell of seaweed, pine and wood smoke.

"And now?" she enquired.

Alan sat beside her, slumped low in the seat. He did not look at her. "You don't seem awfully curious."

"Why should I be curious? I'm not . . . not really very interested, to tell you the truth."

He flashed her a dark glance. "I don't understand you."

"That's possible." She nodded towards the hotel. "Are you going in?"

"Yes."

"Dressed like that?" He was still wearing his faded jeans and reefer jacket, and they were dusty from the stable loft.

"Why not? People come to this place to sail, you know." She shrugged. "Shall I wait here?"

"Yes." He sat immobile, as if unwilling to move. Watching him, she experienced a faint thrill of fear, and with it a kind of exultation. She had not been wrong then: he was still hating himself. She could sense, from this heaviness, this inactivity, that only by a tremendous effort of will was he driving himself to do what he felt must be done. He was nearing the end of his tether. Yes, she knew exultation, and pity, and fear.

He roused himself as if he had been asleep. "Go down to the corner and wait. Be ready to get moving when I come out."

She nodded.

Still without looking at her, he climbed out of the car and walked away among the trees towards the hotel.

Linda, sitting alone in the darkness, pressed her face into her two hands as if trying to blot out something she did not wish to see.

Dear God, she was thinking. *Should I have stopped him?*

238

could *I have stopped him if I had so wished? Would it have been right to do so? Oh, dear God, what is right?*

Alan's mind was a blank now. The cool breeze from the sea and the clean smell of the pines cleared his brain and left it empty of thought. The sigh of the wind among the pine needles stirred a harsh memory of Rocky's savage death, but this only spurred him on. He felt perfectly confident, almost superhumanly in control of the situation, and the empty-headedness was agreeable—like the effect of alcohol, but unblurred. He walked into the foyer of the hotel and up to the young man behind the reception desk.

"A friend of mine is staying here," he said, "a Major Hobart."

"Yes, sir. The two gentlemen went up to their suite after dinner. They were both tired, I think."

"Major Hobart would wish to see me all the same. If you would say I come from Lord Kellandale."

The receptionist had dark eyebrows. They shot up at the mention of Kellandale.

"*Yes*, sir," he said.

Alan, in his mood of empty-headed certainty, had no doubt of the effect that The Name would have on Hobart.

"He says will you go up, sir, or shall he come down?"

"I'll go up."

In the lift he thought that Hobart would be prepared for all eventualities but this one. He would be sleeping with a revolver under his pillow; he would lock all doors and windows and refuse to speak to his own wife—if he had one. But Kellandale . . .

That ordered but not orderly mind, knowing that its master's greatest wish was to be in no way connected with Meister, would panic to hear The Name spoken by a mere hotel employee at this drastic climax in the affair. He would flounder among the thousand possibilities of such an eventuality.

Alan tipped the page boy, watched him out of sight, and rang the bell of Suite seven. After a moment he heard a footstep on the other side of the door, and the handle began to turn.

They faced each other. The major's face went purple. As he opened his mouth to speak, Alan pushed him sharply in the chest, stepped into the room and shut the door. Hobart eyed the gun in the young man's hand and gobbled like an excited turkey.

"I told Kellandale you were a fool," said Alan. "He replied that you were loyal. Doubtless you are. If I had to choose between foolishness and disloyalty, I'd take disloyalty every time. Sit down." He pressed the furious major back into an armchair. "Where's Meister? In the bedroom?"

He could not bear the ridiculous sight of Hobart preparing to say that he didn't know who Meister was, let alone where he was.

"Oh, for Heaven's sake," he snapped. "Call him. Don't pretend. I've got you and you know it."

The major had a certain dogged courage. He shut his mouth and glowered in silence. Alan sighed.

"Meister. Heinrich Meister, come here."

He thought to himself that he sounded like the clerk of a court; in a way he was clerk of a court—an ironic idea.

The bedroom door opened and the German appeared. Seeing the young man, his pale face went suddenly grey. Was it, Alan wondered, that he recalled other young men in other circumstances? A flare of rage leapt up, almost blinding him; then it died down and he was calm again.

"Come in," he said. "I'm not going to shoot you—not if I can help it." He waved the gun, indicating that the Ger-

240

man should stand by Hobart's chair. He himself edged towards the telephone.

"Now," he said. "I don't want to linger over this. It—" he thought of Linda—"it doesn't give me any pleasure."

This was true. He saw in the face of the man he had known as Schröder pure and helpless terror; yet even when he considered those contemporaries, his comrades-in-arms who had been killed so ruthlessly, he could feel no pleasure at the sight. It was as if the experiences of the last few hours had burned him out like a gas mantle, leaving only a bright, efficient shell. He doubted whether he would ever feel anything again.

He said, "Heinrich Meister? That is your name?"

The scientist nodded.

Alan spoke in German now; he wanted no word to be misunderstood. "You are a murderer, Heinrich Meister. In this country murderers are tried and hanged. In a moment I shall pick up this telephone and call the police. I am an adventurer, a crook if you like, but I have never killed a man. You have killed men by the score—defenceless men who had done you no harm. You don't deserve to live."

For a moment he forced himself to meet the other eyes. Then he moved towards the telephone and put out a hand to lift the receiver.

It was all over in a flash. The man had presumably lived with a sense of his own guilt for so long that this was to him no more than a reflex action, feared but in some way desired.

It happened exactly as Alan had visualised it. For an instant, light gleamed on the metallic capsule. Hobart leapt to his feet. The German spun round and fell, breath making a raucous gasp in his throat; he twisted once and lay still, long limbs grotesque in final agony. A faint bitter-sweet smell permeated the warm room.

Alan said, "I don't know how much you've been told about

this fellow's past, but he's a wanted criminal and the charge is wholesale murder."

Major Hobart gobbled, eyes dilated. Already, perhaps, he was facing Kellandale with explanations. He found no words.

"There's only one way," the young man continued, "for this thing to end—and that's for the police to find Heinrich Meister dead."

Again he reached for the telephone.

"What . . ." exploded the major. "What are you going to do?"

Alan paused. "I'm not taking any risks. I don't want you to start disposing of the body—that's what you would feel it your duty to do, I imagine—from the Kellandale point of view."

He lifted the receiver.

"Exchange? Will you call the police, please—a man has committed suicide in this room."

He replaced it carefully, nodded to Hobart and turned to the door.

The major gobbled. "Hey. I mean, look here . . . I mean . . ." The bulbous eyes were wide in fear. "What about me?"

Alan shrugged. "I should take the next 'plane if I were you. Regardless of where it goes. I don't think you'll be owned by Lord K—not after this. Of course, he might give you a helping hand when they let you out, but that wouldn't be for two or three years, would it?"

He closed the door behind him, leaving his old adversary in the close embrace of his conflicting loyalties; but there was little doubt in his mind as to which would triumph. After all, self is important, even to the most faithful of Hobarts. Loyalty, even to the most exacting of Kellandales, must have a limit. Besides, loyalty is a phoenix; and there

242

are men in Australia or America or the Malay Archipelago prepared to accept it—and pay for it.

The hotel foyer was still calm, unaware of the storm about to break over it. Alan crossed it quickly, went out into the cool night, back through the pine trees to the waiting car.

He got in, slumped back into the seat and said, "Drive."

"Where?"

"Anywhere, it doesn't matter. Get moving."

His voice, she noticed, was flat and dead; she knew that it was over.

"You killed him," she said.

"No. He killed himself."

"Compound Angel of Death?"

He nodded.

At the main road she turned eastwards towards London. He said nothing—never so much as glanced up—but sat huddled into the collar of his coat, hands spread flat on his knees.

In Bournemouth the public houses were closing their doors. She took the Winchester road, weariness lying heavy upon her. This day seemed interminable, was interminable. Already fifteen hours had passed since he had put her ashore on the estuary.

He did not speak. It was impossible to guess at his thoughts; she could only pray, earnestly and passionately, that out of this crisis would emerge something new and better. He had sunk into himself and the good God alone knew what he was facing there, islanded in an uncharted sea, lost, helpless. It was the crisis that she had always known must come.

The miles crawled by. Winchester, Alton, Aldershot. The villages were deserted now, asleep. In the towns only an occasional policeman moved beneath a street lamp, or a cat arched against area railings.

Perhaps he slept; she was not sure. In any case, sleep

would not break his mood, she knew that. His was a deeper weariness than sleep could solve.

Once or twice she nodded at the wheel. Then alertness descended on her. She had passed beyond the danger point; she felt almost vital. Bisley, Kingston, the fringes of London. For a few moments, in the centre of the city, there was a kind of hectic sub-life; the life of prostitute and ponce, of night club and no-place-to-sleep. Then, again, out to the suburbs and the long featureless rows of dwellings where slumbered the featureless millions. She felt an infinite aloneness, an unreality.

London broke up into scattered housing estates, and soon it was country again.

At half-past four, in the deceptive radiance of first light, she swung the car off the road and brought it to a standstill on the sandy slope beside her cottage in Wainport.

Alan raised himself, glanced at the estuary, at the paling sky, but never, she noticed, in her direction. He followed her meekly into the kitchen, but would not wait there; he pushed past her and wandered through the dark sitting room onto the terrace beyond. There he stood and stared at the estuary.

She had never seen a face so withdrawn, so vacant of expression; and her awareness of him, standing there in the first glimmering of dawn, grew more and more intense as she went about the business of making coffee and lighting a fire.

When she had finished, it was almost light. A grey, misty radiance lay over river and marsh and the sea beyond. Against it the solitary dark figure, hands thrust deep in pockets, looked infinitely alone. So Adam, she thought, might have surveyed the first dawn. So the last man left on earth might survey the last dawn.

She braced herself and went out to him, carrying a mug

of coffee. He looked haggard and old, but he turned and stared directly at her. Then, miraculously, a faint smile wandered over his mouth.

"You're tired," he said.

Linda choked back an hysterical laugh at the inadequacy of this.

"Coffee." She held it out to him.

He nodded, still staring, took the mug and began to drink. "Have you had some?"

"Yes."

Oddly, there was nothing false in this exchange of everyday pleasantries. It was as if they had fought their way together through a jungle of murky danger to arrive, weary but triumphant, on a cool plateau where there was safety.

When he had finished the coffee, he took her arm and led her back to the cottage. The fire in the sitting room greeted them cheerily. He guided her to the settee and made her lie down, staring always as if seeing her for the first time. Then he took one of the rugs she had brought in from the car and lay down beside her, taking her into his arms and putting his rough cheek beside her smooth one. After a moment, during which he held her tightly as if in terror, he relaxed. Sighed. Fell asleep.

Presently she also slept.

Dawn flowered over the marshes,. and, far down the estuary towards the sea, the first gulls called to each other.

Farquarson stood in the open doorway and watched.

He saw a young woman, radiant in happiness, with her hair, which was cut in short Byronic curls, touched to bright gold by sunlight streaming in through the kitchen window. She was busily engaged, packing tins and bottles into an old wooden sea chest. She was singing to herself.

Presently she glanced up. . . .

Farquarson said, "I beg your pardon." He saw suspicion flood into her face, and the change in expression touched even his jaded heart.

"What . . . do you want?"

He pursed his lips. "To tell you the truth, lassie, I'm not *quite* sure." He removed his hat, and she, seeing how his head was bandaged, coloured violently. Wave after wave of colour.

"The name," he said, "is Farquarson."

She glanced instinctively behind her. Through the door, and the terrace door beyond, Farquarson caught a glimpse of the stocky mast of a small sailing boat.

"He . . ." she began, and faltered. Her legs were giving her trouble, he noticed. She sat down heavily on a hard kitchen chair and stared with grave, frightened eyes.

"I'll be frank," said Farquarson, leaning against the door post. "We *could* pull him in—not for anything very serious, not—" he raised an eyebrow—"for anything half as serious as you would suppose. It wouldn't get us anywhere, from our point of view. The judge would probably tell us off for wasting his time. You see—" he gestured—"there's no proof."

She swallowed convulsively and nodded. The policeman's stare moved from her face to her hand—to the wedding ring on her finger. Their eyes met.

"The day before yesterday," she said.

"Ah." He was silent, watching. Through the two doors he saw a sail running up the stumpy mast.

"You . . . you're thinking of making a journey?"

"Yes."

Again, "Ah."

Suddenly she burst out, "You've *got* to leave him alone. He's happy now, he's all right. Can't you see . . . ?" As if ashamed, the voice faltered. She was standing up, and Farquarson thought that she looked very beautiful.

"Can't I see . . . ?" he queried.

She spread her hands as if the explanation were too big for words. "It was only you," she said, more quietly, "only you, and your 'justice'—" oh, the irony in that word—" which made him what he was."

"Was?" queried Farquarson sharply.

"Yes. Oh yes." She beat her two hands together. "I promise you. . . . No, I can't do that."

"You're an honest young woman," said the policeman approvingly.

"But he won't give you any more trouble, I know it. I could almost promise. Oh, yes, you may smile."

"I wasn't smiling *at* you," said Farquarson, quite truthfully, "but with you."

She stared at him, wonderingly, and then looked away. "I'm . . . sorry he hit you."

"So am I. But not as sorry as I was two days ago."

She said, "There's one thing I want you to know—about the money."

"Yes. He must have been paid quite a lot for that little adventure."

"You know who sent him?"

"We . . . suspect. There'll never be proof. There never has been proof."

"He took his fee," she said, head up. "I made him take his fee because he'd earned it, and he sent a . . . a certain sum to . . . to Rocky's mother."

Farquarson nodded.

"I made him send the rest back." She was defiant.

"You . . . !"

"It was blood money."

For what seemed a long time they regarded each other in silence.

"Yes," said Farquarson finally. "You said that you could

247

'almost promise.' I accept that. You're a remarkable young woman."

"And you won't . . ."

He shook his head. "You can tell him he's damned lucky, all the same. If we'd had proof . . ." He ruminated. "You can tell him that next time. . . ."

"There won't be a next time . . ."

Farquarson looked at her as if a trifle surprised suddenly. "D'you know, I believe you're right." He glanced at the sail, fluttering now in the breeze. "Good sailing to you, ma'am. I'm glad to have met you."

He held out his hand, and she took it—perhaps a trifle awkwardly.

At the door he glanced back. "Pardon me saying so, but if you're as good a wife as you are accomplice, he's a lucky young man." He chuckled and was gone.

Almost at once Alan's voice called out, "Linda, Linda."

"What is it?"

"Here a moment. I want help. I'm stuck."

She smiled, and went out into the sunshine to help him.

THIRD SEASCAPE

ON A SEA THAT WAS ONLY A TRIFLE MORE BLUE THAN THE arch of the sky, a small boat meandered happily, lazily, eastwards.

All day it had been pursuing its apparently purposeless way across the Gulf of Genoa. No one watching could have said whether it was making for Spezia, or for Rapallo, for Livorno or for Corsica, which lay due south—a shadow on the horizon.

During the morning it passed a little fleet of fishing boats.

"Look." A young fisherman laughed. "Perhaps there is no one aboard."

"Or, perhaps," he added, being Italian, "the skipper is in love."